Farhana Sheikh was born in Lahore. She lives in Hackney and teaches in North London. This is her first novel.

FARHANA SHEIKH

The Red Box

The Women's Press

First published by The Women's Press Limited 1991
A member of the Namara group
34 Great Sutton Street
London EC1V 0DX

© Copyright Farhana Sheikh 1991

British Library Cataloguing-in-Publication Data
  Sheikh, Farhana
  The Red Box
  I. Title
  823.914 [F]

  ISBN 0-7043-4260-X

Typeset by Photosetting, Yeovil
Printed and bound by Cox & Wyman, Reading, Berks

One

The house had many rooms and the grounds were big. Raisa was hiding. Her family waited in the hall. The servants promised her huge boxes of the sweetest chocolates and platefuls of the most piquant tamarind if only she would come down. The child knew. This was no weekend trip to her cousins in Islamabad. This day's journey would be of a different kind. It was like the dream – they had come for her, and there was nothing she could do to fight them.

She heard her Nani Amma. 'Achcha baitee. It doesn't matter. Your amie will have to go all on her own, poor thing! She'll be all alone in the big aeroplane with no one to hug her and keep her safe. It doesn't matter.'

The house was silent. Then the little child, small for her seven years, appeared on the wide stairway.

Her grandmother, barely pausing for breath, pressed the Word of God to her heart and recited the sacred verses. Verse after verse she breathed over her daughter and her grandchild.

The grandfather passed a hand over the child's head; he whispered a prayer. He turned to his daughter and his eyes filled with tears. He said, '*Inshallah*, we'll meet again.'

'Abba jaan, I'll come back. Each year, I'll come back.'

This was the moment of parting. The old man wept. His wife stood pale and rigid. No airport farewell for them. She would not watch the monstrous plane carry away her first-born child. He could not watch: his heart was weak; his health was failing.

The mother ran to the waiting car. Her brothers and sisters followed her with the child.

     *   *   *

The airport was busy. Neither mother nor child noticed. They walked through the scenes but they did not see.

Like sleepwalkers they went to their private lounge, and sat waiting for the flight announcement. Silently, they met the last embraces of their family.

In the plane, among the clouds, they both paused and wondered. The child no longer cried, but her heart was heavy. She had left her Nana Abu. She might never again see her Nani Amma, or her aunts, or her uncles, or her cousins. She felt the pain of bereavement and, seven years old, she understood what it meant to be powerless.

Her mother was hushed with emotion. She had waited long for this journey. She had wanted to make it; the alternative was impossible. But her father's parting words overwhelmed her: '*Inshallah*, we will meet again.' She was frightened. The vast distance ahead terrified her. Fourteen years ago she and her family had fled across mountain and plain to reach the new state of Pakistan. Now, aching with a sense of loss, she was making a second migration, where fear lay not in imagined massacres, but in huge, forlorn uncertainty. How would her child fare in a strange Christian land? She prayed that they would soon return.

She wondered about her husband's life without her. She imagined the thrill of meeting again the man she had married, but with whom she had spent so little time. She dreamed of honourable and splendid futures.

She looked at her sleeping daughter.

Two

Voices and laughter filled the study, and then became silent. Raisa labelled the cassette, 'T & N: Int. 3'. She turned her chair away from the desk, relieved that the interview was at last transcribed. Her back was stiff and her head ached.

She could have paid the department secretary to do the job, but her conversations with Nasreen and Tahira had become very private. She did not want a stranger to hear them.

She walked into the living-room. She liked the silence. It soothed her to be alone in her own flat, though it was never quite her own. She had bought it partly with family money, and her father's house lay only a ten-minute drive away. To relatives and family friends, the flat in Fulham was described as a 'family property'. Her father and sister were given spare sets of keys but neither ever used them. Her privacy was respected. There was, of course, the almost daily phone call. The contact was necessary – a reassurance to everyone that everything was as it should be.

Nasreen's and Tahira's words lingered in her mind. Those words must generate meanings and understandings by the time she led the seminar. Now, though, they mingled with other preoccupations. Her father would soon phone. He would expect her to spend the evening with the family. Her cousin and his wife from the States were coming to dinner.

The pain in her head began to vibrate. She opened the balcony door. The gardener was walking out of view; he had finished tending the plants and lawn. The early spring air entered the room. It was soothing, but her headache persisted. The phone rang. It was her father.

'*As-salaam alaikum*, darling. Everything all right?' They always spoke English with each other.

'*Wa alaikum usalaam*. Fine. What're you up to?'

'Oh, the usual, writing, reading.' Raisa waited.

'What time do we expect you?'

She said what had to be said. 'Abu-ji, I've got some work to finish. I can't come this evening.'

'Not even for a few hours?'

'I'm going to the opera later. A friend had a spare ticket.'

'Friends and operas are more important than welcoming my sister's son?'

'It's *Rigoletto!* I'm lucky to have got a seat. Anyway, I've arranged to meet some friends there. I can see Sohail another time.' It was a battle of wills.

'He's only in the country for a few days. He's a busy man. Baitai, his wife, will note your absence.'

'I haven't anything to say to any of them. You and Atiyya can look after them quite well without me.'

She heard the lameness of her argument. Her father heard it too.

'Baitai, where are your manners? He's my sister's son. He brings his wife to my house and my elder child stays away? Where are your manners? As a Muslim you should know these things. You must show consideration.'

She could have said, 'Yes, as he showed consideration for the driver he kept waiting outside our house the last time he visited,' but she did not interrupt her father. She accepted that her relations set great store by manners. He was right: her absence would give offence. But there was a part of her that wanted to offend. After all those years, she hadn't forgotten. She could never forget the way they had been with her mother. It still hurt to remember. Her dislike of them and of their kind was concrete. Nonetheless, she was being swayed. Her presence was important to her father and she hadn't been home. She would play the hypocrite with Sohail as she enquired about relatives and reminisced. The evening would pass though, and she would have done her duty.

'You can't just ignore accepted codes of behaviour,' said her father. 'There's no virtue in making strangers of your own family.'

'All right, Abu-ji, all right.' He mustn't think she had bowed to his will. 'I'll come tonight, as a favour, and for my own reasons.'

4

'We'll expect you in a couple of hours.'

'Yes, yes, OK.' She made no effort to hide her irritation.

She pressed down the receiver. She told Alun she had a migraine. He was a friend on her course. She could not have told him the truth, and it was not quite a lie. The headache was still there.

The curtains were drawn against the afternoon light. She lay on her bed in the darkness. The voices on the tape were still with her. She remembered Tahira's words. 'Well, you know what's right really. Even if you do wrong, you know it ain't right. It's like you've always known what's right. You don't always do it though.'

Encircling the girl's words was Raisa's conversation with her father. She remembered a scene. She hadn't thought about it for years. Her memory was hazy. She must have been about four years old . . . Gulberg, Nana Abu's house. She cannot recall the details of the place. Think. Concentrate. She can see narrow windows; a balcony facing inwards, running the four walls of the third storey and overlooking the cool, marble-floored inner courtyard. Here, there is little awareness of the afternoon heat that is burning the world outside. Nana Abu's house in Lahore has become the grand eastern house she has seen in films and read about in books, and she can see herself, a child, running down the stairs, barefoot, anxious to escape. She wants to be with Muna and the children from the gulley. She fears discovery because it is wrong to wander away from the house, it is wrong not to be wearing shoes, it is wrong to play with the vulgar street children.

The memory becomes clearer . . . She's sure that the women of the house – Amie, Zorah, Azra, Nani Amma – are all in the 'blue room' eating pan and smoking hookahs. She knows that the naukars are in the kitchen cooking the afternoon meal.

She must escape detection from all these quarters. It's frustrating to stay at home with the adults when excitement and danger are outside with the barefoot children who throw cow-dung into the rich people's houses and then hide to see the fun; who steal mithai and kutlummai from old Baba's shop when his back is turned. She's approaching the final flight of stairs; she has to sneak past the busy kitchen before she can reach them. A dry throat, a racing pulse, do not deter her. She takes a deep breath and plunges into light – but she is halted by diabolic sounds, wailings and howlings. She cannot move; she's not sure where the demons are. They are nimble, she's heard, and they can appear anywhere and in any form. They could be above, below, behind. They are not in front of her . . . Could they be in her? Nani Amma did call her Shaitan when she did wrong things. She is doing a wrong thing now. Oh, I don't want the demons to be in my body, she thinks. They will hurt me, and they will take me to a hell of fire.

The howling fills the space around her, and then she sees them. Their faces, with round staring eyes, have red gashes cut into them. Black shrouds cover their twisted bodies. There are three of them. One is upright, beckoning; two are writhing on the floor mouthing words she cannot hear.

Fear gives way to excitement. These demons have visited before. Last time they turned out to be Zorah Khala, Azra Khala and Nani Amma, wearing ripped burqas. She smiles – she'll call their bluff. She runs upstairs to the blue room. As predicted, it is empty. She feels powerful and full of energy. She walks down to the demons, needing to pass them to look into the kitchen. She has to be sure only the servants are there. With waning confidence she edges forward towards the kitchen, and the servants make way for her as she moves inside.

There before her eyes, sitting around the work table, are Amie, Zorah, Azra and Nani Amma. She panics. If they are in the kitchen, and the servants too, who are the wailing women? The truth strikes with an awful clarity. The demons are behind her. Their misshapen tentacles are moving nearer. She runs towards the women she loves, longing to be enfolded in their protecting arms. But Amie turns away from her. Zohra, Nusrat, Akhter, Nani Amma step away. She cries, she screams, she begs. The howling stops. The witches freeze. She hears Nani Amma's voice, 'Little children who do not obey their elders are bad children. What elders tell you is for your own good. You must not wander away from the house. Someone might take you away. Bad children belong to Shaitan. If you don't want to be taken away by these witches, you must promise not to disobey again.'

She promises, and runs into her mother's waiting arms.

Raisa shivered from the pleasure of a good tale. Then, diligently, her mind worked to establish connections. Buried in all the complexity of the day was the possibility of understanding something about the way in which identities – as she had learned to say – were formed and regulated. Intellectually encouraged, but uncomfortable at the way she was responding to her father's call, Raisa dressed, and left for home.

Three

Jamshid gazed ahead as his burger and chips turned cold. A tall boy, he sat at the end of the table, with his legs using the space to the side.

Najum and Ijaz, his closest friends, were keeping away from him. The government wouldn't let his brother stay in the country, and Jamshid couldn't bear to be separated from his brother. His friends understood his desire to be left alone.

'Look at this rubbish food. It ain't even warm.' Tahira squirted ketchup on her chips.

Mumtaz noticed Jamshid. 'Don't Jamshid look sad? Wonder what's wrong. Can't be girlfriend trouble, he's a good boy, he don't go out with girls. What a waste, though.'

'He ain't that good,' said Tahira. 'I had an argument with him last month. He saw me and Tanni with her bloke cousins. Him and his friend were talking, and I heard him say that I was getting out of control and going round with boys. Told him to shut his fat mouth, and guess what he called me? Called me a Kunjaree, the stupid bastard! Thought I never heard.'

'Yeah, but his green eyes; he's got lovely green eyes. You're lucky he's Hussain's friend.'

Tahira saw Nasreen walk into the dining hall. 'I'm gonna call that Nasreen over,' she said.

'Oh, do you have to? I wanted to talk about Bina and her Jamaican boyfriend.' Mumtaz was disappointed.

'Yeah, well, I got to ask her something. Oi, Nasreen! Come here when you get your dinner.'

Mumtaz asked, 'How come you're all chatty with her these days?

You're only with her in social studies and registration. She ain't changed or nothing.'

'She ain't really a snob, you know,' Tahira said. 'Well, her sister might be, and her mum. I don't think she is. It's just she's working hard for her exams, ain't she? Bet you she's been to the library!'

'But she's so boring. What do you talk about?'

'This and that. I suppose we don't really talk, you know, like talk talk. I got to ask her when that woman's coming in again. You know, I was telling you about her, the woman Beeston knows, a Paki woman, the one who don't look or sound it.'

Mumtaz was again looking in Jamshid's direction. 'Why are all them gorees crowding round Jam's table?'

They were too far away to hear anything.

Jamshid's thoughts were interrupted. He saw five English girls surrounding him. He recognised them. They were in the year below him, except for one who was in his sixth form tutor group, the twin sister of a friend.

'That's him, Michelle. He's the one,' spoke a girl called Julie. She was small and blonde.

'Oi, you!' Michelle spat the words. 'You're one of the Pakis who picked on me mate's brothers, right?'

'What?' He felt their hate. He looked at the taller girl, at the acne on her face.

'I said, are you the Paki wanker who picked on me mate's brothers?'

Jamshid thought, can they feel my hate? Do they know how much I hate them, hate them, for their filthy language and their filthy hate of me?

He said, 'We didn't pick on 'em. They were picking on our brothers and sisters, that's what. They started it.'

'Oh come on, Michelle, leave it,' said the sixth form girl.

'Fuck off, Sonya. You talk to 'em, you're friends with 'em, ain't ya?'

'It ain't that, it's just . . .'

'Well then, shut up!'

Jamshid looked at Sonya; she was avoiding his eyes. He had known her since primary school. He noted how she had moved behind the girl with the vicious anger.

Michelle's friend, Julie, said, 'Their dad ain't pleased neither.

They ain't forgotten. Don't you go thinking it's the end of it, 'cos it fuckin' ain't. Four against two!'

Jamshid heard her working herself into the drama. He said, 'What about them, fourth years, threatening first years? They threatened them with knives. What about that? Their dad stood laughing when they threw stones at us on the street. They had no right doing that.'

Another girl joined in. 'Look, you bloody wog, this ain't your country, this ain't your school. "They've got no right!"'

'We was well pleased when you got the cane! Thought you'd bring in a penknife, eh?' Michelle jeered.

The noise of the argument had risen, and a crowd had started to collect. A teacher stepped in. 'Right you lot, what's all this then?'

No one answered.

'Now come on,' he said, 'everyone back to your seats. We don't want to get indigestion now, do we?'

Tahira had moved up to the crowd around Jamshid's table. She shouted across the heads, 'Oi Sonya, what's happening?' Sonya seemed not to hear.

Najum and Ijaz had reached Jamshid.

'There's two more of 'em, Michelle. They were with him,' said Julie, excited.

'OK, you two,' the teacher addressed Jamshid's friends. 'Come with me – I need to see you about something. And you, young ladies, eat your lunch quietly, right?'

The teacher waited until all had returned to their seats, and then left with the two boys.

The white girls sat down, at Jamshid's table, Michelle opposite him, Julie next to her, then the others, with Sonya at the end of the line and out of Jamshid's view.

Jamshid ate his food, though it was cold and tasteless. He waited. The gorees were looking at him, straight at him. They wanted him to know they were looking. He carried on eating, hot-faced and eyes averted.

'It ain't the end of it, you know,' said Michelle.

'He can't look at us, Michelle. He might get all excited. You know what they say about darkies,' said Julie.

The girls laughed. Jamshid, briefly, wondered whether Sonya was joining in. The laughing, the ridicule, continued.

'Yeah, we'd better watch it, he might get really excited,' said Julie.

Jamshid put down his fork and looked up. They were still laughing, and staring.

'Tell us. What *do* they say about darkies?' asked Michelle.

'Well, you know, about their you know whats,' continued Julie.

'What, pricks?' said Michelle. 'Big pricks? Nah, that's about the other darkies. Pakis don't have big pricks.'

The laughter reached new heights. Jamshid met Michelle's stare. He didn't blink. The word was caught behind his clenched teeth, and then he opened his mouth, 'Prostitute!'

Julie said, 'Listen to him. That's what they think of women, dirty pigs!'

Michelle said, 'You heard him, you heard what that fucking bastard said!' She shot up, flinging Jamshid's plate on to him.

He caught her arm. He wanted to punch her, kick her, wipe her out. Instead, he let go of her. But he couldn't stop repeating the word, 'Prostitute, prostitute, prostitute . . .'

'Look, he won't stop, he won't stop!' Michelle screamed out the words, and punched him. They all did. He felt the punches on his head, on his face, on his chest. His face was wet and his vision blurred. He wouldn't hit the girls. He heard someone shout in Punjabi, 'His eye's bleeding.'

The teacher intervened, others with him, extracting the loudest boys and girls.

Jamshid felt ashamed. Everyone had seen it, had witnessed his humiliation. Someone said, 'He went too far, Sir. He shouldn't have called them prostitutes. That's bad, ain't it, Sir?'

Jamshid felt the gaze of the onlookers. Girls and boys who knew his brothers and mother and father had seen the white girls beating him. It was the mark of his weakness. The girls had hit him because they could. He hated everything: the girls, the school, the country, and his family who didn't fight back. He saw the three Pakistani girls. They were looking at him and talking. He ran out of the hall before the tears came.

Mr Symes, the deputy head of the fifth year, took the five girls with him. The students were back at their tables, talking or thinking about the incident, or ignoring it.

The three Pakistani girls remained silent for some moments. Each was hushed by the awfulness of what had happened. Each was suffering the shaming of a brother, and the humiliation of her own self.

Tahira spoke first, 'What happened? What was all that about?'

Mumtaz answered, 'Ijaz just said it's to do with those boys, you know, Martin Ames and his brother. The gorees wanted to get Jam. They heard he brought a knife . . .'

'Huh, shows what they know! It weren't even him. It was Hussain. It was my brother who brought it,' Tahira said.

'Hussain?' Nasreen asked. 'I thought it was Jamshid.'

'Yeah, 'cos he was caught with it. None of them said who brought it in. It was one knife, but they all had it, like, and so it didn't matter who brought it in. Mind you, they might not all have got caned if one had took the blame.'

Mumtaz said, 'And those girls got Jamshid. He was sitting on his own today. Wonder why?'

Tahira's voice quivered, 'But it's bad. They made his eye bleed; it's bad. They shouldn't have done that. Don't it make you ashamed? They shouldn't have . . .'

'I know,' said Nasreen. 'I mean it's not as if it was their own brothers, is it?'

'Yeah, but that ain't what it's about. To think, that bloody Sonya was with them!'

Mumtaz said, 'Sonya didn't hit Jam, I'm sure she didn't. She weren't that near the other girls.'

The three stopped talking again. Nasreen got up to leave – she had arranged to see Mr McCormack about her economics test. She said to Tahira, 'I'll see you tomorrow morning outside the stock cupboard.'

'What, is what's her name coming in the morning? I thought it was later,' said Tahira.

'No, it's in the morning. I wrote it down.' Nasreen left the dining hall.

Mumtaz and Tahira stayed behind, waiting for the end of the lunch-break.

Four

Raisa: What do you mean by 'pride'?

Nasreen: Well, I think of pride, about religion, I'm really proud that I'm a Muslim, because I think it's a true religion, it guides anybody through life, properly, and shows them what they should and shouldn't do so they do not get into trouble, and have a proper, happy life. Well, I'm proud – not in the bad way – I mean, I like and enjoy what I believe. I like to hear more about it and –

(Interrupted by visitor to stock cupboard)

Oh, hello Jane.

Jane: Hello.

Nasreen: I don't know, what do you think, Tahira?

(Jane leaves with book. Pause)

Raisa: OK, you're 'proud' of being a Muslim, is that what you're saying to me? I know when I was at school there were things I was ashamed of. Is there anything about Pakistani-ness that fills you with, er, something that isn't pride at all? You were talking about dupattas and things and walking down the street and feeling embarrassed. What do you mean?

Tahira: Yeah, like, say if you was going out and your friends've always seen you in trousers, and when you have a 'no uniform day' you wear really nice clothes, but when I go out with my mum, I have to put my shalwaar kameez on, and she sometimes tells me to put my dupatta on 'cos someone like my uncle or somebody might see me. On the other hand, if some of my friends see me, that's embarrassing.

Raisa: What's the embarrassment? What's it about?

Tahira: A lot of English boys in this school say, oh look, she's got her night clothes on, that's what they say. They say you've got your pyjamas on; they start teasing you when you come back to school, don't they?

Nasreen: Yeah.

Raisa: How's that different from any other teasing? Lots of girls, English, Pakistani, are forced to put up with boys' teasing.

Tahira: I think that's really a lot different because they're just probably mucking about. When we come back to school we get the teasing whenever we go past them . . .

Nasreen: It's not only you that's being insulted, it's that everybody, all Muslim, Pakistani girls wear them, so it's not just an individual that's being offended or insulted.

Tahira: Yesterday, at dinner time, in the dining hall, a boy – he's in the sixth year – was eating his food, and four gorees, from our year they were, really did beat him up in that hall, especially one of them girls. They were going to him, oh, we're gonna get rid of one Muslim, chuck him out of the country, so the teacher . . .

Raisa: Did they say 'Muslim' or 'Paki'?

Tahira: Paki, they said Paki, we'll get rid of one Paki and chuck him out of the country. It was really bad. All because he and his mates sorted out these two gorrais – friends of one of them girls. Served them right for bullying the Asians in the first year. But them girls couldn't take it. So we went to our teacher; Miss Beeston was helping, and Mr McCormack. But the deputy head won't do nothing. He just had a go at the girls.

Raisa: Did the teachers know the details of what happened?

Nasreen: Yes, I think they must know.

Tahira: The point is really, that deputy head ain't done nothing. We shouldn't really be seeing that girl walking round the school again, the way she beat that boy up. And you know Mr Busby – he's the head of our year – I said to him, about a year ago, I said to him, the deputy head's a racialist. Guess what he done? He slapped me across the face.

Raisa: I don't believe you!

Nasreen: He did.

Tahira: You can ask all the teachers. They all know I got slapped across the face by our head of year. I said to him they shouldn't treat children like that, and he said . . . he got up and slapped my face, and I got a letter sent home as well, saying that I insulted a teacher. But that weren't an insult. It was only pointing something out.

Nasreen: I mean, like, you know these English kids, if they beat up these Asian kids and . . .

Tahira: We have to fight back!

Nasreen: . . . the Asians, they try and fight back but they're stopped. That's what fills you with shame really.

Raisa: That fills you with shame?

Nasreen: Yeah.

Raisa: Say a bit more about that.

Nasreen: 'Cos then it seems as though we can't help ourselves, we can't defend ourselves. That's why it fills us with shame.

Tahira: Yeah, and the English think we're frightened . . .

Nasreen: We want to get them back but we can't.

Raisa: Hitting back can be done peacefully, of course.

Tahira: . . . but they'll probably think we're starting trouble. We ain't starting trouble because then the English can hit you more. Like, if we don't do nothing about that boy that got beaten up, then everytime someone goes in the hall, they'll beat 'em up, won't they, the English girls?

Nasreen: Yeah.

Tahira: So you've got to do something about it. If the teachers can't do nothing about it, then we might as well ourselves.

Nasreen: If you really stop to think about it, it makes you sick. Do you remember the time all of us were locked in the hall?

Tahira: Yeah, last Christmas, in the fifth-year playground, all these Asians were being sworn at and snowed by this huge crowd of gorrais. And guess what the school did? They locked up all the Asians in the hall, with some teacher in front. Teachers couldn't do nothing about them white kids. Half the teachers in this school are racialists.

Raisa: You feel that? Such a large number?

Tahira: They don't help you, that's the only thing they do, they don't help you. That girl shouldn't have been walking in the school the way she beat – there were four or five of them who beat him, but one hit him really hard. Their teacher took her outside his office and had a go at her, and she probably got a letter sent home, and that's it.

Raisa: Is there anything else, any other not so dramatic signs that tell you the school is racist?

Tahira: What do you mean?

Raisa: Is it only in the name-calling, and fighting, and the way teachers deal with it, that you say the school's racist?

Nasreen: It's in everything. You know what most of the teachers are thinking about you. You know who's side they're really on. Some of them tell you they're interested in you and want to know about you, but you can't really trust them.

Tahira: They wouldn't understand nothing, even if you told them.

Nasreen: It would be difficult to explain.

Tahira: Yeah, but I wouldn't anyway. I'd tell them any old thing.

Nasreen: And it doesn't make any difference having Pakistani teachers here.

Tahira: There's one at this school, and he's a right git – Mr Aslam.

Raisa: So school isn't the place where you think about your particular lives. You could call school racist in that sense too, then?

(Pause)

Tahira: If the English hit you, er, when we do hit back, er, like, about five Asians got caned, see, so there ain't much we can do. My brother, that boy who got beaten up, his brother –

Raisa: What did these boys do that they were caned?

Tahira: This was about a few weeks ago. Like I told you, they beat some English boys up at lunchtime. Well, they didn't really beat 'em up, they just had a go at 'em, and said you leave our brothers and sisters alone. I don't see the English getting caned when they beat up Asians. Why didn't Mr Busby slap that girl across the face?

Nasreen: Yes.

Tahira: You know, I never used to think about Muslims and that that much. Like we had a little talk with Mr McCormack once and I said to him – Oh I think it's right, too many Asians do come here. That's what I was thinking at that time. I even said once – I want to be white – yeah, it's bad, innit? But now when I see the English start hitting the Asians, I think we should fight back.

Raisa: Do you feel more of a Pakistani because they're attacking you?

Tahira: Yeah. I didn't, I don't always think that, but these days I do, especially when you think of all the things. You know in Ilford, the Kassim family?

Nasreen: Yeah, they were burnt . . .

Tahira: On Saturday, everyone went marching to the Town Hall and the police were down there thinking we might start trouble, but we were just marching and showing how much we cared for 'em.

Raisa: Yes, of course.

Nasreen: There was a girl in this school, she was in the second year, her house got burned down.

Tahira: Yeah, and the police didn't do nothing. I bet they'd have caught someone quick if it'd been a white family!

Raisa: I'm interested in what you're saying, Tahira, how you didn't used to, or don't always think about being Pakistani and . . .

Tahira: Miss Beeston even knew that. I used to think I was English; I wanted to be a goree. But when my mum goes out, when somebody says something horrible to her, like the time when she was coming home from work, some bastards pushed into her and spat on her, when that happens, well! When she told us, I wanted to go out and kill them bastards, I swear I did. I went upstairs and cried. I was shamed and angry. I was angry. I mean, she was coming home all tired. Now I think, if you really want to know, I don't mind wearing Asian clothes, because I don't care. English people, they can go . . . It don't bother me if I wear Asian clothes now because I am who I am. First of all I was embarrassed: I'd wear trousers and I wouldn't care what my mum'd say, I'd answer her back. But now, it really makes you think. And then I said to myself – I don't care, I'll wear my clothes 'cos that's who I am, a Pakistani.

Five

Raisa walked to the window, the cassette still playing. She had stopped listening. She was thinking of that first visit. At 10.20 on a February morning in 1985 she had walked into South Park School, on the outer fringes of the East End.

She had felt the chill of the long grey corridors, lessons in all the classrooms, the silence occasionally broken by a cough, a door opening, distant words. Raisa had come to meet Nasreen Ehsan and Tahira Rashid, the two fifteen-year-olds who might help her to define an area of study for her MA dissertation.

She had been anxious. How would the girls receive her? As a teacher, or as a fellow Pakistani? Would they approve of her, respect her as an aapa, or would they reject her for her European clothes, her hairstyle and make-up? Should she have put on shalwaar kameez? Her silk ones, sometimes worn at family functions, didn't seem appropriate. She had wanted them to approve of her, to feel pride in her breaking of the myth of the 'plain, austere, humourless Asian teacher', yet she feared that approval would be withheld.

She stands outside the English stock-cupboard, notebook and cassette recorder in hand, waiting for the two Pakistani girls. She's a stranger there and she feels a little clumsy. The corridor is crowded with chattering and laughing and angry children moving between lessons. There's a group of brown-skinned girls to the side of her. She wonders whether Nasreen and Tahira are among them. One comes forward, smartly and modestly dressed, smiling politely. She thinks, this is Nasreen. Tahira doesn't come forward, perhaps she's not there. She notices a girl in the group looking at her in a slant-eyed manner, making eye contact and then swishing her head away. She feels slapped, insulted. The group moves off, leaving the polite girl and the other, who must be Tahira. She thinks, she knows who I am: the fellow Pakistani, someone older, who has come across London to meet her. Has she no manners? Does she not know how to behave when a guest comes to visit? What has her mother taught her? She's shocked by the words she's thinking. The girls are there in front of her. The three introduce themselves. She speaks, laughs easily, and moves into the room.

The gardener saw Raisa at the window and waved to her. She waved back, but quickly moved away, embarrassed. Had she been staring in his direction? They weren't strangers: they always exchanged greetings whenever they passed each other, in the carpark or stairway. Once he had told her she reminded him of an old girlfriend – same chestnut hair, same eyes. Her embarrassment lingered.

Back at her desk, she rewound the cassette. Play.

Raisa: Who are you?
Nasreen: Muslim.
Raisa: What does that mean to you?
Nasreen: Well, it's my faith. I believe in my faith, I believe in my traditions, and, er, you know, like respecting your parents and obeying them and, er . . .
Tahira: Yeah. (Quietly) Not most English people do that really.
Nasreen: Well, they do.
Tahira: Not really, not all of them do.
Nasreen: I think it's more strict in Islam.
Raisa: Do you think that's good?
Nasreen and Tahira: Yeah.
Nasreen: It's good because your parents, they're more wise than you, and if you respect them, then they're going to give you good advice.
Tahira: Yeah, but I think it'd be different if you were back in your own country. I don't think it's good in this country. Like, if your parents say you can't go to a disco or something, you might go anyway. If I was back in my own country, she, my mother, could say that, but because I'm born here and everything, I *should* be able to go.
Raisa: You'd accept not being allowed to go in Pakistan?

Tahira: I wouldn't be allowed in Pakistan. It really would be bad there. People think it's bad there, and you couldn't get away with it really. But I think I should be allowed here.

Raisa: Do you go to discos?

Tahira: You ain't gonna tell none of this to no one, are you?

Raisa: No, of course not. No one will know that it's you who's speaking.

Tahira: Well, I do go to discos and parties and stuff like that, but not with my mum knowing.

Raisa: Yes. I remember I had to lie and be secretive and all that. I couldn't understand, I mean, I don't think I did anything bad, but, of course, I couldn't let my father know because he'd think just going there was bad. I mean, I didn't behave like most of my English friends, not at all. It was only talking and sipping coke. As far as my father was concerned, just being there was wrong.

Nasreen: That's because it's the religion as well, isn't it? That girls should keep their bodies covered, all of it, whereas if you're going to discos, then you're sort of acting, you know, not according to your religion.

Tahira: Yeah, like your parents take your going to discos like you're going with boyfriends and that. It's not really. It's like going with your friends and having big fun.

Raisa: Tell me. Say you're at this disco and you're with your English friends. Do you think they might think you're a bit odd by the way you behave there? How would you behave?

Tahira: Just like my friends, no different, 'cos I don't behave different anyway. Whatever they do, it's OK.

Nasreen: I wouldn't.

Raisa: You wouldn't?

Nasreen: No. I mean, they might drink, they might smoke, and dance with boys.

Raisa: You wouldn't do that?

Nasreen: No!

Raisa: How would they see you, do you think? You're not doing any of these things, and they are ...

Tahira: Probably think we're stupid!

Nasreen: Well, they wouldn't regard me as being the same as them.

Tahira: Yeah, but they wouldn't understand all our religion really, would they? So they'd think you're stupid. 'Cos they don't really know what our religion is. They think you're stupid, like weird.

Raisa: Nasreen, how do you get on with your English friends? Do they treat you as someone who is not one of them?

Nasreen: Yeah. I think so, all the time. I don't know really, it's just their attitude towards you, their behaviour to you. They say things like who they go out with, but never to me because they've accepted it that I'm not going to go out with boys and don't do all these bad things, and so they don't speak to me like that, as sometimes they would do with their other friends.

Raisa: I know exactly what you're saying!

Nasreen: And sometimes, you know, I prefer it to be that way. I would never like to go out all evening. I mean, I don't go out after about five o'clock. Not because my parents never allow it, my parents have never said, you can't go. It's just that I don't think it's good either. So I take my parents' advice.

The meeting had taken place over a month ago, and Raisa was still pondering the words they had spoken. She had heard them, transcribed and read them, and now, here re-winding, there fast-forwarding, once again, she listened.

Tahira: My mum don't really understand my life.

Raisa: Why do you think that's the case?

Tahira: 'Cos parents don't really know school life and all. My mum lets my brothers go to discos and bhungra parties. She lets them go; she don't really care. She does care but she don't stop them from going. Whereas if I go, come home too late, God! She don't really have a go at them.

Raisa: Why is she like that with you and not with your brothers?

Tahira: Well, er, with girls, like, er . . .

Raisa: Go on, doesn't matter, say what you want.

Tahira: Well, you know, girls, they might go out and get married, whereas boys, er . . .

Raisa: Go on.

Tahira: Well, if I wanted to go out and my mum said no, to tell you the truth, I'd really go, but, er, er . . .

Raisa: You'd have to lie?

Tahira: No, I wouldn't lie, but when I come back, she wouldn't talk to me. Sometimes, if I really wanted to go and my friends said, come on, and my mum said I couldn't go, I'd really go, but my mum'd lock the doors up. But your English friends don't understand. They don't know what Pakistani life is like and what their religion is like.

Raisa: Well, if your English friends did, would that make it easier for you?

Tahira: Might do. Don't really matter, though, 'cos I think if I'm born here, in this country, I want to do what the others do.

Raisa: So, would you say you like the 'English group', and you're quite happy to belong to it?

Tahira: Well, I don't like all the things English people, well, girls, get up to, and things like that, not everything.

Raisa: What do you mean? What wouldn't you like?

Tahira: Well, I don't like English girls having kids when they're only about, er, when they're not even married. I wouldn't like to be like that. It's not worth getting married then, is it?

Raisa: Are you telling me you don't agree with the idea of sex before marriage?

Tahira: No. I would if I was English, but I don't 'cos I'm a Muslim, er, no one in our country would marry a girl who, you know . . .

Raisa: You see yourself marrying a Pakistani, of course.

Tahira: Yeah. I have to 'cos, like my sisters, when I leave school and go to work, my mum'll say, who do you want to get married to? If I said someone English she wouldn't agree, but if it was someone like a cousin or something, she'd most probably agree. Pakistani parents are strict, ain't they? They don't want their daughters marrying no English blokes.

Nasreen: Because the religion's different. That's got a lot, that's got everything to do with it. I mean, the way both live is very different. You know it's going to be a stable and strong marriage if you marry someone within your own religion, because they're from the same faith and they believe that it's for life. And if you follow the rules, then you're going to get on well. Whereas with English people, because they drink and do all this, go to pubs, discos, because they see other boys, the boys see them, then they're going to feel more inclined to leave their husbands. Whereas in our religion, in our way of life, it's more strict. I mean, the women cover their whole body so that the men can't even look, can't even think, oh she's beautiful. They have self respect, they won't let other men see them so they go after them and bother them. It's the same with men. If they know their wife is faithful to them, and they can't see other women – their faces, the shape of their bodies – they're going to stick to their own wives as well.

Raisa stopped the tape, and replayed Nasreen's long utterance, once, twice, and a third time. The more she heard it, the more complex it became. Who, Raisa wondered, was Nasreen including in her use of the word 'our', in 'our religion' and 'our way of life'? Again, she remembered.

Islamabad, 1979
Raisa has hardly been here an hour, and Imran, with that American drawl of his, is telling her of the week's entertainment.

It's great, he says, to have her and Akhar at the same time. Maybe he'll go back to Paris with his brother, though he's not sure what company Akhar would be, busy swotting for his finals. That guy was running the risk of being as big a drag as Sohail.

Phuppo Razia speaks to Raisa, as always, in Urdu – she uses English only when essential. She insists that she keep free enough daytime hours to visit her father's old friends and relatives. It wouldn't do at all to idle away the whole week with her cousins and their cronies. And it is such a short time.

Shahzia, stroking her mother's forehead, says to her that they haven't seen Raisa since early '73. She couldn't possibly expect her to spend too much time with relations and Ahmed Mamoo's friends.

Phuppo Razia leans back on the chaise longue; Shahzia massages her temples. The mother tells her second-eldest to keep control over his excesses, as indeed his friends should over theirs. She knows they were boys, but they often have their sisters with them. Remember, there is such a thing as becoming, decent behaviour, and family name. Alas, there are those only too willing to point the finger at their family. With all those TV programmes as well on true Islam – all right, she knows it isn't their idea of Islam – but with Zia and his army and all that talk of Islamisation, there are people who think they can judge others, and so brazenly.

Soraya looks up from her book, 'Like that father and daughter. All they were doing was going for their regular walk, and every day for a week, those mother-fucking police were making all this shit about "Who are you?" "Why are you walking together?" "Do you know each other?" '

23

Displaying no irritation, Phuppo Razia continues, 'Yes, only last week or so, can you believe it, an educated woman was slapped by a man in a shop, a stranger, for not covering her head? Imagine, this was in a well-to-do area!'

Hussein knocks at the open door.

'Come in Hussein.' Phuppo Razia speaks in that singsong, slightly louder than normal manner reserved for trusty servants. 'Meet my beautiful niece from London.'

Raisa shakes hands with him. He looks taken aback, almost embarrassed. She is pained to see an old man – he has her grand-father's face – standing there with eyes lowered.

'Begum Sahiba,' he says, 'Janab Tayyib Ali and BegumTayyib have arrived, and are waiting in the drawing-room.'

Phuppo Razia leaves the room. Imran lights a cigarette and passes the packet to Soraya.

'. . . Well Imran,' says Raisa, 'what about this evening? What have you arranged for tonight, you the efficient organiser?'

He laughs, tells her not to worry. Her evenings are booked for the whole week. This evening they are all invited to a soirée at Omar Qureshi's house. He's a good friend. He and his family are return-ing to Europe next week: his father's a first minister at the embassy in Rome. The parents won't be there, of course. And Akhar's been persuaded to leave his serious-minded friends to come with them.

Shahzia is simply dying for Raisa to meet her friends, and some very interesting – she stresses 'very interesting' – acquaintances.

Soraya takes a deep drag of her cigarette. She tells her sister to wear less make-up to the party, her eye-stuff makes her look too tarty.

Three pathans, with rifles hidden under their chadurs, guard the front of Omar's house. The rooms are large and graciously furnished, more Louis XV than Mogul, though there are rich eastern carpets here and there. One of the rooms has been transformed into a dimly-lit dance floor. Music played in the London and New York clubs blares from the concealed speakers. People relax on the sofas, chairs, and at the tables. Some stand talking on the balconies, some by the paintings, and others by the ornate mirrors. A group of men and women laugh and lean on one another at the bar. They sip their scotches and mint juleps. The guests are mostly Pakistani, but there are embassy people there too. Everyone seems to breathe style and importance, self-consciously so.

The host greets them; they talk through the noise. He takes them to the seats near the dance floor. Raisa feels a wave of heat sweep over her: the space is bulging with hot, dancing bodies.

Shahzia nudges Raisa. 'See that girl with the straight, long hair, the one with the white sarong, doing those sexy movements? Remind me to tell you about her and a guy called Ali. Her name's Marium. She's the sister of that Zeenat I was telling you about. Look to your right, the guy with the beer, the one talking to the Nigerian, he's looking straight at you now, the badtameez!'

'You mean that hero over there?' says Raisa, 'Mr *passé* John Travolta? Just look at those hungry looks!'

'That's the one, he's Ali. You know, he's quite old, thirty and still a student. But what the hell, he's a nawab's son,' she laughs. 'He used to go out with Zeenat. It was really serious. She went off to study in the States. And when he visited her, he caught her with some American!'

Raisa asks her how she knows all this.

'Oh,' she says, 'Marium told me. You won't tell anyone, will you? Anyway, they don't really care. Zeenat, she left that American, and this is the funny bit, Ali's going to marry Marium. Marium's had boyfriends and everything. Ali knows all that, but she comes from an old family, loaded they are. Her father's some bigshot with the BCCI, in New York at the moment.'

Raisa says, 'I can't believe they do it all so openly. You make it sound as if they do.'

'Not really openly. But people talk and people get to know,' Shahzia says.

The music changes. Marium sees them and comes over. She's unsteady on her feet; her eyes don't quite focus. 'So you're the cousin from London! How nice to meet you.' She hugs Raisa, a little too long. Her breath smells of tobacco and alcohol. There's plenty of alcohol. But although numerous women are slurred of speech and flushed of face, you don't actually see them drinking substances that are unequivocally alcoholic.

Soraya, it seems, has become a chain smoker. In London she hardly smoked. She points out a Yusuf Said. 'That's Imran's bosom friend these days,' she says. 'He nearly always comes on his own. Sometimes he brings his younger brother. You never see his sisters. They're totally hidden away. His family own a lot of land, not much water under it though. He's a complete asshole.'

Imran brings Yusuf to join them. Yusuf asks the usual questions about London and the nature of Raisa's visit. He speaks deliberately, clearly. His speech has a transparent quality so that you can almost see the layers of history in it: below the American accent is the Oxonian, and below that, the sounds of Pakistan. He asks if Raisa would like something to drink. She says that fresh fruit juice would be nice. He looks at her in surprise.

The early hours of the morning, and Imran has had too much to drink. Soraya insists that he sober down before Phuppo Razia sees him. Knowing he drinks is one thing, seeing him falling about is another.

They have a reason to prolong the evening – a drive up the Marghella Hill, with the magical nocturnal view of Islamabad. Yusuf will drive. He can hold his drink like a man; he smiles. They fit comfortably in the limousine.

The windows open, and travelling at 100mph, the wind blowing through their laughter and hair, they could be in a Hollywood movie, or an Indian one: wealthy, stylish, privileged youngsters go for a wild fun drive after the late, late party. Raisa watches the two men – Yusuf with his Cartier watch, cigarette in mouth and single-hand driving, Imran drowsy and singing. Is that what they are, happy heroes of a celluloid fantasy? She thinks of Akhar, and likes him for staying with his friends that evening, even as she slips, mindlessly for the moment, into the film set.

On the hilltop they stand. The car doors are left open, George Benson is singing. Raisa clenches her teeth; the wind is so fast, and suddenly icy. It stirs everybody.

Yusuf hovers around her. 'Before you go back to London, you must let me drive you through my family land – Pakistan really is a magnificent country.'

Shahzia wants to tell a joke. 'It's hilarious, but perhaps I shouldn't tell it. A girl at my old school in Surrey told it to me, and you can imagine why it isn't really suitable for proper company.'

Raisa wants to hear, but keeps quiet. Yusuf is interested.

Imran says, 'If it's anything like your last joke, don't bother, 'cos no one'll laugh.'

Shahzia tells the joke. It is about James the chauffeur who likes to dress up in women's clothes. It is told slowly, teasingly: it makes use of pause and suggestion; it titillates. They all laugh – Yusuf the loudest, with tears running down his face.

Raisa is cold, and says, 'I'll wait in the car. I want to go back.' There is something shocking about it all.

Imran, now more alert, wants to drive; he won't take no from anyone. His eye-lids are heavy. The car speeds down the hill.

Raisa: And girls in Pakistan don't do the sort of things English girls do?
Tahira: No, I went there. We're allowed out much more than they are over there. When they go out, because of the lots of men, they put their burqas on. But, you know, even if they thought it weren't bad or nothing, they still wouldn't go to discos (laughs) or nothing. My cousins in Pakistan are sort of, you know, they live in the village and that. Even the children, when they finish school, they've got to help their mum and dad with their work. The work's got to be done, for food and things and paying the rent for their bit of land. So, you know, even if it weren't bad in Pakistan to go out and all that, I don't reckon they would.
Nasreen: Yeah, and you'd really feel bad leaving the work for your parents to do.
Tahira: I know. I mean it's the same here really. My mum goes out to work. Me and my sister do the work at home, mostly. My brother's busy looking for work, the other'll probably do the same when he leaves school this year. So I do feel more bad going out, 'cos if me and my sister don't do the work, it's left to my mum. It'd be the same if my dad were alive.
Nasreen: And your Ilford cousins work in that factory after school, to help your uncle . . .
Tahira: Yeah, but (laughs) Shireen still finds the time to muck around! But if you stop to think about it, it's tough for my mum, you know. Makes me angry really.
Nasreen: I have to help my mother with the housework, not that much though – she and my dad say I have to study. But some of the English kids in my class, they work after school. And there's this Greek girl who works at her father's restaurant. She's even had a week off school because he needed her full-time.
Tahira: But that's 'cos her dad can't afford to pay someone else to do the job. And you know you was saying English girls might be

working after school and all, and might not have much time for a laugh? Well, when they finish work, they don't get no hassle about going out afterwards, do they? We do though, 'cos it's badmaash and all that.

Nasreen: Like swimming. My sister wanted to go swimming, but my father said there's no way she's going to go swimming. So she didn't, because . . .

Tahira: My mum said I couldn't go swimming. I couldn't go to the headmaster and say my mum won't let me go swimming because she doesn't want me showing my legs.

Raisa: You didn't tell the headmaster?

Tahira: No. You feel funny telling people that, 'cos all girls've got the same legs and that.

Raisa: What would the headmaster have done or thought if you'd told him?

Tahira: He'd have thought we're sick or something.

Raisa turned the cassette over.

Nasreen: I go on Fridays to the mosque. They teach me about faith. You should believe in the message of the Qu'ran and the angels. I found it quite interesting. I thought it was useful. You know, I really needed that. I think more Muslim girls should have gone because if we were living in Pakistan we would have known that ages ago. But because we're here, I learned to read the Qu'ran at eleven or twelve, whereas there I'd have learned it by six.

Tahira: My mother says I should read the Qu'ran Majeed but I don't really take much notice of it now. I don't go to mosque, but I do read it sometimes.

Raisa: Why don't you go to the mosque anymore?

Tahira: I dunno. I've read the Qu'ran. I don't think I should go to mosque no more. I don't want to learn no more, because I'm not gonna go back to my own country. This is really my country, so I should really do what English people do, but . . . (pause) I wouldn't do everything the English do, not everything.

Raisa: Do you think English people will allow you to be one of them?

Tahira: Yeah, my *friends* would. If I was allowed to go to discos and that, then they'd gradually, er, I reckon we should be allowed to be together.

Nasreen: Tahira wouldn't mind following the English ways, but I would. When I have children, I would like to teach them everything about Islam.

Raisa: Why is there such a difference between you and Tahira?

Tahira: Maybe her parents are . . .

Nasreen: Maybe Tahira doesn't take an interest in her religion. I really do take an interest in Islam because I think it's good. What's going to happen when you die? This is like a test to see how obedient you are. If I'm obedient to my parents and do everything good, when the Day of Judgement comes, I'll live in eternal happiness.

Raisa paused, and then pressed 'fast-forward'.

Tahira: I would really like to be treated the same as my brothers. Girls are asking boys out now (to Nasreen), innit? Asian girls at the college.

Raisa: Is that true?

Tahira: Yeah. At the college, it used to be Asian boys asking Asian girls out. Now that ain't no more. The girls ask the boys out, some of them.

Raisa: Pakistani girls? Muslims?

Tahira: Yeah. You're surprised?

Raisa: Do their parents know?

Tahira: Parents don't know nothing (laughs).

Fast-forward.

Tahira: My mum don't get no pension, no nothing, because my dad was married twice. So if they give it to our mum, they've got to give it to the other mum. So they don't give it to none. And then my mum's working for my brothers and things like that, and one's going with an English girl and one's . . .

Raisa: She's working for your brothers?

Tahira: You know, making gold for their wives.

Raisa: Oh, I see.

Tahira: She's making, getting stuff. She bought suits and things like that. She don't wear them now. She's getting them for them, isn't she? But they don't think of her that way. They just come in at night and they worry her too much. But then, I've been a worry to my mum. I can't say I'm really good as well. She's all tired and working hard, no husband or nothing, and England's still a foreign country to her really, and there I am giving her a bad time. I should be good, but you know, I mean, well, you know what's right really. Even if you do wrong, you know it ain't right. It's like you've always known what's right. You just don't always do it though (laughs) . . .

Raisa walked absently to the window. The gardener had gone in now. Tahira was still speaking. Raisa heard the girl's questions and challenges; she was impressed by them. She thought of her own adolescence; she understood Tahira – the pulls on her, the guilt.

And Nasreen. There was nothing so disjointed in her world. Her religion made sense to her; she affirmed the values of home. No doubt there was comfort in that: the model daughter and sister, the happy family. But it couldn't be that smooth. Raisa hurried back to the table and rewound the tape.

Tahira: . . . When you say bismillah, that means we start in the name of God, so something'll come out right.
Nasreen: It gives you confidence, doesn't it?
Tahira: Like when I have to go to Mr Busby. I say bismillah, so I'm not going to be that frightened.
Raisa: It gives you strength?
Tahira: Yeah, it does.
Nasreen: Like God is hearing you and He will help you.
Tahira: But it don't work out all the time, does it? (Nasreen and Tahira laugh) I always say it though. I wouldn't say it in front of nobody at school!
Raisa: You say it at home though?
Tahira: Yeah. My mum gets happy when I do, so I please her. She gets pleased when I say that.
Raisa: Yes, I know!
Tahira: I don't think my mum is strict. My dad died, so I've just got my mum. I've got a cousin in school. Her dad and my dad were brothers. If I wanted to go to a party at night and want my cousin to go as well, *I* could go, my mum'd let *me* go. My cousin would have to ask her dad, my chacha, and then he'd come up to my house and tell me off. If I had no relations in this country, I'd have my hair cut, wear skirts and things like that.
Raisa: Your hair is long because you're not allowed to have it cut?

Tahira: Yeah. I can't have my hair cut. My mum won't let me have my hair cut. If I had my dad right now he'd be really, I mean, really strict. One of my sisters got married when my dad was still alive and she had an arranged marriage and she had to wear things like shalwaar kameez. When my other sister got married, my mother got her a langa, booked a hall for her and a big reception, with lots of guests. But my first sister didn't have that because my dad was strict. Like my dad would've liked us to carry on with school and go to university, but no one wants to do that. I don't want to study. I want to leave, but my mum can't do anything about that. She can't control, my brothers stay out, my mum can't do much about it. One's eighteen years old – the one with an English girlfriend. My mum, what can she do about that? If it was my dad!

Raisa: Why is it that mothers are . . .

Tahira: Mothers can't do much. If my dad was alive, my brothers wouldn't dream of having English girlfriends.

Raisa: So you don't think it's really your mother that keeps you in line?

Tahira: Say my mum said I could stay out late, and say some uncle or relative saw me, they'd go round to my house and say to my mum – your daughter's wandering round the streets – and things like that. They're really good at getting to her. Sometimes my mum don't really mind if I go out, but she worries that other people will see me and come round the house and say things like – your daughter was out and wasn't wearing a dupatta. My mum ain't really strict with me. She don't really think I'm doing bad things or nothing, but it's all the others.

Raisa: That's it, isn't it? All the gossip and things!

Tahira: Yeah. They start talking. If they see you talking to a boy, they go home and phone your mum up.

Raisa: Why does your mum get upset at this? Why can't she tell them to mind their own business?

Tahira: My mother don't feel guilty. It's 'cos we have to live with our relations, and say my mum wants to arrange a marriage for her kid, she can't really answer 'em back. She has to be polite with 'em. I don't think my mum feels guilty. She don't want to hear their talk. (Pause) I bet your mum wouldn't have worried. Rich people don't have to, do they? . . .

*   *   *

Raisa recalled the sideways look that had accompanied Tahira's words. And then she remembered the day the girls had come for lunch. They had been talking about Ayesha and Hind, about the good and bad women of Islam; they had compared stories – some familiar, some not so familiar.

For the past hour, Tahira had hardly spoken or moved from her armchair. Her smiles were gracious; her politeness exaggerated. Raisa offered her profiteroles, Tahira said she'd eaten enough, thank you. She left her chair, suddenly, to look at the shelves of books and the Léger prints on the wall. She asked whether Raisa paid someone to clean the huge windows. And the garden, did she have a gardener?

In the car, as Raisa gave the girls a lift to the station, Nasreen conveyed her mother's message – her mother wanted Raisa to come to dinner, with her family.

Tahira asked if it was true that Raisa lived on her own. Raisa looked ahead and gave a vague answer. She told Nasreen to thank her mother for the invitation; she'd phone and arrange something.

Tahira opened the car door. She said nothing; then smiled, displaying the effort involved.

Raisa said she'd phone their parents when she got back so they'd know when to expect them. Perhaps she'd catch Tahira's mother this time. She'd love to meet her. Tahira said her mother wasn't well. She couldn't really talk to people, you know, get to the phone.

The girl had irritated her.

The tape still running, Raisa stretched, and walked across the room. She thought of her most recent seminar, with its discussion of 'regulation' and 'resistance' and the other useful, but by now unsatisfying, commonplaces of her course. Would those be the themes of her dissertation? She could already see how they applied, in the anger and resignation of Tahira and Nasreen. Real lives would provide the material which her new-learned theories could explore. But not – she blushed with shame at the thought – in any simple way. Somewhere, those lives had to include her own; and she knew that embedded in her life were complexities beyond the reach of the terms of seminar discussion. It would be the same with the two girls.

The tape had come to an end. Raisa looked at her watch, and remembered. Atiyya would be around in an hour with her new friends from college.

Six

They sat eating in the kitchen. Nasreen was the first to finish. She looked up and noted the silence. She opened her mouth to speak, but instead let her fingers trace the pattern on the vinyl table-cloth. Her sisters and brother were lost in their own thoughts.

Her father and mother had gone out for the evening. It was a rare occurrence; they were visiting a relative in Wandsworth. Nasreen imagined their journey across London: the long walk, through streets that were never quite safe, to Barking station, her mother heavy and out of breath, and then the cold wait for the train to Wimbledon. Her father had taken time off work; her mother would make up for lost time when she returned, with her children's help. Mr. Khan's son would call for the blouses the following afternoon.

All the sisters had now eaten; Rezwan was helping himself to more rice. Rehana, the eldest, pinched his cheek just as he swallowed a morsel. She said, 'Babu, you fatty . . .'

'Don't call me that! My name's Rezwan.'

'Hai, hai, listen to him.' She spoke in Punjabi, '*Juldi kur*, finish your food and clear the dishes, it's your turn.' She turned to her youngest sister, 'Samra, it's your turn to wash up.'

'Yes!' she answered. 'Babu, hurry up so I can start. Remember,' she addressed Rehana, 'you've got to help me finish my option form. It's Wednesday tomorrow, Miss wants it in.'

'Yes, yes, all right,' Rehana said. 'It's only seven. Hurry up all of you!'

Samra was annoyed. They should know that choosing exam courses was a serious business. She looked at her brother. She watched him chewing, so painfully slowly. Exasperated, and knowing that she could do it in a fraction of the time that he would take, she started to clear the table herself.

Nasreen got up to leave the kitchen. Everyone was downstairs; she'd have the bedroom to herself.

'Nasreen,' said Rehana. 'I'll join you with the blouses in half an hour. I'll have to stop by nine. Make sure you do the labelling properly this time or Amma'll only have to do it again.'

'I've got to do my homework first. I'll come down at nine and work till about ten-thirty,' said Nasreen.

'Right!' Rehana left the room, slamming the door behind her. She felt burdened. She hadn't even begun her physics essay. How would she ever get the grades to enter the school of medicine?

Upstairs, alone in the bedroom she shared with her two sisters, Nasreen looked at her watch. It was eight-twenty and she had already completed her homework. There were still the three chapters of *Jane Eyre* to be re-read, but there was no urgency to read them that night.

Rehana was busy with the blouses; Samra had joined Rezwan in front of the television; and her parents wouldn't be back until past ten. Nasreen had the room to herself, possibly for a full forty minutes. Behind the drawn curtains and closed door, she would shut out the world.

She sat on the floor, her back against her bed, *Jane Eyre* on her lap, and her feet warming to the old fan heater. Always, this had been the position of relaxation, of chores at least nearly completed. She understood the young Jane Eyre with her hidden window-seat and her imaginings. Ever since childhood, Nasreen had realised the pleasures of daydreaming. Of late, the pastime had become a passion. She sought out the time and silence to concoct the scenes of which she was the subject. An alternative life would unfold over days, over weeks.

She leaned back her head so that it rested on the bed's edge. No one could reprimand her for what she did in her mind: it was its own place, no one could look into it. There, nothing was really forbidden.

'Mr Rodriguez,' she murmured the words.

Mr Rodriguez, the art teacher. There had been stories about him, and his dark-room. People at school talked of his friendliness with the sixth-form girls, with one in particular, an Yvonne. She had long blonde hair. Like the other girls, Nasreen had liked Mr Rodriguez. She wanted him to see beyond her staid uniform. She had wanted him to find her beautiful, irresistible, but in a pure way, not in the way he might like Yvonne Marland.

She hadn't thought about him, or about the mirror, for a long time. She recalled the scene clearly; it was like remembering an event, not an imagining.

Her mother out, the house empty, Nasreen stands in the bathroom. The door is locked. The mirror is there in front of her. Behind her eyes – now being seen, now seeing – stands Mr Rodriguez. Black hair, firm arm, gentle eyes. She sees him. He looks at her: Nasreen and not-Nasreen. Her lips and cheeks are rouged. A large silky scarf is swirled tightly around her slim body – hers, because she feels the quivering in her centre, and not hers, because she isn't an Yvonne. She slides her palms down her sides, pausing by her breasts and moving on to her waist, her hips. For a second, the hands are his, but only for a second, because the ending must be put off; the second of his touch must be erased, and it is. He still looks, from behind her eyes. She wants to tighten into a ball.

Had words been spoken, or whispered, inside her head? Had he, had she, said 'I love you', 'I want you'? Real sound would have been impossible, though no one was there. Clothes, make-up, movement. That was as far as she had dared to travel beyond her secret thoughts, in that silent room.

She walks into Mr Rodriguez's dark-room. Innocently. But the body, tightening into a ball, tightening until she thinks she'll burst, knows. Who is she? Why does she enter? The plot moves on. In the mirror, she enters the dark-room. He sees her and not-her. She lies on her back; holds her father's shaving mirror to her face, to her shoulders and below, and back to her face. This is how she looks lying down. How lustrous her hair looks, dark and loose around her head; how enticingly high cheek-boned she has become! She sits up suddenly, and puts away her father's mirror. The shaving foam smeared in one corner hasn't even dried.

The point of bursting never arrived. Though she possessed the room somewhere in her mind, she never quite saw what lay inside. And yet, in the silence and darkness of her bed, the scene in the mirror was revisited and remade so often.

The bedroom had become uncomfortably hot. Nasreen leaned

forward to switch off the fan heater. *Jane Eyre* had slipped from her lap. She marvelled at the clarity with which she recalled those minutes in the locked bathroom.

Her daydreams had changed since, but her yearnings were constant. Nasreen looked at her watch for the second time in ten minutes. It was only eight-thirty; she still had plenty of time before she worked at the sewing machine. She brought out her thoughts of Zahid, a Muslim and a Pakistani, with Brian Harrington's face and smile and warmth. She saw Brian Harrington every day, but it was Zahid, born and nourished in her mind, whom she knew.

Zahid and Nasreen have been married for nearly a year. Nasreen's parents wanted him as their son-in-law because they knew him to be good and from an excellent family, and because he was clever and successful. Nasreen chose him for all these reasons, and because her parents approved of him – love could not split her from the wholeness that was the family. She chose him too because he loved and wanted her above all else, and because he had Brian's shiny dark hair and watery brown eyes, and Brian's height, strength and gentleness. All the girls, or rather, women – time has passed – liked him. Zahid has a powerful job with a big company. He and Nasreen live in a large, detached house in a private road.

Nasreen thinks, when her parents come to visit, would they feel at ease there with no other musulman nearby? But that wouldn't matter, because she and Zahid would also invite other relatives and friends to stay, the house was large enough. Maybe the English neighbours wouldn't like that, you know what they say – 'these people, living ten to a room'? Again, not a problem, because where Zahid and Nasreen live, the English neighbours are nice and don't think like that. Maybe her parents could come and live with her where it was safer? That meant Zahid's own family would have to be living abroad. Yes, they lived abroad . . .

In Zahid and Nasreen's house, in a special section reserved for Zahid's western friends and business acquaintances, there is a bar, just as they have them in films: golden and red liquids in elegant bottles, sparkling crystal decanters and glasses, wood-panelled walls and thick carpets. Sometimes, Zahid joins his western friends in a drink. Nasreen doesn't approve, of course, but husbands aren't perfect and, as she's heard, it's up to wives to set the example and teach their husbands, quietly . . .

Zahid was her own creation, yet, to Nasreen's mind, he and the life she imagined with him were not impossible, for such a being and such a life did exist in the world. And there had to be something of the possible in her mental dramas. But even as she thought this she understood that the 'not impossible' was unlikely to be, and in many respects should not be, the stuff of her life. She continued, though, to watch and talk with her imaginary lives.

The young husband and wife were always there in Nasreen's present imaginings, a shimmering backdrop to her thought. She would occasionally summon forward particular scenes to occupy her whole mind. There was no narrative chain that connected the episodes of Nasreen's drama. Individual scenes leapt out vividly from a hazy background in which circumstances and explanations were hardly defined. To one such scene, Nasreen, with intense pleasure and concentration, returned again and again.

The car stops outside the house. They've returned from an important dinner party. Zahid taps Nasreen's elbow. She opens her eyes and smiles.

'Nasreen! Nasreen!' She heard her elder sister's voice, and then her footsteps. Nasreen quickly picked up a book.

'Nasreen, are you deaf or what?' Rehana came into the room. 'I've been calling you!'

'Oh, I was miles away. Sorry. Nothing's wrong, is it?' She became worried.

'You cleared up the kitchen cupboard; where did you put the bulbs? The light in Amma's room's gone out. Tell me quick, will you. Amma and Abba'll be here soon, the work won't get done, and Amma'll be too tired after the trains.'

Nasreen saw the strained look on her sister's face; she didn't look well. Nasreen thought of her parents' lonely walk home from the station.

'I know where I put the bulb. I'll go find it and fix the light.' Nasreen felt the pain of love, and guilt. 'You might as well leave the sewing now,' she continued. 'It's already gone ten to nine. I'll start as soon as the light's fixed.'

'All right then.' Rehana smiled. Nasreen sensed her tearfulness.

She sat on the sheet covering the carpet. She picked up the last of the sewn blouses and checked it carefully. Mistakes meant loss of pay.

Then she organised herself around the sewing machine and set to work on the unsewn garments. Twenty minutes passed. Her back and shoulder began to feel the strain. The room became oppressive. She was amazed that her mother was able to work for much longer stretches of time, even as she complained of cramps and aches. She moved her neck from side to side; she yawned and rubbed her eyes. She returned, irresistibly, to Zahid and Nasreen.

She's wearing a black chiffon sari, close-fitting and elegant. She's beautiful. He's handsome. There's a casual air about his dinner suit and cashmere scarf. They've returned from a dinner party.

She steps out of the car. He has opened the door for her. She's pleasantly dizzy and unsure of step. She takes Zahid's arm but falters still. He props her up by her waist. She laughs and insists she can walk alone to the door. He moves aside and smiles. She turns to him, suddenly and imperiously. Her words slide into one another as she orders him to put away the car. He stands leaning against its shiny body; his arms are folded. He looks amused, but is ready to catch her, should she fall.

Briefly, Nasreen paused to consider how the woman in her head had come to be drunk, and why Zahid wasn't incensed by the sinful lapse. She must have sipped the wine unknowingly. Was that possible? Perhaps she drank the wine to stop her husband from taking alcohol, however occasionally. 'If you can drink, so can I,' she'd say to shock him into abstinence. She started to weigh the plausibility of such motivations, but the lure of the plot was too great.

Nasreen has reached the door. She fumbles for the keys in her clutch bag. The search is soon abandoned, and instead, she yawns luxuriously. Then she closes her eyes, and with her back against the door, she slides down until she's seated on the doorstep. Zahid returns from the garage. Softly, he places his thumb and finger on her chin and lifts up her face. Her mouth forms a smile, wide and soft. The love in his eyes warms her. She stretches out her arms to him. He draws her to him. The door has opened; he carries her in. The door closes.

Nasreen watched the door close and, back in her parents' bedroom, she saw the bulk of flimsy material that had yet to be worked into finished garments. She'd have to concentrate on the sewing and leave Zahid and Nasreen until all were asleep. This time, she promised herself, she'd go beyond the closed door, to the drama she always anticipated but hadn't yet entered. Then she thought of her father, and of her mother, and of the collector who'd be there the next morning. Carefully manoeuvring the cloth through the whirring machine, Nasreen vowed not to stop until she had completed at least three blouses.

Seven

That Saturday afternoon Nasreen's father had stayed in especially to meet Raisa Ahmed, the researcher from the university. After the proper introductions and enquiries, he left Raisa to his wife and daughters.

The gold and onyx centre table was laden with sweets and biscuits. Wearing her Jaeger jacket and trousers – a present from her aunt – Raisa sat next to Mrs Ehsan. Both were drinking hot tea, stewed in the pan, the desi way. She hadn't sipped that aromatic tea since 1979, when she and her sister had visited Lahore. In its scent and sweetness lay memories of childhood.

She had known Nasreen's mother only an hour, and the woman was sitting close to her, almost touching. There was a softness between them. It was as if Raisa had known her all her life. Her physical nearness, her smile, the way her children moved around her, conjured up images of her own mother, though Raisa knew those images masked so many other realities. Still, the woman communicated a mother's warmth, and Raisa knew her. Sitting with her in a terraced house in a crowded street in Barking, she was being returned to the blue room in Gulberg.

'It gives me such happiness to see one of our own daughters doing well in this country.' Mrs Ehsan spoke in Urdu, but with the sounds of a Punjabi speaker. Even Raisa, whose knowledge of both languages was rusty, was able to recognise that she wasn't comfortable in the language.

'That's very kind of you to say so,' Raisa replied in Urdu. Then in English she continued, 'But I think you're exaggerating my success.' The woman seemed not to understand. She had exposed Mrs

Ehsan's uncertain English. Raisa resolved to return to Urdu.

'Look, I've lived in this country for more than twenty years, and I still can't speak the language!' Mrs Ehsan said.

'Well,' Raisa replied, 'my Urdu isn't good, the language of my parents!'

'That's not surprising – you live here, you study in English, and you're doing well,' she said. 'Don't worry about the Urdu. You can speak Urdu and English. I'll understand, even if I don't speak English.'

Rehana said, 'Or we can translate.'

They all laughed. Nasreen offered mithai to Raisa. Her mother said, 'Go and make fresh tea.'

'Oh, no, no. This is fine, thank you,' Raisa said. Nasreen left for the kitchen anyway.

'You don't speak Punjabi?' Mrs Ehsan asked.

'Yes, I do, but not very well. As children we spoke Urdu and English, but people around us spoke Punjabi.' She remembered Sarwar, her grandfather's driver, and the servants. She said, 'I can understand it. Please speak in Punjabi. It'll be good practice for me. It's a beautiful language. My mother and aunts used to speak to each other in Punjabi.'

'But not to the children, I know.' Mrs Ehsan switched to Punjabi.

Nasreen came in with a fresh pot of tea. She filled Raisa's cup, then her mother's, her sister's and her own.

'Look at her. Can you imagine, this girl, when she's got even five minutes to herself, locks herself away. I tell her, studying is good, but she mustn't ruin her eyes. Rehana's done her A levels.'

Rehana, smiling, corrected her, 'They were O levels. I'm doing my A levels now, Amma-jaan.'

'Yes, yes, O levels. I tell her, Rehana's passed her O levels, but she didn't lock herself away all the time.

Nasreen looked down at the crumbs on the carpet. She didn't speak. She could, without offending or overstepping good manners, go up to her room, until called. But she did not want to leave. She wanted to hear the conversation, and watch Raisa.

Passing Raisa a ludoo, Mrs Ehsan said, 'You must have studied hard as a child?'

'Well, yes, I suppose so.' The one spoke in Punjabi, the other answered in Urdu.

'Your family, they have settled here? You studied in England, of course?' she asked.

'Yes,' Raisa smiled. The enquiries had started once again. She wanted the Ehsans to approve of her, to accept her as one of their own. And so there were details of her life that she did not want to divulge.

'Nasreen has told us your father is a barrister here.'

Raisa, in one of their conversations, had mentioned it to the girls. She said, 'He used to practise. Now he's a legal adviser.'

'You must be from a good family. You have sisters, what do they do?' Mrs Ehsan spoke in Urdu.

'I have a younger sister. She's studying law,' Raisa said.

'Yes, you are from a good family. From Lahore?' She returned to Punjabi.

Raisa, still speaking Urdu, said, 'Well, branches of my father's family are based all over Pakistan – in Karachi, Islamabad, Lahore.'

Mrs Ehsan asked, 'And your mother's people?'

Raisa became nervous. She did not want to say the wrong thing. She said, 'My mother's family live in Lahore.'

'Whereabouts?' Nasreen, as always, spoke to Raisa in English, 'My mum's uncle lives in Lahore.'

'Oh, around the Jinnah gardens,' said Raisa, 'my grandfather's house is around there.'

'Yes,' Mrs Ehsan said, 'you are from a good family. The houses near the Jinnah gardens are like palaces, just like palaces.'

Raisa relished the woman's praise, even though it embarrassed her, sitting there in that cramped living-room. 'My mother's grand-father was not a rich man,' she said. 'We have lots of relations in Kasur, God-fearing, hard-working, and still poor.'

'Your mother's grandfather, your great-grandfather was a good man, and he worked hard, and his family after him have done well. I work hard, their father works hard, and that's what I tell my children – work hard, don't forget who you are, and you'll get the best in this world.' And then, quietly, as if speaking from a distance, she said, 'But life is still very hard.'

Rehana and Nasreen sat quietly while their mother talked to Raisa.

'My family are from a village in the Punjab, near Gujranwala,' she said.

'Yes, I know Gujranwala,' Raisa interrupted, 'it was there we had the best kutlamai I've ever tasted. We drove through it on our way to Lahore, from Islamabad, in 1979.' Raisa spoke as if the two had discovered a mutual friend.

Mrs Ehsan continued, 'In our village, like his father before him, my father worked on his piece of land rented from the zamindar. To live like that, it was too difficult.'

'It was the same for my relations. Yes, I remember life in Kasur,' Raisa lied. She had never been to Kasur, and she had only occasionally met those Kasuri relatives, who had settled in Leyton. Her desire to be included was strong.

'Zamindars are always greedy, you know,' Mrs Ehsan said. 'But, if you think about it, if we were zamindars, we'd be like that too. It's the way money is made, isn't it?'

'Did you leave your village and come to England?'

'Oh no, no. I was only a girl then. It was a long time ago, thirty years. Is this what you want for your university work?'

'Once she starts talking about the old days, there's no stopping her!' said Nasreen.

'It's really interesting though. We love hearing about those days in Pakistan,' added Rehana.

'Yes, I know. The past has always held a fascination for me too.' Raisa had not switched to English. 'Please, go on. It doesn't really matter whether it's useful for the research or not.'

Mrs Ehsan was proud of her knowledge. 'Around the late fifties, or maybe 1960 – yes, around that time, Ayub was in power – my father, mother, brothers, all of us left the village and made our way to Lahore. We had heard there was more chance of finding work in Lahore. All types of factories were springing up there. But that wasn't why we left. Ayub had promised help to people like my father. Instead, the zamindar pushed us off the land and put his own relatives in charge of working it, all because Ayub said if zamindars weren't going to work their own farms, they wouldn't be allowed to own them. So what they did, they got rid of some of the poorer tenants, and took over the land for their own families. All of Ayub's promises and good words didn't help us. My father had no rights over the land he rented.'

'This happened during Ayub Khan's years as president?' Raisa enquired.

'Yes,' Mrs Ehsan said. 'And to think of all the problems we had after partition. To think we suffered through all that, only to lose everything.'

Rehana said in Punjabi, 'Nana and Mama Ashraf and Mama Abid didn't go straight to Lahore, did they?'

'No, we didn't just go. Your Nana and uncles didn't have any land, so they worked for money, to stay there. So many did.'

Nasreen asked, 'Nani didn't work, did she? Women didn't, did they?'

'Women worked as they've always worked – they helped the men, they worked to keep their families together. The men earned the money, the workers were men.'

Raisa said, 'The ordinary people of the world, women and men, didn't get it easy!'

'No, that's very true.' She returned to the past, 'Life was difficult, unless you were rich, from one of the rich families. When the English left, that's what it was like: there were the rich families, and the poor. But that's the way life is, isn't it, even in this modern country?'

'So, you settled in Lahore, and became Lahoris like my family,' said Raisa, helping herself to a ludoo. Mrs Ehsan nudged Nasreen to assist her guest, and continued, 'Yes, we did leave for Lahore. People from our village had already left, some for Pindi, some for Karachi. But we had people from our baraadri already in Lahore; they helped us. My future husband's father, who was also my mother's cousin, worked for a jeweller in those days. He learned everything about making jewellery. He saved his money and he's now a good jeweller, and rich.'

Nasreen added, 'He must've worked very hard, because in those days it was very difficult to do things.'

'Yes, in those old days especially, life was very hard.' Mrs Ehsan sat back and absently adjusted a bra strap. 'It wasn't easy to find work. There were so many people ready to work, and the wages got lower and lower. My older brothers, my father, took all types of work – from day to day, whenever they could find it. My father,' she stopped to cough, 'my father, he was a good man, a haji. He made sure that we received education and a better chance in life.'

Nasreen said, 'One of my uncles is a lecturer now at the university in Lahore.'

Raisa asked, 'So when did you come to England?'

'Oh, in 1966. Their father was already in England. He came here with his two older brothers in 1959 or 1960. Do you know, their father studied engineering at London University! But only for a year. He couldn't work and study, and he had to work to live.'

'Yes, I know,' Raisa said.

'I married him in Lahore in 1966. Then he brought me here to his home.'

'And you've been here since?'

'Yes,' Mrs Ehsan answered, 'and you always think, one day we'll go back, when we have enough money, to make our life out there. But here I am, with my children, who, *Inshallah*,' she stood up and passed a hand over both their heads, 'who, *Inshallah*, will lead good, successful lives.'

'*Inshallah*,' repeated Raisa, 'but, as we know, life is hard in England as well.'

'For some, it's very hard,' Rehana said.

Raisa wondered whether the girl was aiming a specific anger at her. But there was no malice in Rehana's gaze or smile.

'My mother's cousin,' said Raisa, knowing that the relationship was much more distant than that, 'the cousin from Kasur, who has settled in Leyton, he and his family live hand to mouth, in shocking conditions.'

'And they're from your family!' Mrs Ehsan marvelled at the quirks of fortune. 'Yes, it's like us,' she continued. 'My father-in-law is a famous jeweller in Lahore, my brother is a professor at the university. I'm an FA pass.' Raisa felt embarrassed. Mrs Ehsan hadn't finished. 'My husband went to London University, Beer-beck College . . .'

'Birkbeck, Amma-jaan,' Rehana said.

'Yes, yes, Burrbeck College. He went there, but he had to leave and work as a bus conductor.'

'There's no shame in that,' Raisa said.

'But what about the long night work, the drunken men, with their 'paki' this and 'paki' that? What about the little money?' She spoke passionately.

Rehana said, 'My father will lose his job soon because he's over forty and because of the driver-only buses.'

Nasreen was listening silently and intently.

Mrs Ehsan, smiling again, said, 'You are going to put all that in your research?'

45

Raisa laughed, 'Oh yes, and solve life's injustices!'

'Life is full of problems,' Mrs Ehsan breathed deeply. 'But that's our test on earth, isn't it?'

'Amma-jaan,' Rehana lowered her voice to her mother, 'I'll start the work now.' Speaking Punjabi, she appeared older to Raisa, and Raisa felt excluded by her.

Her mother smiled apologetically at Raisa. She explained, 'You must forgive my daughter, but work makes us forget our manners.'

Rehana blushed. 'Oh it's not that, but my mum has got to . . .' She stopped and looked at her mother, uncertainly.

Raisa said, 'Please, don't worry at all, there are no bad manners.'

Mrs Ehsan said, 'I work from home. You know how it is, bills and things have to be paid.'

'Yes,' said Raisa. She thought she saw Rehana looking at her Enny handbag.

Rehana said, 'My mum sews clothes. Mr Khan's son'll be around at six to collect them. She's had to work twice as hard this week. Mr Khan's got to have the right number of blouses by the end of today.'

Mrs Ehsan said, 'Yes, if we don't work fast, the store won't give him another order, and if he doesn't get orders, we don't get the work.'

Nasreen spoke, 'It's really hard work though. All this week, she's even had to work through the night.'

'What are you saying?' Her mother answered, 'It isn't as bad as that . . .'

'But it is really,' Nasreen persisted.

A look passed between mother and daughter, and the daughter kept quiet. Suffering is shameful, Raisa thought, and so we hide our suffering.

Mrs Ehsan said, 'Mr Khan works very hard, and his sons. Salma Khan, his wife, goes every day to their factory in Whitechapel. She works like the other women, on the machines.'

Nasreen said, 'They've moved into a big house on Longbridge Road.'

'Yes, that's true,' the mother conceded. 'They're having a big milad sharif next week. We've all been invited. No one can deny that they've worked hard and saved every penny. They used to live in the poorest part of Whitechapel. I've heard they have lots of money to pay back.'

'Yes, but paying you 25p for a blouse!' Nasreen said. 'In the big stores they sell them for twenty, twenty-five pounds each.'

'Meri-jaan, the big stores make much more money than he does. And that's the way things are, that's how money is made.' Mrs Ehsan laughed, as if to say 'How naïve the young are'. She said to Raisa, 'Mr Khan is helping me by giving me work at home. Who will look after this home if I go to work outside? My small son has to be taken to school and my English – well, you know.'

Raisa said, 'Lots of people learn English by working outside, and there must be classes you could attend.'

'No. I know where I am at home. And it's not easy outside. There are lots of problems – my friends tell me,' she replied. 'And do you know, the Khans are our friends and I don't have to pay tax or tell the council that I work from home. They can stop you using your houses, can't they?'

Raisa said, 'But if you don't pay tax it means you're invisible as a worker. No one will help you get better pay or fight if you lose your job.'

Mrs Ehsan said, 'Who will help me anyway? Who's helping my husband?'

Raisa said, 'If you're hidden, you haven't a chance of fighting and helping yourself.'

Mrs Ehsan turned to her daughters, laughing. 'She wants me to be like your dadi-ma.'

Rehana explained, 'My father's mother felt strongly about the English ruling India, and about the Muslims having an Islamic country. She used to go out on demonstrations with lots of other girls and women and once she had to spend a night in prison. She was on the demonstration where one of the girls climbed up on to the roof of the government building and pulled down the British flag.'

Raisa said, 'Oh I know about that, my mother told me. Didn't the girl put up her dupatta instead of the union jack?'

'Yes,' Rehana answered.

Mrs Ehsan said, 'Their dadi-ma was a brave woman.'

Raisa was about to speak, but Rehana stood up and asked, 'Can I make you some tea before I start the sewing?'

'Oh goodness, no. I think I've taken too much of your time already.' Raisa repeated in Urdu, 'I've taken too much of your time. Anyway, I have to be getting home soon.'

Mrs Ehsan wouldn't hear of it. 'No, no, no. What are you saying? It's such a joy to meet you, a girl like my own daughters.'

Rehana left the room quietly.

'No,' Mrs Ehsan said, 'the work will take care of itself. It will get done because it has to be.' She leaned back on the sofa, but with her heaviness found it uncomfortable, and sat forward again.

'You're not eating.' She moved the plate of sweets in front of her guest. 'You must stay for dinner.'

Raisa moved to speak.

'You must,' said Mrs Ehsan. 'You have come to our house, how can I let you leave without eating?'

The mother and daughters were sparing no effort in making her feel welcome, and yet the work for Mr Khan had still to be done. Raisa felt uncomfortable. Without the research, she would not be in that house in Barking. She said, 'It's kind of you to welcome me so warmly, and you hardly know me . . .'

'What do you mean, "know me"? You are like my daughter,' said Mrs Ehsan.

'Yes. Thank you.' Raisa was moved by the woman's words, and again, she thought of her own mother. She cleared her throat and continued, 'It's so kind of you to ask me, but I know you have work to do and I . . .'

'You must stay! It's no problem.' Mrs Ehsan was forceful. 'Nasreen,' she said, 'start the cooking.'

'No, really,' Raisa answered. 'We can arrange it for another time, at my house. You see,' Raisa lied, 'I've got to be home by four. My father's having some guests, relatives, and there won't be a female at home to receive them – my sister is visiting an aunt.'

'Your mother's away too?' asked Mrs Ehsan.

There was the slightest of breaks in the conversation. Raisa said, 'Yes. I mean, my mother died some years ago.' She laughed nervously. 'It's difficult, even now, to talk about it.'

Mrs Ehsan murmured a prayer. She did not pursue the subject. She said, 'All right, you go now, but you, and your father and sister, must come with us to the Khans' milad sharif.'

'But I haven't even met Mr and Mrs Khan,' answered Raisa.

'*Baitee*, you'll be with us, and it *is* a milad sharif,' said Mrs Ehsan. Raisa was again embarrassed. Mrs Ehsan must have noted her ignorance.

'Yes, that's final. It's next Sunday,' the woman said, and to make the invitation irresistible, she added, 'there will be many musulman there. You can talk to them, you know, for your research.'

Raisa asked, 'Will Tahira's family be there? Her mother?'

Mrs Ehsan said, 'Well, we don't really meet and the Khans don't know them very well. You see, the Khans are a different type of people, Mr Khan comes from a good family. He has a degree from London University.'

'It doesn't matter, of course,' said Raisa, 'I'd love to come. It's just that, I mean, I thought you knew Tahira's family well.'

Nasreen said, 'We used to meet more years ago, when I was in infants with Tahira.' She addressed her mother, 'Didn't you and abba-jaan know them well when you were all new in this country?'

'You *used* to be friends?' Raisa asked.

'In those days we used to meet, but, you know how it is.'

'Yes, people drift apart. It happens.'

Mrs Ehsan continued, 'I know Nargis, Tahira's mother, has had a hard time with her husband and his family, but she should make sure her children remember their mashriqi ways. She should keep them under control. It's difficult without a husband, I know, but what are her children learning? You hear all sorts of stories about them. I've seen, with my own eyes, her daughter laughing and shouting in the street. Maybe they have all become English now, the children *and* Nargis.'

'All right, Amma-jaan,' Nasreen interrupted.

Mrs Ehsan seemed not to have heard. She said, 'Our families don't meet anymore. People change.'

Raisa nodded in agreement.

Eight

The large, musty cupboard and the two beds left little room for movement. The clashing prints on the walls, and the curtains, and the carpets, made the room look smaller. Tahira rushed in and covered her dishevelled bed. She caught her breath, then gathered the strewn items of clothing and threw them into the bottom of the cupboard. A minute later, her cousin walked in, holding two mugs of tea and her bag of clothes.

'I can still smell the damp, you know. You should get it treated properly, not just cover it up,' said Mumtaz. She sat on the bed by the window.

'I reckon I've done a good job with the paper, thank you very much!' Tahira swallowed some tea. 'Anyway, shut up about the damp – we've got to be out of the house in an hour. Ashraf'll be back by then.'

'I thought he got himself a job,' said Mumtaz in Punjabi.

'He did, but it only lasted three weeks. Mama Abbas finished doing up that Sikh's house and he can't keep Ashraf till he gets another place to do,' Tahira replied, also in Punjabi.

'Why don't you get your mama to fix your damp? He wouldn't ask for much.'

'Yeah, but it'd still cost. Anyway, Amma's saving up to go to Pakistan. She wants to see her mum – reckons she'll die soon. I hope not.'

Mumtaz stood in front of the cupboard, looking at her image in the tarnished mirror. 'Don't you think these dhoti shalwaars are great?' She held the garment to her body.

'Yeah, they're OK, though I don't fancy wearing them down the street,' Tahira answered.

'You're mad. The posh boutiques have clothes like these – you look in some of them magazines. Anyway, lots of girls at the college wear them now, and all them girls down Solly.'

'That's different, ain't it?' Tahira said.

Mumtaz picked up a photograph of her late uncle, with his wife and children. The two married sisters and the two brothers stood on either side of their parents; Tahira and her sister Munty sat at their feet. They all looked so smart, and happy; and the luxurious back-drop didn't for a minute resemble the cheap nylon curtain that it really was. Her father had taken the photograph; he was clever with the camera. They had sent a copy to Pakistan and Mumtaz had seen it there.

Mumtaz said, 'Wonder if this bhungra disco's like the one they showed on that telly programme?'

Tahira was busy taking out a small suitcase from under her bed. She said, 'Shut up and get ready, will ya? We've got to hurry.'

Mumtaz seemed not to have heard. 'It's great having a disco during the day, ain't it? Don't have to make no excuses to go out in the evening.' Then she said, 'You're right about hurrying up. I don't want to bump into Ashraf right now. God, he's a right old drag! Don't know what that English girl sees in him.'

Tahira laughed, 'Ah, poor little Mumtaz. Might have to marry that boring old fart.'

'Shut your mouth! You can talk. You'll end up with Sakib, Amma's ladala. And he's a bigger boring old fart!'

Tahira said, 'He'd have a heart attack if he knew we was going to a disco, and on our own.'

Both girls fell back on the bed, shrieking with laughter. Tahira stopped laughing. 'Look, you stupid cow, you've spilt your tea over Munty's bed. She'll go mad. Now get up, we've got to get ready.'

Mumtaz stood up to draw the curtains. Looking out over the worn roof-tops and the uneven back gardens, she said, 'Come on then, let's get ready. You can tell me about Tanni's party and what's his name.'

'No,' Tahira said, 'I'll save it till after the disco.'

'When did you last see him then?'

'Last Saturday.'

'What's he look like?'

'No. You can meet him first and tell me what you think.'

Mumtaz gave up. She asked, 'Is Tanni coming today?'

'No, she only bunks off now and then. She ain't like us, I mean, like me.'

'Ain't it funny,' said Mumtaz, 'I only met her that one time at the college, and it's like I really know her? Do you talk to her about me?'

'No,' answered Tahira. 'I don't see her that much, you know.'

Tahira and Mumtaz walked quickly along the road, alert to women in desi dress and men with desi faces. They had their excuses ready for any friend or relative: 'We're out on a geography assignment.' They hoped their made-up faces and their spray-tinted hair would not be noted.

They reached the end of the road and stopped. Mumtaz's shoes were new and ill-fitting; she had to rest. She leaned against the wall and adjusted a shoe strap.

'Up your arses!' said Tahira.

'What?'

'"SMASH THE RACE ACT! NF",' Tahira read the graffiti.

'Oh that! Right, that's better.' Her feet eased, the two walked on. The early afternoon traffic had started to collect in East Street.

'Walk quicker. I want to get to Ilford and change these stupid trousers,' said Tahira, a little out of breath. 'Bet my skirt's getting all creased up in the stupid bag . . .'

She saw that she was walking alone. Mumtaz had stopped by an Our Price record shop. Tahira walked back.

'Bloody hurry up, will ya!'

'Do you think she's pretty?' Mumtaz asked, pouting her lips like the Madonna of the huge poster.

Tahira looked around for familiar, prying eyes. She said. 'Yeah, she's pretty. Looks a bit cheap though.'

'Sakib has a poster of her in his bedroom.'

Tahira tried to imagine Mumtaz's brother in his bedroom. 'Millions of blokes have posters of her,' she said. 'Don't mean Sakib'd marry her.'

'Madonna wouldn't care, would she? She's famous, and rich, and she don't have to marry.'

Tahira said, 'Anyway, all blokes don't think like Sakib.' Then she added, 'I ain't sure, you know, that Sakib wouldn't want to marry her – if he could.'

Mumtaz was still looking at the poster.

'Wouldn't it be perfect if you could be sexy like Madonna, and not be cheap?' Tahira thought of Raisa.

'Yeah, and be rich!' said her cousin.

Tahira took her arm, and together they laughed and walked towards the bus stop that lay at the end of the road.

Mumtaz was the first to notice the car. A dented Ford Escort, 'R' registration, had started to cruise alongside them. 'Hurry up, Tahira. Those four blokes in that car, they're looking at us.'

Tahira turned to look at the car. 'What's that filthy pig doing with his tongue?'

'Come on, don't look at them. Quick, let's go into that shop.' Mumtaz pulled at her.

'No, I ain't going into no bloody shop!' she shouted, and, raging, she gestured back with two fingers.

'Dirty Paki slags,' the man's voice lashed out.

The car drove off. Tahira screamed. 'White trash, pig, bastards! Hope your car blows up! Dirty, dirty, filthy bastards!'

Mumtaz continued to pull at her. 'Run, come on,' she said. 'If they heard you, they might come back.'

'They've spoilt it. We're going out, I was looking forward to today, I got dressed up. They've spoilt it.' Her eyes filled with tears.

'Don't cry, Tahira. Your make-up'll smudge.' Mumtaz tried to make light of it.

'They're bastards, bastards! It's like Jam and them girls, ain't it?' Tahira wouldn't let go.

'So what if it is? You know they're what they are, and they'll get punished for it.' Mumtaz wanted to comfort her cousin, and herself. 'Worse things can happen. What about that plane crash?'

'But that don't make it right. It ain't right!'

'Are we gonna go to this disco or not?' Mumtaz asked. 'The way you're carrying on, we might as well not go.' She looked at Tahira, and in a parody of an Indian accent said, 'Au ddarrling, lett uss gau tto the partty andd meett aul the heerroes!'

'You sound so sexy when you talk like that, Mumtaz.'

'Yeah, I know. Can't wait to see your friend. You worried he might fancy me?'

'Don't make me laugh – with me there, you got no chance.'

Nine

The people in the street thought that it might be a religious festival, some sort of coming of age, perhaps.

The youth of Asia were arriving in large numbers, but there was no queue outside the old cinema house. Just as well, thought Mumtaz, someone was bound to see that most of them were school kids; some were still in uniform. Tahira walked in ahead of her cousin.

Inside the main entrance, the rose-coloured electric lighting hid the disrepair of the building, but not completely. The fraying carpets, the fading walls, were still visible; and the air fresheners couldn't mask the pungent smell of age and neglect.

Michael Jackson blared above the sound of voices.

'All right?' Two girls and a boy greeted them.

Tahira asked, 'Seen anyone else from school?'

'Nah,' said one of the girls. 'Most of them'll come after lunch.'

'Right,' said Tahira. 'We're going to the loo. See you later.'

A line of girls, clutching bags of party make-up and clothing waited outside the toilets. A few would go in as others came out, magically transformed.

Their hair came in long shiny tresses; in chignons decorated with flowers; in corkscrew permed bobs. A few boasted near-shaven crops. There were chunky gold-plated ear-rings and Anarkali glass bangles. There was flamboyant stage make-up, kajal-eyed make-up, understated make-up and no make-up. They wore mini skirts with thick dance tights; shalwaar kameez of various styles, in denim, in lamé, in PVC; and trousers that were tight or baggy, long or short, classically cut or ripped at the thighs and knees. They squashed their uniforms in bags and left them in the cloakroom.

Clusters of boys waited nearby – Michael Jacksons and Govindas, and some Asian skinheads. Some were chatting and looking around, before they walked into the dance hall. Others were waiting for their girlfriends.

The two cousins left the cloakroom.

'Well where is he? Can you see him?' Mumtaz asked. She held on to Tahira's elbow; there were so many people around them.

'No. I told you, he won't be here till later. His half day don't finish till one and then he's got to drive here all the way from Stratford,' said Tahira.

'Has he got a car?'

'No. It's his dad's – he sleeps in the day and don't use it, see. His dad works nights even though it is his own bakery,' said Tahira. 'They make nans and kulchai and stuff.'

'God, Arif – is that his name?'

'Yeah.'

'God, he must like you, coming specially with his dad's car,' said Mumtaz. 'It's already quarter to twelve, you know.'

'Come on then.' Tahira took out their tickets. 'We better go in.'

The girls meandered through the crowd.

'Look, there's Jayesh, the bloke collecting the tickets. Remember him?' Tahira made her way to the door of the dance hall, Mumtaz following close behind.

'He was in the sixth year last year, weren't he?' Mumtaz asked. Tahira was already at the door. She gave her tickets to the lanky boy in the hat.

'Right, Tahira! How's it going?' He saw Mumtaz. 'You're her cousin, right? Your brother was in my class.'

Mumtaz smiled. 'Watcha,' she said.

Jayesh directed his talk more to Tahira. 'It's great you all came.'

Then he turned to the brawny youth next to him, and with the authority of a proprietor, told him to collect the tickets.

'Can I get you something to drink?' He led the girls to the bar area. They asked for cokes.

'Nothing stronger? Ah, you're good little girls, right?'

'That's right,' answered Tahira, noting the close dancing of one or two couples.

'Then how come you're not at school?'

Mumtaz answered, ' 'Cos we ain't boring like all them others, that's how.'

'School ain't my scene. Exams and all that shit ain't gonna get me what I want.' He gestured to the barman for attention. The man was still busy. Jayesh leaned against the bar, and continued talking. 'I reckon in a year or so I'll be earning more in a week than my dad did in six months. It's sad, man, I mean for my dad, but it's his fault for taking all the shit.' The barman took their orders.

Mumtaz asked, 'You didn't organise this disco, did you?'

'I've had a lot to do with it. It's only a start,' he said, 'I'm thinking big, man. You know, we got the band cheap, and look at all the kids who're coming in.' He pulled at his jacket, and shirt. 'Pure cashmere, pure silk.'

'Yeah, all right, all right,' said Tahira. 'But it ain't just the band that's got everyone here.'

Drink in hand, Tahira moved towards the dance hall, apparently enticed by the jumping colours of the disco lights.

'Hey Tahira,' Jayesh moved nearer, 'tell your uncle I might be putting some business his way. This Indian guy wants an extension built.'

'Yeah, all right. Tell Gita when you know.'

A tall man with two others behind him walked towards them. Mumtaz thought, this must be Arif, he's good looking. The man said to her, 'Hello, I'm Anwar. I hope you're enjoying yourself.' His eyes sought Jayesh; his words still addressed the girls. 'We're thinking of making this a weekly disco. Tell your friends about it.' The man walked away, Jayesh following behind at his silent command.

'What a prat!' said Tahira.

'I thought he was nice,' said Mumtaz.

'God, you've got to be joking. He was a prat!' She looked at her watch.

Mumtaz said, 'Did Arif say what time he'd be here?'

'Oh bloody hell, do you have to keep going on about it? He'll come when he comes, and if he don't, then that's his problem!'

Mumtaz felt slapped. She left the subject. A table had cleared a few yards ahead.

Tahira said, 'Come on, I told Gita I'd save her a place if I got here first.'

The two pushed their way towards the table, only to be stopped by loud whistles and calls.

'Hey, over here! Tahira, Mumtaz, over here! We've got you seats.' Gita was calling them over to a large group of boys and girls who had placed three tables together.

Most of the boys were from the college. Tahira recognised them. Two had been in the fifth year the year before, and the others moved in the same crowd as her brother, Hussain.

'Tahira, we ain't seen you in the refectory for some time. What's the matter?' one of the boys asked.

'I got better things to do than spend all my time there, ain't I?' she answered.

'Hey, but Tahira, we really miss you, you know what I mean, yaar,' said Imran, winking at the others as he drank his lager.

'Piss off! We go there visiting our mates, girls, that is,' she said, 'so don't go getting no ideas, right?'

'That's not what we heard,' Imran persisted.

'Well you heard wrong then, didn't you?' Gita jumped in.

Imran grinned at his friend and said, 'Don't worry, we don't care, we won't tell.'

'Get lost!' Tahira turned away to face Gita. She touched her friend's leather mini-skirt. 'Looks good, and your spiky hair-cut.'

'We heard about Jamshid and those girls. That was bad,' said Suleiman. Tahira had always been impressed by his seriousness. He continued, 'Those gorrai are still hassling him.'

'Yeah, and the school don't do nothing,' Tahira said. 'They say Jamshid shouldn't have called that girl a prostitute, but they ain't really listening to what them girls said to him first.'

Gita added, 'And the teachers don't do nothing when the English boys call girls slags. Makes you sick!'

Tahira said, 'Hussain told me Jam's carrying a knife now, in case the Ames' dad and uncles come for him. It's bad, someone could get hurt, and if Jam gets caught with the knife, I mean, he's already always in trouble these days.'

'When you get down to it, this ain't our country, yaar,' said Imran.

Suleiman put down his coke. 'It bloody is,' he answered. 'We pay our taxes, we do the jobs the gorrai don't want, and you say it ain't our country!'

'The English ain't gonna let it be our country,' said Imran. 'An

English girlfriend is making you soft in the head.'

Suleiman didn't correct Imran and tell him that Norah was Irish. He spoke slowly, 'What're you saying?'

'Hey, cool it! I wasn't saying nothing against your friend.'

The moment passed. Hussain, Najum and Ijaz arrived carrying two drinks apiece.

'Oh, so you're here,' Hussain addressed his sister.

'So bloody what? You're here an' all,' replied Tahira. 'What time did you get here?'

'Just now. We saw you all and brought some drinks. Here, you two,' he spoke to his cousin and sister, 'take the cokes, if you want.'

'Looking after your sisters, are ya?' said Gita. 'Mustn't have them drinking bad stuff, eh?'

The boys sat down. Ijaz asked, 'Who wrote "Barking Badmaash" on the wall outside? The manager's really angry, man. It was one of you, weren't it?'

'Why do you say that, yaar? We ain't written on no walls today – we've been together all the time.' Imran lit a cigarette and threw the packet to the others.

Hussain said, 'Well, it's probably the guy who first writ it on the wall in the park.'

Imran mused to himself, 'Great name! Suits us fine.'

'I wonder who that was,' said Suleiman, answering Hussain. 'Was it someone from your school?'

Tahira answered, 'Dunno. I reckon it was some little old lady.' Everyone laughed.

The English music suddenly stopped. An electric-loud voice came through the speakers: 'Hello y'all! This is the Cool Dude from Southall. Now for the R.E.A.L. music. Let's dance.'

The cheers, whistles, screams became deafening.

'Everyone up!' the voice spoke on, 'Don't want no one sitting down, NO ONE!'

The drummy beats of the bhungra filled the hall. Tahira felt the loudness in her chest. Here and there, a girl and boy, a girl and girl, a boy and boy worked their spectacular improvisations. They packed the dance floor, their arms flung out, their shoulders jerking up and down. But the age-old folk dance of the Punjab remained at the heart of the disco twirls and leaps.

Mumtaz and Tahira had stayed in their seats, though the rest of their group had tried to pull them up.

'They're good, ain't they?' Tahira said, watching a boy and two girls who had worked out a routine.

'Yeah,' replied Mumtaz. 'You feel daft trying to dance next to that.'

'I know,' Tahira agreed. 'I'd feel an idiot out there. Gita don't seem to mind.'

'No, she's good.'

Through the smoke and the sweat and the drums, Tahira saw Arif's friend. Tahira moved to the edge of her seat and waved. The friend left his group and walked over to their table.

'Hi, you're Tahira, yeah?' he asked. His skin was shiny with perspiration. 'Yeah, Arif told me to tell you if I saw you – he can't make it today. He had to do something for his mother, yeah, he had to do something. Enjoying yourselves?' He looked at Mumtaz.

'Is that all he said, then?' Tahira asked.

'Yeah. No, he said, since he can't phone you, he said to tell you he'll meet you at the kebab place in Southall, the day after tomorrow, three-thirty.' A girl called him. He said, 'I'd better get back. See you around, yeah?'

Mumtaz watched him join his friends on the dance floor. She said, 'So you've already been with him to Solly?'

'You're not jealous, are ya?' asked Tahira.

'You must be joking. I'm pleased you've got company for when you next bunk off!'

'Don't make out I force you to bunk off.'

There was a moment of silence. Mumtaz said, 'Looks like I won't be meeting your Arif today.'

'Yeah, it does.'

Another pause.

'Tell your mum to phone up my mum and dad so I can stay at your house tomorrow. I want to hear about Tanni's party,' said Mumtaz.

The bhungra records made way for the DJ's voice, announcing the band from Birmingham. Mumtaz stood up to catch a better view of the six men. Tahira stayed in her seat as the hall resounded.

Ten

Munty was too proud to speak her feelings. She told her sister not to rearrange her things, nor to mess up her area of the room. She said nothing to her cousin.

Mumtaz watched her leave the room. 'She thinks she's been kicked out. She's angry at me.'

'Oh, leave her. She's always angry about something.' Tahira loosened her shalwaar, and lay under her blankets.

Mumtaz stood in front of the tarnished mirror of the cupboard, brushing her long hair. Tahira watched her, soothed by the rhythm of the brush. Mumtaz walked away from the mirror.

'Open the curtains, will ya? Tahira said. Tahira always slept with the curtains drawn back. In the daytime the window revealed other windows of rooms like her own. In the dark, it opened up the room, and relieved the clutter; it eased the night-born tightness in her chest. Lying in her bed, in the near silence, she could look out at the sky and contemplate the small scale of human life and conflict.

Mumtaz switched off the lights and drew back the curtains. Both girls lay quietly in their beds. Tahira blinked and waited for the blindness of night to pass. Mumtaz, propped up on her elbow, turned to her.

'Are you asleep?' she whispered.

'No,' Tahira whispered back.

'Don't be boring. Are you gonna tell me or not?'

All their night-time talks began like this.

'Tell you what?'

'What happened at Tanni's party – as if you didn't know!'

'Don't talk so loud.'

'Can I get in your bed?'

Tahira made room for her. In the secret cosiness of the bed, the one lived her evening anew, the other made her own pleasurable sense of it.

'Well, you know it was a birthday party – she's sixteen – and I got invited,' Tahira started.

'What did you tell your mum?'

'I told her it was Tanni's birthday party. She thought it'd be like in Pakistan, you know, only family and mostly girls and kids. She didn't know Tanni's mum and dad stayed out of it, and, you know . . .'

'I didn't know aunty was friends with Tanni's lot?'

Tahira thought about her family, and the Chauderys. They knew each other. In the old days, when Tahira was a little girl, they had lived next door. They used to meet all the time. As a child, Tahira had thought Tanni's mother and her own were first cousins. She had often heard the grown-ups talk of the days before England and remember their old village, an age away. But things had changed. The Chauderys had made some money and moved away to Ilford. They'd sold their souls to make money, people said. It wasn't through drug dealing; but they had still forgotten who they were. They sold alcohol in their restaurant and their children had too much freedom. Tahira's and Mumtaz's mothers would talk about the parents. The father was always at the restaurant – all right, you've got to earn money, you've got to eat, but Chaudery was rich now, he could afford a manager. It seemed money was more important than his name. The families had drifted apart, though there were the meetings at Eid where Tahira noted how their critics were keen to sit and talk with the Chauderys and congratulate them on their big house and their business success.

Bumping into Tanni in the refectory of the college, recognising each other, discovering mutual friends – Tanni knew Suleiman and Imran – and mutual interests, had led to a closer contact. Hussain had been given weekend and holiday work at the Chaudery restaurant, and Tahira's mother spoke less critically of that family. It did rankle with Tahira that her brother worked in their kitchens but it was in Tanni's house that she had met Arif.

'Amma wouldn't have let me go, even if your friend had invited me,' Mumtaz said.

61

'You could've said you was coming round here for the night. Ma would've kept quiet about us really going to the party. I mean, she'd be too ashamed to admit to your lot that she'd let me go to Tanveer Chaudery's party!'

'No, if it ever got out that I went to Tanni's party!' Mumtaz emphasised the name. 'You know,' she said, 'she goes to the Hippodrome, and not with her brothers neither. She sees some English bloke.' Before Tahira could interrupt her, she hurriedly added, 'Marium reckons her mum and dad know about it an' all!'

'There *were* some gorrai at the party – some girls and a bloke. He was quite old, about twenty, I'd say. That must've been her bloke. Come to think of it, it must've definitely been her bloke!'

Mumtaz wondered what Tahira knew. The whole night lay ahead, and a lot of talking. Mumtaz left the bed to fetch some sweets from her bag. Returning quickly, she adjusted her pillow and laid the sweets on her lap.

'Yeah?' she urged the flow of talk.

'They didn't do nothing, nothing like that! It's just that,' Tahira paused to work out her ideas.

Mumtaz said, 'She met the bloke at her dad's restaurant. He and his mates eat there, every week, I think.'

'Right! It's definitely, definitely him then,' Tahira said, her teeth crunching on a pear-drop, ' 'cos he said he goes to Tanni's restaurant a lot. It is him, fancy that.'

Mumtaz said, 'But, you know, I don't think her parents know about it. They might sell sharaab at their restaurant . . .'

Tahira spoke, 'They drink it as well, the dad definitely does. Even the mum might, I reckon. They've got drinks in their house.'

'Yeah, that's bad, ain't it? Still, it doesn't mean they let Tanni have boyfriends, and English ones!' Mumtaz answered.

'They can't like it, but they don't really stop her, do they? I mean, look how they let her have parties and invite blokes.'

Mumtaz said, 'I still don't think they know. They must think those boys are really her brother's friends.'

'They might say that. If they think that, they must be stupid!' Tahira thought of her own mother, who was anything but stupid. Her words of anger, her suspicions, showed just how much she knew of Tahira's secret life. And yet, she also took the lies. Did her cleverness have its limits, Tahira reflected, or did her mother sometimes choose to believe the lies? Perhaps she didn't really see any harm in going to parties where there were boys and where parents stayed away, as long as, of course, nothing bad happened.

Tahira asked, 'Marium reckons she does naughty things, eh?'

'Don't know,' said Mumtaz, a little embarrassed.

'You know, I reckon Tanni might do it.' Tahira was weighing up all that she knew about Tanveer Chaudery.

'Parents can't really do anything, can they?' Mumtaz tried the idea.

'Yes they bloody can!' said Tahira. 'Unless it don't matter to 'em. But it must do. The mother says her prayers, they send Tanni to a girls' school in Ilford, and anyway, who'd marry a used up girl? Not a Pakistani!'

The digressions of their talk were so much a part of their involvement in that evening.

'Yeah, well,' Mumtaz sounded thoughtful. 'Tell me about the party,' she said, 'and about Arif. What were you wearing? What was Tanni wearing?'

'Tanni lent me a really nice dress. It was really nice, something out of *Dynasty*, it looked. Blue, it was, and silk. It had this 'V' at the back. I couldn't wear my bra with it, 'cos of the straps. Didn't look rude though.'

'What about Tanni?'

'She looked good. You ain't seen her new hairstyle. It's a really nice, smooth bob, just like in that Vidal Sassoon advert. She's had it highlighted. It looked really good with her creamy shalwaar kameez, didn't look an ordinary shalwaar kameez. Looked sort of expensive, not gotta or nothing, just sort of expensive. All the girls were dressed nice.'

'Who else was there?'

'There weren't no one there we know. Mostly her cousins and friends from her school,' said Tahira. 'To tell you the truth, I felt a bit out of it, just a little. Some of the people there were friendly.'

'What about Arif, then?' Mumtaz sat up more comfortably, offered a sweet to Tahira, and took one herself.

'Well, I was there.' She used gesture to elaborate her words. 'I was sitting and the door was there, and he come in. I just stopped and stared.'

'Oh great! Did your eyes meet?'

The two laughed. Mumtaz waited for the story to unfold.

'He stopped and stared. God!' Tahira's words were barely audible; there was almost a shyness in her laughter. 'And then, what happened after that?' she asked herself. 'God! Let's see, I moved away. I was sitting talking, and he was up there dancing, to Luther Van Dross. Really good dancer, my God! Tanni's mum and dad, all the old people were upstairs.'

'Yeah, go on.'

Tahira had become a character in a teenage romance. 'And, he was dancing, I just couldn't get my eyes off him. And I asked Anita, this girl called Anita, Tanni's friend . . .' Tahira paused for a second.

'Go on,' urged Mumtaz.

'I go, "What's his name?" She told me it was Arif, and she goes, "Do you fancy him?"'

'Yeah?' said Mumtaz.

'She goes, "Do you fancy him?" I go, "Yeah, yeah, I do." You know, the party went on like and . . .'

'Where was he all this time? Was he sort of looking at you? Eye contact?'

'Well, well,' Tahira's voice became shrill. 'It was just normal. He was just dancing in there, and talking to this girl.'

'But were you sort of thinking, you know, he might be looking at me . . .?'

'Yeah, yeah,' Tahira said, 'he might be looking, yeah.'

'He might be looking, so everything about you was very, you know.' Again, they both laughed.

'Shh, they'll hear!' Tahira nudged her cousin, then said, 'Yeah, you know everything you do is sort of, you know.' They shared a knowledge.

Mumtaz said, 'I hate that! 'Cos when you think someone's looking at you, you . . .'

'You do something stupid!'

'Yeah, go on.'

'So the party went on, and we took a few photographs, and you know, they cut the cake. It was really big, in the shape of a sitar – Tanni likes all that old music.'

'Yeah yeah, what happened to Arif?'

'I sat on the stairs, there were some others there as well. Anyway, I was waiting for Suleiman and Norah to bring me a drink, and *he* came outside.'

Arif had returned, at last. Mumtaz munched another sweet. 'Come on!'

'And I just sat there, right, and he was just by the door near the stairs, and I dunno, everybody around me, they sort of like, one by one went away.'

'Yeah.'

'Then Suleiman and Norah came with my coke. I felt a bit nervous with Suleiman there. Don't know why.'

'Could be you thought he might tell Hussain and it might get round to your mum.'

'What, Hussain might make trouble for me?' asked Tahira.

'It wouldn't be just to make trouble, would it? I reckon, deep down, he don't like you going out, bunking off school, talking to boys. He's probably worried about you.'

'Well, he can't stop me. I ain't scared of him!' said Tahira.

'You know what, the way he goes all quiet when you mention her, I think he fancies Tanni, and she's no angel, is she?' said Mumtaz.

'I know. He'd have loved to have got invited to the party.' Tahira laughed, and then felt guilty. She loved her brother. She shouldn't be laughing at him. She was angry that Tanni had no interest in Hussain. She thought of him in the Chaudery kitchens.

'Anyway,' she carried on, 'Suleiman was called away, and the others went away as well, to take photographs or eat some cake, I'm not sure. And I was by myself, just staring, sort of looking ahead, at nothing really. He was just there.' Her hands placed Arif. 'He was there with his friend, the one we met at the disco. He turned and looked at me!' There was thrill in her voice. 'I thought, God! What am I gonna do? And this is me, I just went like this, stiff.'

Mumtaz was living the moment. 'You were all shivery and nervous, right?' It was pleasurable to recall the evening, and to recreate it as a grand romance.

'And after that, nothing much happened. The party ended and people left.'

'What d'you mean, it ended! Didn't you talk to him or nothing?'

'The next day, he asked Tanni about me. We all went out that night – me, Tanni, Suleiman, Norah, Arif and Hussain. I had to take Hussain, Amma was getting a bit suspicious,' said Tahira. 'We went

65

to that nan-kebab place in Solly. The day after that – when you had to stay at home for your mum – he come round the school and we drove around, him and me.'

Mumtaz said, 'Yeah, I heard all about that. But, God, he works fast, don't he?'

'He was supposed to come to the disco yesterday, and I'm supposed to be meeting him tomorrow – if I bloody turn up!' Tahira remembered Arif's friend, and Arif's message, which might or might not have reached her. Her memories of the party faded. Neither girl spoke for the moment.

Then Mumtaz said, 'But Arif had a good reason for not coming.'

'Yeah.'

'And you saw him Saturday.'

'Yeah we went to this flash coffee place where that Raisa woman lives.'

'What were you doing down there?'

'Somewhere to go.'

'I saw her in school the other day.' Mumtaz lay back. 'She's pretty.'

'Yeah.'

'What's she like?'

Tahira looked up at the window and the wide dark sky. 'She's got nice clothes and a nice flat. She talks nice. She drives a car. She's clever and all that. She looks happy, know what I mean?'

'Do you like her?'

'Dunno.'

'What do you mean?'

'I like meeting her, you know, and I reckon she likes me. I can't really explain it. She ain't like us. She don't really mix with people like us. I don't know no one like her.'

Mumtaz yawned. 'I bet she's got boyfriends. And she must have done it by now.'

'Do you think?'

'Yeah, definitely. Better keep Arif away from her!' She turned on her side.

Mumtaz drifted into sleep. Tahira carried on looking out of the window.

Eleven

It was half-past eight in the morning, and the doors were still locked. Ijaz and Najum waited outside the sixth-form block, their backs stiffened against the cold gusts of April. The two friends rarely came in for morning registration.

Ijaz, never particularly talkative early in the day, spoke first. 'If Hussain can't stop Jam, think he'll listen to us?'

Najum kicked a stone. 'We'll have to make him.'

'What, make him listen when he's so mad?'

'We'll have to. It's getting out of control, yaar,' said Najum.

'Hussain says it's only a kitchen knife, but a kitchen knife can do a lot of damage.' Ijaz counted the contents of his packet of Silk Cut.

'What, he's thinking of using it?' The idea stunned Najum. 'He's mad,' he said.

'The Ames lot carry flick-knives,' Ijaz answered. 'We're wasting our time trying to stop him. No way's he gonna stay away.'

'So why're we here, then?' Najum was losing patience with his friend. 'Might as well've stayed in bed. Tuesdays, don't have no lessons before dinner.'

'What's wrong with you, man? I know we got to stop him. It's just that, it's, it's . . .' He had much to say. 'Jam's angry, he's angry, man. Those gorrai, it ain't right what they do.'

Najum was moved, but he said simply, 'He'll get in trouble. He should go to Miss Beeston, or Mr McCormack. They'll . . .'

Ijaz interrupted, 'You're mad! What can they do? They're only two teachers, not the whole school. Jam's right – we got to show those bastards.'

Najum said, 'People get hurt with knives, yaar.'

'Yeah, I know, but . . .' Ijaz didn't finish the sentence. They both wondered how they would persuade Jamshid to stay away from school.

'Have you seen Ames' dad?' Najum lowered his voice as a group of fourth-year students walked past them on their way to the main building. 'He's like a tank.'

'So bloody what! Have you seen Jam's dad?'

They both knew that Jamshid's father had the physique, and stamina, of a wrestler – how else could he work in a factory by day and drive a mini-cab by night? But his father also believed that arguments should be settled legally, peaceably.

'Have you seen all the gundai at the college and in East Ham and Southall if we need them?' said Ijaz. He doubted his own words. Wasn't he really exaggerating everything? After all, a fight between schoolkids wasn't exactly a war between people, was it?

Najum asked, 'Do you think the Ames'll come for Jamshid? That's what the gorrai reckon.'

'Don't know.' Almost instinctively, and barely conscious of it, Ijaz understood threats and injustices to fill the very air that he breathed. 'If Ames' dad comes, the school won't stop him. And say we do get the police, what're they gonna do?' He finished with the short laugh of repressed anger.

The grounds around the buildings were filling with children impatient to move into the warmth. Most were ill-dressed for the cold wind, and the first spots of rain.

Barry Woolf, in the same tutor group as Ijaz and Najum, approached the two boys. 'How're you doing, Ijaz?' Barry punched him on the arm. 'Ain't seen you all week.'

Ijaz smiled faintly.

'Is there really going to be a fight?'

'Dunno,' said Ijaz.

In discussions or conversations Barry always took their side. But could they trust him? He was still a gorra. Whose side would he take in a fight?

Najum said, 'We heard there's gonna be a bad fight at break. Jam against Terry and Martin Ames – them geezers in the fifth year. They're bringing knives.'

'Shit! That's going a bit far ain't it?' Barry noted a group of white fifth formers, most of them girls, within hearing distance. He raised his voice. 'Those bastards are still beating up the Pakis in the first year, right?'

The briefest of looks passed between Ijaz and Najum. Barry saw and understood it. But he hadn't meant anything bad, just an abbreviation.

Barry said, 'Why don't the Pakistanis and the Indians in the first year all get together and go to the teachers?'

'That's a stupid question,' said Ijaz.

A teacher pushed through the crowd and unlocked the doors. Tahira, Mumtaz and Gita followed the boys into the common-room. They had been running.

'Is it true about the fight today?' Tahira asked, catching her breath.

'Yeah, it is,' said Ijaz. 'Did Hussain tell you?'

'No. That stupid git came home late last night. I ain't seen him yet. He's gonna be in the fight ain't he?'

'We hope there won't be no fight. Hussain's gone to Jam's house to put him off coming to school.' Najum didn't look directly at Tahira; only rarely did he do so, and then very self-consciously. He moved to the window. From there, he had a clear view of the school gate.

'The teachers don't know nothing about it do they?' Tahira asked the others.

'Some of them must have heard,' said Gita, 'but what are they gonna do? They must think it's just another fight, you know.'

Barry almost shouted, 'Then we got to tell them it ain't just another fight!'

He felt Tahira's stare; it made him uncomfortable. He said, 'It's about time Martin Ames got sorted out. If the teachers can't do it, well then.'

Tahira asked him, 'How come your twin sister's so friendly with Michelle's lot these days? Terry Ames' girlfriend, if you didn't know.'

Barry answered, 'Sonya talks to them. She ain't friendly with them.'

Najum was still standing by the window, diligently keeping watch. He was praying that Jamshid would stay away. In case his prayers failed, he was also rehearsing powerful arguments. He didn't hear Barry's sister come in with her urgent news. Tahira moved away.

Sonya said, 'Terry and his brother are in school. They've brought knives.'

'Where are they now?' asked Ijaz.

'They've gone in for registration. They've got loads of kids behind them, you know. They're all talking about Pakis and how Jam calls white girls prostitutes.'

'Yeah,' Gita added, 'Terry's saying Jam tried to chat up some gorree. That's really getting them worked up.'

'It's getting really serious, you know.' Sonya looked at Tahira.

Suddenly, Najum rushed out of the common-room. After a second of incomprehension, Ijaz and the others ran after him. Hussain, and Jamshid, had come to school.

In the aftermath of the clash, amid the confusion and the mistrust, the girls sought the privacy of the toilets. Trips to the loo – at breaktimes, and between and during lessons – were nothing new to Tahira and Gita. But today Nasreen had been swept in with them.

Earlier she had gone out in the playground to talk to Tahira about the homework for Raisa. They had barely exchanged greetings when Jamshid and a white boy had started to unleash the fiercest of abuse at one another. Huge crowds of students encircled the combatants, leaving them just enough space to move from threatening words to dangerous contact. And Nasreen had stayed with Tahira and Gita throughout the events that followed, even after the ambulance had arrived, and the teachers had spoken of alerting the police, and the brothers, sisters, cousins and friends had been dispersed to their various rooms.

In the toilets, the girls were silent. Tahira pushed at the doors of the cubicles to ensure that the place was empty. They listened.

'It's only English – we won't miss no work. Come on.'

Michelle Ryan was approaching the toilets along the noisy corridor. Julie Webster hurried to catch her up. They heard them coming. Tahira recognised Michelle's voice. With one mind, they ran to the last cubicle.

Michelle's words came out furiously. 'I hope he's got it. I hope that bastard's got it this time. Thought he could flash his knife about! Yeah.' She continued, 'Don't it make you sick the way them teachers are gonna gang up against Terry, like them Pakis never done nothing wrong?'

'Yeah and that bloody Sonya. I didn't see her helping. What was she doing next to that big-mouth slag, and the rest of them Pakis?' Julie was flushed and out of breath. She proceeded to answer her own question. 'She likes them, don't she?'

'She ever comes near me again, or me brother, and I'll bloody spit in her face!'

Julie said, 'We'd best tell the teachers what happened. You know that McCormack'll side with them, and them Paki girls were talking to that old cow Beeston, telling her God knows what.'

Michelle elaborated for her friend, 'That's right, how they're always picked on and weren't doing nothing and didn't want no fight.'

'Well, we'd best go to Mr Busby and tell him what happened.'

'That's right,' agreed Michelle, 'and tell him he shouted "prosti-tute".'

'Did he?' Julie's tone expressed the pleasure of confirmation.

'Yeah,' said Michelle, 'I heard it with my own ears. He never shouted it, he said it, like – when you pushed that Paki girl on to him.'

'Oh her, that slag who was all mouthy to Terry!'

'Gita, I think,' answered Michelle.

'They all stick together they do, talking in Paki, calling us dogs. That's what "kuta" means, "dogs". You've heard them.'

'Yeah, tell Busby that.' Michelle kicked at the door of a cubicle.

Julie continued, 'They're always saying it – "ku-ta ku-ta"! Ugh, makes you sick the way they all stick together. It really . . .'

'Tell Busby everything, before them Pakis get their words in. They just love them in this school, they do. You can't say this, you can't say that against them. God, it's like it ain't our country no more!'

'Well come on then.' Julie was impatient to reach the head of year's office, before the others did.

Michelle said, 'Terry was just walking down – Kevin in the fourth year told me – Terry was just walking down by the shed and they was waiting for him, all of them, sixth formers against a fifth year. Kevin saw it all. They had him up against the fence, by his neck!'

'What, all them Pakis were hitting Terry? Loads against one?' Julie asked.

'The way that bastard was hitting at Terry. It was horrible, the

71

blood on Terry's face. I wanted Terry to kill him. But Terry weren't doing nothing. He was just taking it.'

Michelle said, 'Thank God Martin was there. He just blew! Served the bastard right when the two of them went for him. He asked for it.'

'It was that Jamshid pulled out a knife. Terry didn't even have one,' Julie added.

'That's right,' Michelle said. 'They searched Terry after and never found nothing. He couldn't have had one, could he?'

'When I think of Terry,' Julie was remembering again, 'him in an ambulance, and that bastard not even getting hurt!'

'Well that Jam-shit better get out of this school. 'Cos if he don't, it ain't right.'

Michelle was shouting, 'If you're a darkie, you can say what you like, you can beat us up, you can. Remember when that teacher took our register?' Michelle raised her voice in an attempt to mimic the student teacher, ' "It's not the same as when a white person says it".'

Julie took up the theme. 'That's what that mad McCormack says. He thinks us saying Paki's worse than them calling us dogs. Even the other teachers think he's mad.'

Michelle's voice trembled with anger, 'I suppose Paki's worse than prostitute!'

Julie said, 'The way he beat up Terry. It weren't right. Terry never really beat up them Paki first years.'

'No,' said Michelle, 'and if he's been beaten bad and can't do his paper rounds, well, he's gonna lose his job, ain't he? Course, it wouldn't matter to Jam-shit. He's all right, he don't need no jobs after school.'

'Come on, Busby's probably teaching next lesson.'

Julie and Michelle ran out of the toilets. The girls in the far cubicle waited for the rush of footsteps to fade into the distance. When all was still, they left their hiding place.

Gita spoke first, 'It's sick. They're telling all these lies, and they'll all gang up against him.'

Tahira said, 'They're not all lies though. I mean, it is lies really, they're just not all lies.' Beyond her words was a fullness of thought that evaded expression.

Nasreen shouted, 'What do you mean? They *are* lies, they're bad lies. They've got things back to front. They're not saying the truth!'

Gita and Tahira had never before heard her shout.

Tahira attempted to find the words, 'I know, but, what I mean is, they ain't saying that Terry and his brother weren't scaring the first years. I mean, it's true they've never really beaten them up either, and Jam did take out his knife, and he most probably did say prostitute!'

'Yeah, he did. I heard him,' Gita spoke quietly, and then added, 'but you should've heard what that bitch Julie Webster said to him first, when she shoved me on to him.'

'Yes,' said Nasreen. 'What about all those things? And what about all the other things as well?'

Tahira understood Nasreen's meaning. She said, 'Well, they're gorrai and they hate us. Why would they say all them other things?'

Nasreen seemed not to have heard her. 'It's lies. It didn't happen like that.'

'I know,' answered Tahira.

A moment passed.

'Should we go to Mr Busby and tell him?' Gita asked.

Tahira answered, simply, 'He wouldn't believe nothing I said. He thinks I'm bad.'

'Well, what's Michelle then?'

Tahira said, 'You go with Nasreen. Never know, he might believe you two.'

Gita asked Tahira, 'Are we gonna meet at dinner time, or are you seeing your friend?'

For a second, Tahira was puzzled, and then, remembering, she looked pointedly at Gita.

Gita said, 'You know, I mean meeting your cousin, Mumtaz.'

Tahira answered, 'Nah, Mumtaz ain't at school today. She's going to social security with her mum.'

Tahira looked at Nasreen, who seemed not to have noted any deception. In a strange way, after that long morning, Tahira was pleased not to be meeting Arif.

Twelve

He stood waiting on the polished floor. The green rug and the wide desk separated him from the headmaster. The swelling under his eyes tingled. Mr Kern had neither looked up nor spoken. It was the first time that Jamshid had been in his office.

Jamshid thought, Mr Kern, my father wants me to become a doctor. The words rang in his head. Alarmed, he wondered whether he had spoken them aloud.

Mr Kern seemed suddenly to notice the boy standing above him. He rose from his chair, waving Jamshid's file. 'Jam-sheed Iq-bal? Right, sit there.' He pointed to a high-backed wooden chair in a corner of the room.

Jamshid sat down silently and looked into the man's eyes. The headmaster was irritated by the sixth-former's manner. The window behind him now, he leaned against the corner of his desk and faced the seated boy. He folded his arms and shook his head in a gesture of worn exasperation. He appeared merely as a silhouette to Jamshid, and the messages of facial expression were wasted.

'You do understand the gravity of the situation?'

Jamshid didn't answer; he wasn't even sure that he'd been asked a question.

'Ah, I take it that you do understand the gravity of the situation.' He continued, 'You've already been through the business of the knife, haven't you, with the police officer? The police have decided to take a lenient attitude and leave the matter in my hands to deal with. And that's what I'm now going to do – from the point of view of the school, where we treat each other with respect, wherever we come from.'

Then the phone rang. He moved back to his seat behind the desk. 'Yes, Jane. Well, it's rather difficult at the moment. Well, OK, go on . . .'

Jamshid focused his gaze at the beige walls and the posters of Switzerland. He thought of Saeed and felt a pain in his chest. His elder brother would soon be wrenched from those who loved and needed him.

Mr Kern was still at the telephone. Soon he would pass sentence on him. 'Listen, Jane, do you think you could hold all calls for the next, say,' he looked at his watch, 'ten minutes? I'm dealing with a rather serious matter here. Right. Thanks.' He put down the phone and immediately dropped his smile. 'Right, Jam-sheed, before I have my say and present you with the facts that I have here,' he waved the file for the second time, 'what have you to say for yourself?'

Jamshid looked directly at him. 'They started it. The police should talk to them, you should talk to them.'

'I would prefer it if you left what I should or should not do to my judgment. And the police did talk to the others. The fact is, you brought a weapon to school.' The headmaster noted the boy's stillness. There was an infuriating truculence about him. 'Do you have anything to say for yourself before I state the school's position? Perhaps you'd like to give me your story?'

'It's not a story. It's what happened,' said Jamshid.

The boy really was exasperating. 'Well, perhaps you'd like to tell me and leave me to decide.'

Jamshid didn't speak. The headmaster's reprimands, though probably no different from the words used with the white children, took on added meanings with Jamshid. He did not trust the man. It had already been decided that he was guilty; he knew the punishment that lay waiting for him. Why, he thought tiredly, were they still going through the motions of 'fair play'?

'Since we don't have all day, and it seems you're having difficulty explaining yourself, I'll tell you what happened, shall I?'

The headmaster's eyes refused to make contact with Jamshid's for longer than the briefest second. Self-consciousness hung in the air between them.

'Right,' he started, 'it seems that you and your friends, a large group of you, pounced upon and attacked a fourth-year boy, Terry Ames. By the shed, wasn't it?'

'We didn't pounce on him.' Jamshid paused; he remembered Ijaz and Najum and Hussain, and Barry. He said, 'Others, other Asians and – others – joined in, but not all against one. It went out of control, lots of people were fighting, Asians and English.'

Jamshid thought, he's got a file on Terry Ames, he knows he isn't innocent.

'Whatever your version is of this totally unacceptable event' – the man's voice became louder – 'the fact remains that it was you who brought a knife to school, and you who pulled it out in the fight, and I dread to think what would have happened if the teachers on duty had arrived a second later.' He paused for breath. His face had become flushed. He continued, now looking directly into Jamshid's eyes, and incensed that the boy would not turn away, 'It seems that you don't understand some of our ways in this school.'

Jamshid leaned back in his chair and continued to meet the headmaster's look.

'It's a criminal offence, in this country, to carry weapons – you do know that?' He paused and added, 'I've also heard that you've taken to carrying a knife around with you all the time.'

Jamshid said, 'Terry Ames had a knife on him. At break, when Mr Fairfield, and the others, stopped the fight, Terry passed his knife to someone else. He did have his knife. He and his mates carry them, so do his family. His father . . .'

He was interrupted, 'You can say all this, but the fact remains there's little or no evidence to support your claims. There's no doubt, however, that you had a knife, and that you were angry enough to use it, and that is something that cannot be excused!'

Jamshid said, 'Ames and his friends carry knives, so do Ames' family. They scare, they try to scare us after school, they throw stones at us in the park, come down our streets with knives and poles and throw things down letter boxes – leaflets about Pakis, and other things and . . .' He stopped, suddenly. There was no point.

No one spoke. Jamshid moved his gaze to the icy slopes of the travel poster and breathed deeply to control his quickened heart-beats.

'Jam-sheed, I'm afraid the school has little say or power over what happens in the streets and outside of school hours. Hopefully, we are teaching tomorrow's adults the right way to behave in the world, but what you're describing is a matter for the police.'

Jamshid turned away from the poster. The headmaster was irritated by the boy's detachment.

'I'm afraid,' he said, 'I still cannot allow you, and the others, to think that knives, or any other weapon, are acceptable! The fact remains, you brought in an offensive weapon, and you might have used it. You caused a boy to be hospitalised and you forced us to involve the police. You've left me no alternative but to exclude you from our sixth form . . .'

The headmaster faded into soundlessness, and Jamshid saw his father in his cab, driving through the night-time streets of Barking. A painful tickle had developed under his swollen cheek. He scratched at it, tearing the skin.

The headmaster was now skimming through the boy's file. 'It's not as if this is the first time you've been involved in violent incidents, and all this year, it seems.' He closed the file and looked up. 'You're past the school leaving age; we are under absolutely no obligation to keep you here. We don't have enough teachers as it is. Classes lower down the school are larger than they should be, while your sixth-form classes are kept smaller. Why should you be allowed the privilege of an excellent education when you cannot follow our basic rules?' He folded his arms and added, 'I don't think I'm being unfair or unreasonable, do you?'

Jamshid didn't answer.

The headmaster asked, 'Are your parents on the phone? Your mother, at home?'

His mother was at home. She knew enough English to be dev-astated by the news of her son; but not enough for much else.

Jamshid answered, 'No, no one's at home.'

'In that case,' the man spoke with full authority of office, 'as soon as I've finished with you, you will leave the school premises. The school will be sending out a letter to your parents, explaining to them why you have been expelled, and how they can appeal, if they so wish. They're welcome to make an appointment to see Mr Larkins or me.'

Jamshid stood up to leave the room.

'Here,' said the headmaster, putting pen to paper, 'take this to reception before you leave the premises. We don't want anyone thinking you're playing truant.'

Jamshid took the note and turned away.

That afternoon, a memo was pinned on to the staff noticeboard of South Park School:

> Following an incident earlier today Jamshid Iqbal, L65, has been expelled from the sixth form.

But before the appearance of the official note, the news had already spread amongst the students.

'They've got rid of that flash Paki, for good. Serves the bastards right!'

'The gorrais kicked Jam out 'cos he fought back!'

That evening bright red daubings appeared on the walls of the main corridor and of three offices: the headmaster's, Mr Busby's and Mr Larkin's. The caretaker had been unlocking the building for the evening classes when he saw the graffiti. The crimson gloss was still dripping. As he dialled the number of the local police station, he wondered why South Park School, of all places, should be the site for terrorist graffiti. Who would believe it, the walls of his school covered with 'PLO! PLO! PLO!'?

Thirteen

They walked quickly out of the rear entrance without attracting attention. Fifty yards past the school, they slowed down to their usual saunter. In the lonely daytime streets of terraced houses and empty gardens, they had no need to keep their voices hushed. That morning, though, as they made their way to the bus shelter, Mumtaz and Tahira were not very talkative.

School had become a tense place after Jamshid's expulsion. Playing truant was a special relief, but neither of the girls was thrilled about the assignation with Arif and his friend.

Mumtaz said, 'Ain't you supposed to be seeing your woman today?'

Tahira said, 'Raisa. No, she had to cancel it. It ain't till next week.'

A thin, sandy-coloured dog ran up to the girls, sniffed around their feet and then scampered away. The two carried on walking.

Mumtaz remembered her first meeting with Arif. She had wanted so much to go with Tahira to the Southall cafe. She was longing to see the hero of their night-time conversations. It had been two days after the bhungra disco, and they had both told their parents that they were going that evening on a school trip to the theatre. Arif had looked the part of the tall, stylish, good-looking hero – just as the girls who'd caught sight of him outside the school building had reported. But Mumtaz hadn't liked him. There had been something rude and insulting in the way his eyes had lingered over her all evening. His knees had touched hers under the table; he had passed her a note, with his phone number, and he had looked and smiled at Tahira. She could never discuss these things with her cousin.

Tahira, walking alongside her preoccupied companion, recalled another meeting. They had been driving along the Uxbridge Road, all packed tightly into Arif's Datsun: Arif at the wheel, her brother Hussain next to him, and Suleiman, Norah and Tanveer alongside her squashed in the back. Suleiman and Hussain discussed the way the school had treated Jamshid. Hussain described the shock that Jamshid's family had felt, and their shame. Suleiman insisted that the events at the school were all part of the same system that had set up immigration controls against black people and that kept them in low-paid jobs; that the Asians in South Park School shouldn't just sit back and accept things. Arif, driving his father's shabby Datsun, had talked of his foolproof plans to expand the family business, and of the expensive Rada watch that he would soon buy.

'To tell you the truth I ain't that pleased about going out today,' she said.

Mumtaz, called from her own thoughts, answered, 'Yeah, I know. What time are they supposed to be here?'

'We're still five minutes early,' Tahira said, leaning against the plastic wall of the shelter.

Once again, the girls fell into silence.

'You all right?' Mumtaz asked.

'They better hurry up,' Tahira spoke quickly. 'I ain't gonna wait around for them.'

Mumtaz said, 'Look! Ain't that his friend, what's his name, Faisal?'

Tahira squinted her eyes to get a better focus. 'Yeah, that's him. Can you see Arif?'

'No, I think he's on his own.'

Tahira was disappointed – with Arif, for not turning up, and with herself, for still being bothered with him.

'But look at him,' Mumtaz laughed, 'don't he look a right prat?'

There, walking towards them, was Faisal, wearing a suit and dark glasses, like a hit-man.

He nodded to the girls. 'OK?'

'Hello,' said Tahira, 'Arif can't come, right? And you've come with a message?'

'Oh no, he'll be down soon.' He took off the dark glasses. He said, 'I've been at a friend's house – I had to check something out, and Arif had to finish some business in Stratford. We arranged to meet here.'

He had barely finished the sentence when Arif's ageing, though recently washed, car drew up beside them. 'Hi! How're you doing?' he asked Tahira, and smiled broadly at Mumtaz.

Mumtaz said, 'I've got to get home at home-time. My dad's getting a bit suspicious.'

Two hours later the Datsun drove down Southall High Street. They drove past the jeweller's and the video centres, past the shops selling fabric for saris and shalwaar khameez, and those that displayed, at one third of the price, the sequined garments they sold to Harrods and Selfridges. The grocers and the cash-and-carrys were left behind as finally the car slowed down and squeezed itself into a small space in front of the 'Nan-Kebab House'. At night, its neon-lit name flashed like the stalls at a fairground; in the glare of daylight it remained lifeless and shabby.

Their conversation was loud – a blend of English and Punjabi. Tahira watched as Arif smiled at Mumtaz, and complimented her. She watched as Mumtaz squirmed in discomfort. A group of girls came into the café and made their way to a nearby table. Arif looked at them appreciatively. Very calmly, Tahira rested her gaze on him. She thought, I don't like him, I really don't like him.

Arif, still looking at the girls, said, 'Hey, Tahira, you should teach your cousin to be more friendly, you know what I mean?' he moved closer to Tahira, suggestively. She pushed him off.

He knows I can't stand him, she thought.

'Tahira, hey, what's wrong? You're so different when we're alone. The last time – remember?'

'Shut your bloody mouth!'

Tahira ran out into the street. Mumtaz ran after her.

'We'd better get back to Barking. You know what'll happen if we're late,' Mumtaz said.

Tahira didn't look at her cousin. She didn't want Mumtaz to see her watery eyes. 'Yeah, you're right, but I've left my bag in the café.'

'Come on then, let's go and get it.'

'No, I ain't bloody going back in there,' Tahira shouted.

'It's OK. I'll go. You wait here.' Mumtaz turned to walk back.

'Hey, what's wrong? Can't you take a joke?' Arif called out. He had her bag.

Tahira walked on ahead, Mumtaz a few steps behind her, and Arif and Faisal gradually catching up.

'Oh, come on Tahira. I was only messing about. I didn't know you were like that.'

Tahira stopped. The four were standing outside the Gifto Cash-and-Carry. The entrance was busy with shoppers. Boys in stained overalls were carting sacks of rice and flour to customers' cars.

Faisal said, 'We can't stand out here, yaar.'

Mumtaz said, 'We've got to get back before home-time.' She remembered that she didn't have enough money for the fare home. She had assumed that Tahira's friend would drive them back. Now, after the argument, she prayed that Tahira hadn't made the same assumption.

Arif said, 'Let's go back to the car. The way I drive, I'll get you back in no time.'

In the back seat of the Datsun, while the boys were laughing and talking in the front, and the sound of Azad Pardesi was blaring from the stereo, Mumtaz asked Tahira, 'Did you have enough money to get home?'

'No, I didn't.'

Fourteen

'How are you, darling? We don't see you these days. You can't find a few hours to visit your father and sister?'

This was the father who had always told her to put her studies before everything else. 'Seek knowledge, though it be at the ends of the earth.' Those had been the Prophet's sentiments, he had told her as a child.

'Abu-ji!' Raisa sighed audibly. 'I saw you last Saturday, only days ago.'

'Three whole days,' he replied. 'We worry about you . . .'

'You know I'm busy with the research.' He wouldn't argue with that. 'If you could see the work I've got to get through!'

'Are you eating well, sleeping on time?'

'Yes, yes. I'll come round. I'll try to come round. Tomorrow afternoon maybe.'

'Will you be staying for the night? We'll freshen your room.'

'I doubt it. I'll let you know tomorrow.' Why couldn't she be emphatic, and just explain? Instead she always left him a margin to fill with his whisperings.

'All right darling,' he sounded old. 'I'll wait for your call. *Khuda hafiz*.'

She groaned in exasperation and kicked shut her study door. She had been out all morning interviewing the girls. She was already tired. She wanted to be left in peace. She rewound the tape a fraction and pressed play. Elbow on the table, forehead leaning on her hand, she listened, shaping experience to theory.

Raisa: Hi!

Nasreen: Salaam alaikum.

Raisa: Wa alaikum usalaam. Where's Tahira?

Nasreen: I don't know. She was in dinner. I think she's coming. She must be talking to a teacher or something.

Raisa: You don't have to make excuses for her, Nasreen! What you mean is, she's probably chatting to her friends. (Laughs)

(Pause)

Well? How did you get on with the surah?

Nasreen: It's here. I brought it, and my ideas. They're just notes, not much really.

Raisa: That's great. I didn't expect you to do all that work – you've obviously worked hard.

Nasreen: Not really.

Raisa: Should we wait for Tahira, or should we just carry on?

Nasreen: I don't mind. I've got to leave five minutes early today. It's book week and I'm one of the library monitors.

(Sound: door opening and shutting loudly)

Tahira (breathless): Sorry I'm late, had to see Mr Busby.

Raisa: Salaam walaikum, Tahira.

Tahira: Hello. I had to see Mr Busby. He's a right idiot. Asking me why I weren't in his lesson yesterday afternoon.

Raisa: We were waiting. I mean, we didn't want to start without you.

Tahira (still breathless): Oh yeah. That your homework?

Nasreen: Just notes. Nothing much.

Raisa: It wasn't homework exactly. You make it sound like boring old schoolwork.

Tahira: Well, I ain't got mine with me. I ain't really done it.

Raisa: Oh, did you find it difficult? I probably didn't make myself clear – my questions and things.

Tahira: I ain't had time to look at it even.

Raisa: Oh, doesn't matter, we can look at it now. Perhaps Nasreen'd like to start us off?

(Pause)

I know. I'll read the 'translation' to start us off. OK then, here goes – '*Bismillah-rrahimi-rrahim* : I begin by affirming Allah to be the Sole-Creator Whose limitless mercy manifests in being Ever-Bounteous,

84

Ever-Rewarding.' Right, the 'Charter of Male–Female Equality' –
Are you two all right? You both seem a bit, a bit distant.

Tahira: Do we have to do this today? Can't we leave it to next time?

Raisa: Well, yes, of course. It's just that ideas from this conversation
would be useful for what I'm working on at the moment, but don't
worry. If you'd really like to leave it for now – is it the same for you
Nasreen?

Nasreen: If it's OK with you, yes.

Raisa: Right then! Perhaps we can arrange another time – very soon,
I hope. That's if your teachers don't mind. Do they?

Tahira: Mine's glad to get rid of me, I reckon.

Nasreen: Miss Pilecka doesn't mind. She wants me to do a long
assignment on all this for my English. She says it will help me with
the exam.

Tahira: Yeah, Miss Beeston wants me to do the same. They don't
mind, and we don't mind.

Raisa: Fine – same time next week then. I'll check it with your
teachers.

Nasreen: You've wasted your journey, haven't you?

Raisa: Oh, don't worry about that. I can do something else – look
around the school, meet your friends. But before you go maybe I
should explain the work to you again. I was a bit waffly last time –
no wonder you want to put it off!

Tahira: It ain't that.

Raisa: Are you lot all right? There is something wrong, isn't there?

Tahira: Everything's bloody wrong.

Raisa: Something's happened?

Nasreen: The boy we told you about, the one the English girls beat
up, he was in a big fight. Jamshid.

Tahira: God, it was over two weeks ago, and it don't seem like it.
Everyone's still talking about it. The whole school was there – them
and us, and 'cos the gorra had to have stitches or whatever, they've
thrown Jamshid out. He had a knife.

Nasreen: So did the gorrai, but the teachers weren't interested
in that ...

Raisa pressed fast forward. She knew enough about the fight from
the earlier play-backs.

Nasreen: . . . painted over them now.

Tahira: Funny how quick they rubbed all that out. They ain't so quick with 'Paki' or 'Jacks' or 'Slag'.

Nasreen: He shouldn't have said 'prostitute'. He just made things worse. He confused things.

Tahira: He wanted to hurt her, and he did.

Nasreen: He hurt himself more.

Raisa: Why did Jamshid write . . . ?

Tahira: He weren't there. It was Suleiman and his friends from the college, and my brother and two other blokes in the sixth form. This bloke called Ijaz was caught that night – they bloody called the police. They were all running away, and Ijaz got caught. He never grassed 'em up or nothing.

Nasreen: He was severely cautioned by the police and he had to clean up the walls and pay for the paint.

Tahira: In front of everyone! He got caned the next morning as well, but that weren't enough for them.

Raisa: Why did they write PLO?

Tahira: The people in the college – Suleiman and all that lot – they're into PLO and that kind of stuff. You know, politics and that. Suleiman, he ain't posh or nothing, but he's always talking, and reading. He belongs to some group. 'Young' something or other.

Raisa: But why write PLO in the school, after a playground fight?

Tahira: It weren't just a playground fight.

Raisa: Palestine Liberation Organisation.

Tahira: It was more than a playground fight . . .

Nasreen: PLO's us, isn't it?

Raisa: What do you mean, Nasreen?

Nasreen: I mean, they're the same as us, Muslims. They're Muslims like us, and we should stick together –

Raisa: Just because they're Muslim? You're talking of 'international Islam', like the Khilaafat movement in India.

Nasreen: When I think of Pakistanis, I feel all these Muslim countries are just as close – Saudi Arabia or Libya and Palestine.

Raisa: I know what you're saying. I'm trying to understand all that. But all Palestinians aren't Muslims. There are Christians and atheists.

Nasreen: Most of them are Muslims and . . .

Raisa: When I was at college, the International Students' Society – students from all over the Middle East and Asia, Latin America and

Europe, all over the world, Muslims and Christians and atheists – they all supported the PFLP – Popular Front for the Liberation of Palestine. Their leader was a Christian, George Habash. I mean, I was a Pakistani, but here, in my heart, I was a Palestinian. Why did we all support the Palestinians, and why do your friends write PLO?

Nasreen: Maybe because Paki is part of Pakistani, sort of, and Pakistani is only small and only heard of when it's bad things. Deportings, drugs, that's when you hear about Pakistan.

Tahira: 'Cos they're the same as us. Not just 'cos they're Muslims a lot of them. I mean, Sikhs and Hindus ain't Muslims are they, but they're with us here. I mean, I know we all probably get stories told us about Hindus and Muslims and stuff about fighting in the old days and I know we don't talk about them kinds of things – it's like embarrassing and that –

Nasreen: I don't have Hindu or Sikh friends outside of school . . .

Tahira: I do, there's Gita and others, but what was I saying? Oh yeah, over here, in this country, Hindus and Sikhs are all Pakis ain't they, and you don't say PLO 'cos they're Muslim? You might, but lots of people don't.

Nasreen: I don't just 'cos they're Muslim.

Tahira: We wrote PLO' 'cos, well, on telly they're always the bad lot. You know, bombs, terrorism. It's like no one wants to hear them, the PLO and all that . . .

Nasreen: Your friends in that college society, they were from the poor countries, not advanced countries, and the Palestinians haven't even got a country.

Tahira: No one wants to hear any of us. The gorrai want to shut us up like . . .

Nasreen: The PLO won't be shut up . . .

Tahira: But them boys – that's right, and that's why we wrote PLO It means we ain't going to give up and we ain't just little schoolkids being naughty.

Nasreen: We're against being called Pakis and being picked on as Pakis, because if we aren't it sort of means we're accepting it and we might as well accept everything else we get in this country that's bad – that our parents get, that we'll get when we grow up.

Tahira: We're not just being naughty kids.

Raisa: No, we're bigger; we're part of a bigger thing.

Tahira: Gives you strength, don't it?

Raisa: It's like all the downtrodden seeing themselves in the PLO, and that gives them strength.

She stopped the voice in mid-sentence. Had she, an adolescent in the sixties, ever made such direct connections between the great public movements that she had supported with such energy, and her own oppressions?

As she sat at her desk, surrounded by books and files, Raisa's memories stirred with all the force of metaphor.

The fight with Judy Butlin. They were twelve years old. Judy had called her a fucking half-breed. In the playground, they had scratched and punched and pulled at each other's hair.

Rezwana Shah. Quiet Rezwana. She had looked on while Rezwana was bullied and humiliated by the English girls. She was thirteen at the time, and she had looked on.

And when she had come upon her mother's red box – how the memory pained her still! – had she then made connections of the sort that Nasreen and Tahira had made so swiftly? Perhaps not. But that was all part of who she was, and who they were. And there was more. There was always more – like Tahira's ambivalent revelation at the end of the interview, and Raisa's clumsy response. She hadn't yet reheard it; she had avoided hearing it, hoping, somehow, that it hadn't been recorded.

She needed a rest. She would return to the tape later that evening. She would have to return to it if she meant to work beyond her timetable. The following night she would spend at her father's house. She couldn't keep putting him off.

Fifteen

At midnight Raisa, achingly tired, switched on the recorder. Rewind, play.

Raisa: It's like all the downtrodden seeing themselves in the PLO, and that gives them strength.

(Pause)

But what about the English children, the gorrais? How is it they're not able to see a meeting point between them and the PLO? Many whites here are really poor. You've only got to see the way some of them are dressed in this school, and the flats they live in. They're not exactly your powerful gorrais.

Nasreen: You're right, they are poor. Some of them are poorer than some Pakistanis or Indians here. You're right.

Tahira: My mum ain't poor. We've got a big house. You could sort of feel sorry for them gorrai if you like, but they don't help you, they don't let you . . .

Raisa: You were saying how the school shuts you up, well, as a teacher, I can say it shuts them up as well. Remember what you said before. I bet few of them bring their lives into school, even when some teachers ask them.

Nasreen: They'd never support or see themselves with things like PLO. PLO, to them, is just foreigners and terrorists.

Tahira: Some do. There's this boy in the sixth form, his mum's a teacher, he's sort of with us . . .

Nasreen: Whose mum's a teacher?

Tahira: Barry Woolf. But a lot of the gorrai, you know, like that

Michelle and Julie and them boys, they might be like us in them kind of things you said, but it's like they just hate us and don't want to know any of that.

Nasreen: Being racist sort of blinds them. It stops them from seeing things.

Raisa: Yes, that's a very interesting point.

Tahira: If they don't want to know any of that and do horrible things, well, they can just take what they'll get. I think it's right what the Newham Seven done – them gorrai asked for it.

Nasreen: This girl, she really likes the Newham Seven.

Tahira: They fancy them, don't they?

Nasreen: This English girl says, 'Who's Newham Seven?' She says, 'They beat up English people, like you!'

Tahira: The Asian girls in our school, Sikhs, Hindus, all of them, they really fancy them.

Nasreen: They're just defending themselves, aren't they?

Tahira: I think they're good-looking as well.

Raisa: The thing is, their way of defending themselves is considered criminal . . .

Tahira: But what if the Barking Badmaash joined with them and all the other groups, and Africans and West Indians, it wouldn't be so easy to put them in prison.

Nasreen: You'd have all blacks against all whites then. That's bad.

Tahira: The way this country carries on, I mean take this school, with caning and teachers slapping kids, and kids fighting – what do you expect?

Raisa: I agree with Nasreen though. Can you imagine? But who are the Barking what?

Tahira: Haven't you seen it written round Barking? It's all over the place. You don't go round here, do you? It ain't your sort of place though, is it?

Raisa (laughs): I'm a South Londoner, I'm afraid.

Tahira: It's just something written on walls. We don't know who wrote it first, but we've sort of picked it up. It's like a group. The boys at the college write it on walls now. It's good because the English think we're frightened . . .

Nasreen: We want to fight back but we can't.

Tahira: No, they make out we're the trouble-makers and they call the police. We get stopped by the police. It ain't just the West Indians that get stopped now. Did you see that programme they showed on telly about the Asian boys in Booth Street?

Raisa: No, I don't know about it.

Tahira: That was my brother. The police took him because they reckon he threatened them. My brother, and all them others, his friends and that, they were having a go at the racists, them people who'd burn up houses, like the Kaseem family in Ilford. But the police . . .

Nasreen: We want to fight back but we can't . . .

Raisa: There are different ways of fighting back.

Tahira: You mean like petitions and marches and stuff like that? (laughs)

Raisa: Why not?

Nasreen: We should have lots of gorrai with us. It will be dangerous. Anyway, a lot of them are all right, especially on their own.

Tahira (still laughing): You got to meet Suleiman! How would kids get a march together?

Raisa: You have to have a licence from the police.

Tahira: Oh yeah, they're really gonna let kids march through the streets, Paki kids.

Nasreen: That's impossible. How would children know how to organise things like that?

Tahira: I suppose if enough of you did get together, and you got everything together properly, you wouldn't need no licence, not if there were a lot of you and you didn't do nothing violent. I mean, being kids, you could pretend you didn't know you had to have permission. Can you see it – a big march like on telly, to scare them, to tell them you ain't scared . . . ?

Raisa: This is the Tahira who was embarrassed to be seen in her shalwaar, who wanted to be white! Remember you told me . . .

Tahira: I meant . . .

(Interruption: Miss Beeston – Cathy – comes in for books)

Raisa: We're talking about the Big Fight.

Cathy: The way it's been handled, amazing!

Tahira: Oh Miss, you know when we had to write about our life, what book was we reading? I can't remember nothing.

Cathy: That doesn't surprise me. She wrote one page. She doesn't do anything. You should be ashamed of yourself.

91

Tahira: OK Miss, thank you.

Cathy: Her folder is worth looking at.

Tahira: She's seen it.

Cathy: I mean it's a real credit, isn't it? One year's work and all that.

Tahira (indicating folder): This ain't gonna do me no good, is it?

Raisa: She's got to have things that do her good.

Tahira: This English, everything in this school – it's all junk ain't it?

Cathy: Tahira, what is going to do you any good?

Tahira: I ain't thought of that yet.

Cathy: It's about time you did.

Tahira: I've got plenty of time yet. We're reading *Kes* now.

Cathy: Do you like *Kes*? She doesn't like anything.

Raisa: I think life's too exciting, isn't it?

Cathy: I'm not crazy about *Kes* either.

(Laughter)

Tahira: I don't know what it's about, Miss.

Cathy: You don't? What have you been doing?

Tahira: Reading it.

Cathy: Is this being recorded?

Raisa: It's going to get rubbed off. I haven't got enough tapes as it is. I keep using the same ones!

Tahira: I haven't even read the first page of it yet, Miss.

Cathy: What do you mean, Tahira? Are you serious?

Raisa: She told me she's been spending three weeks reading this thing, but she hasn't finished yet.

Cathy: You haven't read the first page? What have you been doing? Staring into space? This is what she does!

Raisa: Yes.

Tahira: She asked me about that book we've read, but I said we haven't read it.

Raisa: It's interesting actually to think why you did forget.

Tahira: That book's so boring! Everyone thinks it's boring!

Cathy: That's all she ever says, 'boring'!

Tahira: I still do the work though, don't I, Miss?

Cathy: What?

Tahira: I still do the work though, don't I?

Cathy: Obviously not if you've been sitting staring at a book and not reading it.

Tahira: Yeah, but I did the work. You know I've given my work in, haven't I?

Cathy: Oh, you hand it in!

Raisa: Oh, filling up pages.

Cathy: Anyway, I'll go. I've got her for an hour after this. Or are you keeping her?

Raisa (laughing): Why do you look so gleeful?

Tahira: More boring . . .

Cathy: It's not boring.

(She leaves with the books)

Tahira: She's gonna get me now.

Raisa: You like her.

Tahira: She's all right. A bit soft really, but she's all right.

Raisa: You hid what you were talking about from her.

Tahira: It ain't stuff you talk in school. All this is getting rubbed off, ain't it?

Raisa: Yes, yes, Tahira.

Nasreen: Is it two-fifteen yet?

Raisa: Nearly.

Nasreen: I've got to take my books back to the library.

Raisa: Yes, of course. Give my salaams to your mother and father.

Nasreen: Yes.

Raisa: Khuda hafiz.

Nasreen: Khuda hafiz. (Leaves)

Tahira: What are you gonna do with this tape, before you rub it off?

Raisa: Listen to it, think about what we've said, relate it to what I'm reading and discussing. Learn from it.

(Pause)

Tahira: You ain't really like us, are you?

Raisa: What do you mean?

Tahira: You weren't brought up like me, or Nasreen.

Raisa: How was I brought up then?

Tahira: Different. You look different. You speak posh. I reckon you had more freedom.

Raisa: Well, that's worth going into!

Tahira: I reckon you have. (Pause) It ain't just racism stuff that gets people, is it? I mean, other things get people as well. There's a lot to worry people with. Bad ain't it?

Raisa: I suppose you're right. For many people – when you think about it – that's exactly how it is.

Tahira: Bad, ain't it? How you can't just be nice and happy.

Raisa: Yes.

Tahira: I've done bad things, you know.

Raisa: Hasn't everyone?

Tahira: No, I mean really bad.

Raisa: Oh yes.

Tahira: Shall I tell you? You won't tell, say nothing to no one, will you?

Raisa: You don't have to tell me if you don't want . . .

Tahira: Oh, Miss, I was going out with this boy, right, and . . .

Raisa: A Pakistani?

Tahira: Yes. And, Miss, I'm not a virgin.

Raisa: Oh.

Tahira: I've done something bad and now he won't leave me alone. When I go home from school he says if I don't meet him he's gonna follow me home and he's gonna get me into trouble. So now I'm stuck.

Raisa: Does your mother know?

Tahira: No! She'd kill me, she would.

Raisa: Yes. These are problems, aren't they?

Tahira: That's really a big problem. I mean, my brother gives problems to my mum, but this is really bad.

Raisa: Yes, it's bad, it'll be seen as bad.

Tahira: I've done it now. I regret it but he won't leave me alone now.

Raisa: I have to rub this off. I'll do this today, I'll transcribe it, cross that bit out. What was I going to say? Right, obviously you can't really talk about these things.

Tahira: No. I can't say nothing like this to my mum. She'd be so ashamed, she'd kill me. I don't want to see him no more but he comes outside the school and follows me home in the car. He's met my brother, so in a way he's trying to blackmail me. If I don't turn up, so and so. If I don't do this, he's gonna do that.

Raisa: Is he really!!

Tahira: Yeah, and he's just a flirt.

Raisa: God. That's a nightmare. You poor thing. . . .

Tahira: It ain't something I can get people to march about, is it?

Raisa: You poor thing.

(Pause)

Tahira: You believed me, didn't you? (Laughs) You believed me!
You should see your face! So serious and bothered! (Laughs) It ain't
true you know, I was only having you on! You should see your face!
Raisa: That isn't funny, Tahira.
Tahira: But your face, you . . .

The tape had reached its end. It had been a long day. The drive across
London. The interview. Her father. Tahira. She rested her head on
the table-top and slept. Sleep protected her from the knowledge of
the rifts that widened between herself and the young girl.

Sixteen

She had left school straight after her meeting with Raisa. She stood at her bedroom window, her forehead leaning against the glass. She was still in her uniform. Her breathing threw waves of mistiness over the late afternoon scene. The backs of houses with their concrete yards and strips of grass moved in and out of focus. Tahira didn't move.

She shouldn't have told Raisa. Raisa who had everything. Why had she told her? Had she thought that Raisa would understand her and console her, tell her that going with boys was not so terrible? Had she thought Raisa would show her a way out? It was weird, but sometimes during their conversations she would feel very close to the woman. Then, Raisa would become more than an attractive, clever woman. She would become also the mother and the older sister and the closest friend, all in one; and when that happened, Tahira would imagine she had cut through Raisa's glamour, and also become part of it.

At such a moment of tearful closeness Tahira had made her revelation. But the woman who had responded had patronised her and judged her.

Yes, Raisa was posh, rich – you could tell she was rich – and she was good. Mumtaz must have been wrong about her. She had everything, and she had found Tahira to be bad.

Had she believed Tahira when she had denied the whole story? Tahira could have retaliated with the thought: so what if the cow knew that she was lying? She wouldn't tell anybody, nobody who could get back at her. And it wasn't as if she knew any of her relatives. She hadn't met her mother or anything like that. But the dissatisfaction wouldn't leave. It lingered and it nagged. Raisa must believe her because Raisa had everything, and Tahira couldn't do with so much less.

She tried hard not to think about the other thing. A feeling near to panic gripped her every time the memory came back.

Night-time. Car windows steamed up . . . She moved her face away from the glass and grabbed hold of the curtain as a feverish ripple moved through her body. Her skin was cold and sweaty, and she wanted to rush to the loo.

Night-time. Car windows, steamed up but still showing the derelict factory grounds beyond. Tight space. Frayed vinyl seats, aftershave. Calloused hands grazing her skin, and the noise, the noises he was making.

She felt disgusted; she felt sick. He had other girlfriends and didn't care for her. He had used her – she knew that, she had known it all along. She hated herself for ever having imagined that it might be otherwise. How could she have gone on seeing him for so long? The shame was unbearable. She pulled at the curtain and moved away.

'Bastard!' she shouted, and immediately worried that Munty or Hussain would run up to find out what was wrong. She listened for footsteps, and hearing none, fell on to her bed. Her eyes scanned the room. The damp around the ceiling had returned, and the cupboard door had slipped open again. She rolled on to her front. 'Bastard,' a whisper this time.

She could pretend to Raisa that nothing had really happened; that it was a silly story from a loud-mouthed schoolgirl who was just trying to shock. But Arif – she couldn't pretend him away. His threats were too real. All the risks she had taken and that's what he was – a dirty flirt and a blackmailer. She saw his crafty face; she heard him. 'Come on yaar, we've got to meet again. This is too good, and, you know, I'd hate to let your family find out what you've been up to.'

'Haram zaada kuta!' Her teeth were clenched. Who did he think he was, that ignorant pig? What had she ever seen in him? She couldn't meet him that evening. It was too revolting. She wouldn't meet him. That was it – she wouldn't turn up. What would he really do? She would push him and find out.

Then she remembered her mother, and the shame, and her resolve faltered. She needed security. If he really meant to tell on her, she would say she hadn't turned up because she'd been ill. That's what she'd say. If only she could find a way of getting back at him, if only she could terrorise him. One thing was sure though – she wouldn't meet him that evening. She'd go instead to Suleiman's house, to the meeting about Jamshid. That was a hundred times more important. Hussain was going, she'd go with him. Raisa would like that . . .

Tahira jolted up on the bed, and sat with her back to the wall. She couldn't contain her belligerence against the woman. So what if she'd like her going to meetings and things! The way she had treated her, why should Tahira care? She might decide never to see Raisa again.

But she knew that wouldn't happen. She might not keep her next appointment with Raisa, nor the one after that, but she would see and talk to her again, if only to convince her that the shocking confession was a lie. And there were other reasons. The talking and those moments of closeness had become too seductive to be given up. The fascinating, unanswered questions were too many. How could a woman who didn't have a husband, who was posh and good-looking, who lived alone, not have boyfriends? No, Arif and Raisa could not be placed together: the one she had to escape, the other she must seek out.

She loosened her hair and walked lethargically to the cupboard mirror. She felt better. She had made decisions, of a sort; some of the confusion had been cleared. The talking in her head was becoming more and more like the conversations with Raisa and Nasreen. Tucking in her long hair to shoulder-length, she looked over her shoulder and pouted in the mirror.

The front door slammed shut; her bedroom shook with the vibrations. That would be Ashraf. In a few minutes, he'd make his way to the bathroom and wash away the paint and grime. When their mother got home, they would all sit down to eat.

Tahira took out a clean pair of jeans and a sweatshirt. Her mother was coming home early that day and the whole family would be in. She knew she'd better hurry downstairs to help with the cooking. She looked forward to work in the kitchen; it might distract her from everything else.

Seventeen

Most of the students had finished their lunch and had gone to the playgrounds behind the building. The dining hall was almost empty. Mr Busby looked idly out of the window. He was eating his dessert, anticipating the end of the day when he could get into his car and drive away home. The noisy afternoon classes that lay between him and the leafy roads of Essex were forgotten for a while. He thought of his garden.

The Asians outside the main gate, clearly in view and growing in number, did not disturb his daydreams. After all, you often saw clusters of pupils moving in and out at lunchtime. But this group continued to swell in the tidy suburban street.

A man with a cat basket crossed over to the other side of the road. The woman tending her rockery stopped to see what was happening. They were always fighting in that school. In the old days it was different. What were the teachers doing about it? she asked herself as she shut the front door behind her. Curtains twitched at one or two windows. The white neighbourhood seemed to be holding its breath.

The three girls pushed their way to the front. They were dressed identically. Each wore a black shalwaar kameez with the dupatta, blazing red, tied around her waist. They stood out among the uniforms.

'How many d'you reckon are coming?' Mumtaz rearranged the knot in her dupatta.

'It'll get bigger,' said Gita. 'Loads of people from other schools are coming.' She gave the evil eye to a boy who pushed past her.

The first and second year students moved about confidently,

cushioned among the older ones. Anticipation shone on their faces.

Tahira said, 'If you think about it, there was two hundred leaflets we give out, and they said to tell others about it. Loads more are bound to come.' She stood tall, aware of her loose hair flying in the wind.

'Maybe we should have waited longer at the park and come here together. You know, really big – loads and loads of us.' Gita played with her spiky hair. 'You know, really make them gorrai shit themselves.'

'No, this is better,' said Tahira. 'Remember what Suleiman said about the cops. If they saw us in the park, we'd never have got here.'

'Well maybe, but this shouldn't get any bigger, not before Suleiman's lot arrive. The teachers'll come out thinking there's a fight, and we won't all be here, will we?'

'Yeah, yeah.' Irritation rang in Tahira's voice. 'But it's done now, ain't it? I mean, we've never arranged nothing like this before.'

'Don't go mad! I was only saying in case I should run down the park and tell 'em to hurry up.' She was hurt at being misunderstood.

Tahira was contrite. 'That's a brilliant idea. If you want, I'll go.'

'No, it's all right. I'll go.' Gita hurried away.

'Bloody hell – you should listen to the two of you.' Mumtaz showed her exasperation by moving further into the crowd, towards the school gate.

Tahira followed her cousin. 'Them blokes over there . . .' she indicated some youths leaning against the wire fencing. 'They ain't from our school, and I ain't never seen them at the college.'

'Yeah,' said Mumtaz. 'Just look at them, the fat one.'

'They look weird.'

'Well put it this way. They're better than the lot that ain't here. Like your friend Nasreen.'

'She ain't exactly a friend, is she?' said Tahira. 'Anyway, you know what her mum and dad would think of this.'

Tahira looked again at the unknown youths. 'They'd better not do nothing stupid, you know. Nothing we ain't planned for.' She remembered the story of the boy who would close his eyes and jump backwards off trees. How like that boy they were themselves, she thought. Though they had discussed and planned this and that and had imagined all kinds of outcomes, today, like the boy in the tree, theirs was also a leap in the dark. Tahira repeated, 'They'd better not do nothing stupid.'

Mumtaz started to speak, then checked herself. She would only have said something frivolous and out of place. It was strange that she should feel like this about a cousin who was three months younger. She had always been a little in awe of Tahira, but never quite like this. For the past weeks all she had seen of Tahira was her total devotion to the planning of the day. She missed those endless chats they used to have, long into the night.

'Look, there's Hussain,' Tahira nudged at the people in front of her to keep her brother in sight. 'Hussain!' she called. He waved at her. Mumtaz folowed Tahira's gaze. 'I can see him, he's with Najum and that lot and them two gorrai.'

Tahira said, 'I thought Barry and Raymond were at the park.'

'That means the others will be coming soon then,' said Mumtaz. 'Don't those gorrai feel a bit out of it?'

'They must do – a bit.'

Tahira felt the excitement; in her veins, she felt it. She smiled.

Mumtaz took the risk. 'Do you fancy Suleiman? He was always at them meetings, right?'

'What?' Tahira was taken aback. 'Don't be daft, he's got a girlfriend, and anyway, it ain't like that.'

'I reckon you fancy him. I don't blame you. He's nice. Not like what's his name. What a pig he turned out to be. Thank God he's stopped pestering you.'

'Yeah,' Tahira's words were slow and quiet, 'just let him try and bother me again.' She hadn't turned up that day, and he hadn't contacted her since. She'd been busy with other things. She hadn't had the time to think about his threats and their terrifying implications. She'd heard he was chasing someone else. Anger and bravado aside, she was grateful to be forgotten.

'Suleiman ain't a bit like that pig,' said Mumtaz. 'I thought you went to all them meetings 'cos of him . . . Well, partly.'

'You're daft.' Tahira noticed the two boys from her class. Brian Harrington, the gorra, and Daniel Dixon, the West Indian boy, were walking up the road towards them. 'I had more important reasons.'

Brian and Daniel were now meandering through the crowd. 'Why are you all out here?' Daniel asked.

'Waiting,' said Tahira.

Daniel smiled; he and Brian walked on into the school.

'What if a teacher comes out?' Mumtaz said. 'The park lot ain't here yet.'

'Well, then, think yourself lucky no one's come out yet.'

'I'm surprised that beady-eyed caretaker ain't come out. Can't see him in his office.' Mumtaz squinted her eyes at the glass doors of the main entrance, and through them at the glass hatch of the caretaker's office. 'He must be out or something.'

There was no time to pursue the conversation. The girls turned to the giant lorry that was rumbling in their direction. It would soon pass the school, and some of their friends were standing dangerously close to the road.

'Fucking get out of the way!' boomed the driver's voice. Shouts pursued him as he sped by.

Tahira saw her younger sister. 'Munty! Get over here now!' Munty and her friend moved away from the pavement's edge.

The woman sat at her bedroom window. If it got any worse, she would call the police.

Assured that her sister was safe, Tahira observed the scene calmly – the expectant sounds and stances of those around her; the unnatural stillness in the road; the school that hadn't yet woken to them.

Someone tapped her arm. 'Oh, wotcha!' It was Hussain. She greeted Ijaz and Najum. 'What's happening over the park? They should be here by now.'

'Yeah,' said Ijaz, 'we're gonna be too many, man. They'll get the police.'

Tahira said, 'There'll be too many of us, they'll have to listen. They'll have to at least listen.'

'It's gonna be great, innit?' said Mumtaz to Hussain.

'Yeah.' He looked about him, eyes wide.

'Ray and Barry are running over to speed them up at the park.'

Ijaz shook his head. 'The minute Sulli and the others get here – there's so many coming with him, man – the minute they get here, them teachers'll phone the police, or someone will.'

Mumtaz was irritated by his gloom. 'What if they do call the police? We'll just have to make sure we say what we've come to say.' She was impressed by her own outburst, and pleased that Tahira was looking on approvingly.

Ijaz grinned as he shrugged his shoulders.

Tahira said, 'You can take that stupid look off your face! Even if we don't get to speak today, Busby and that lot'll know we can get together if we want, and say things and God knows what else. It won't look good on them and they'll be worrying what we might do next, cops or no cops.'

Najum, not quite looking at her, spoke quickly. 'She's right. We should remember all that; we should remember the meetings.'

Tahira spoke to her brother. 'Is Jamshid over at the park? We didn't see him earlier.'

'He should be here soon. His shift ends at twelve. He'll come straight here.' Hussain ran both hands over his head from forehead to neck – a mannerism acquired to tame his shoulder-length hair.

Mumtaz saw Jayesh. He was laughing loudly and greeting his old friends. He looked like a celebrity attending a party laid on especially for him. He rubbed his palms as he appraised the group. 'I read your leaflet. Thought I'd come along to my old school and see what's happening.'

'Nothing's happening yet, man.' Ijaz stared at Jayesh's gold watch and rings. He wondered if they were real. 'We're waiting for someone to call the police.'

Mumtaz moved away.

'I'll be gone long before then,' Jayesh assured everyone. 'I got too many important things on my hands.'

'This is important.' Tahira wouldn't let him trivialise their efforts.

'I'm here, right?' Jayesh stretched out his arms. 'I'll stay, man – for a while, and shout things, right? I got a lot to say to this school.'

Barry Woolf came out from behind a group of younger students. His eyes were bright, his skin flushed. 'They're coming now, they're on their way. You can just about see them over there.' He pointed along the pavement to beyond the trail of students.

Word soon got round. Tahira could hear the rushing of her blood. 'We'd better make sure no one runs to the park. Make sure they stay put and don't do nothing daft.'

Mumtaz said, 'It's a good job there ain't much traffic.'

Their group spread out into the crowd. The white students near the main gate kept a cautious distance. Even those who were 'all right' stayed away. They knew something was happening; many sensed a connection with the fight last month. In their pairs and clusters they all stood back – all, except one girl. She was alone. Her friends were waiting for her in the senior playground. She had been on her way to persuade them to bunk off the afternoon with her. A lunchtime detention and a late lunch had confirmed her hatred of the school and the teachers. She wouldn't have stopped but for the two white boys.

Julie Webster approached Barry and Raymond. She kept to the school side of the gate. 'You make me puke!'

The boys were stunned by the tremble in her voice. She walked away.

A second later, Barry shouted after her, 'Racists and fascists make me puke!' His friend bit on a finger-nail and wondered if the people around him really trusted him.

The unknown youths had not moved or spoken. They were still standing by the wire fence. There were four of them. One resembled a pahlvaan with his shaved head and bulbous body. The other three could have been caricatures of meanness: brooding stances, leather jackets, spiky pieces of metal on their boots, chokers and wristbands.

Friends of friends, they had come along to lend support, though they had no urge to reason with an enemy. It didn't matter that South Park School had not been their school. It wouldn't have mattered where or what the place had been, because the rot was everywhere. Out of their pockets and now on the ground before them, lay their stones and bottles.

Mr Busby had finished his dessert. He laid his green and private Essex in a corner of his mind and got up to leave. It was tiresome that he had to teach that afternoon.

He saw the crowd. It was big. The lines of students ran nearly the whole length of the left-hand side of the school fence. All Asians; at least sixty or seventy of them. There wasn't an English face among them. Not another fight.

Tiredly, he left his table to walk the corridor to the front entrance. He hoped that someone else had raised the alarm and that someone else was taking care of it. He'd had enough of it.

Cathy Beeston and the new student-teacher in the history department were standing by the closed glass doors, observing the students at the gates.

Mr Busby, once again the public man and head of the fifth year, gave out his instructions. 'I'm going out there. Get someone else – in case it gets nasty.' He stepped out.

'There goes your man,' said Cathy. 'Now there really will be a fight.'

The woman at the window could not believe what she was seeing. Who were all those other people coming towards the school, and what were they carrying in their hands?

About fifty yards from the school gates, and on the opposite side of the road, Suleiman and Imran – ex-pupils of South Park School – and Gita led a multitude of girls and boys, at least a hundred of them. The placards that Tahira and Gita had made the night before bobbed above the heads of the marchers. Some of them had brought along drums. The deep, hollow beats accompanied their chanting: 'South Park School is racist! South Park School is racist!' The voices rang out louder and louder as the drummers beat their drums.

The crowd at the gate moved aside. A car was forced to stop as the procession marched across the road and through the gates.

The road with its neat line of semis maintained its reserve. If it had anything to say, it would say it in the right ears.

The woman was no longer at her window. Furious, she was phoning the police. It wouldn't be allowed in their own countries and here they were, bold as brass.

The bell for the end of lunchtime had been sounded, and the front of the school was out of bounds to the children in the playgrounds. Those already in the area were quickly herded into the building. Form tutors had been told to keep all pupils in class until further notice. To the school's relief, few of the white children knew what was happening. The Asians who had ignored the call to demonstrate were quiet. Heads lowered, they courted invisibility. There was no danger of them giving any information.

Mr Kern, his deputies and his heads of year stood outside the glass doors of the main entrance, face to face with the crowd.

'Go home, all of you! Go home and there won't be any trouble!' Mr Kern was shouting. The crowd was hissing him. 'There are too many of you! You can't all fit in . . .' The shouts and the hissing drowned his voice. He tried again to speak. 'No! No! No! No!' spat the crowd.

It was impossible. He couldn't make himself heard above the noise. He saw their unhearing faces, challenging him, and beyond his control. Should he have called the police? Perhaps someone in the neighbourhood already had, and his efforts to settle things quietly were pointless to begin with? His mind was a jumble. A headmaster must be in control, must be seen by all to be in control. The police might mean bad publicity for the school. He had to avoid any dramas. What was happening to these children? No child was treated worse than any other – not if he had anything to do with it.

He tried again. 'Listen to me! Please listen!' This time hushes to silence from within the crowd quietened the students. 'What must the street think – all of you out here like this? What name are you giving your school?'

'It ain't our school!' someone shouted back.

'We don't want a riot here, do we? Now do what I . . .'

'We want to talk to you lot.' Tahira had moved to the front. 'Let us into the playground. The street won't be so bothered then, will it?'

'We'll have to refuse,' said Mr Busby, pulling up the waist of his trousers. 'What if the other children come out?'

'If we refuse it could get worse,' said Elvira Mason, the deputy head.

The hissing had started again somewhere in the midst of the crowd and was spreading outward. 'We'll have better control,' she said, 'if we let them in and talk to them.'

Mr Busby persisted. 'For God's sake, there are too many of them. I've never seen some of them before. We should call the police.'

'That's right, Bob,' said Andy Larkins, the head of the sixth form. 'There are kids out there who don't come to this school.'

Elvira Mason would not give up. 'It's not safe for them out there. They could easily fall into the road. Look, we know most of these kids. We've taught them for years, we should be able to talk to them.'

It was always the same waffle and nonsense, thought Mr Busby. No wonder the school was falling apart.

Imran spoke next. The hissing stopped. 'Let us in! We ain't going till we've said what we've come to say.'

'All right, all of you, listen to me!' The headmaster adopted his most authoritative tone. 'When I give the word, you may enter quietly and slowly. You will follow the teachers to the senior playground. You will not, under any circumstances, enter the school building. I want one of you to answer me – the boy who spoke just now. Do you understand and will you follow these rules?'

A murmur passed through the crowd, followed, once again, by

energetic hushings to silence. Tahira looked at the faces near her; and at the mass of people that had filled up all the space. What would happen next? Would one speak for all? There were so many points of uncertainty.

Gita turned her back to the teachers, faced the students and waved her placard to loud cheers. She said, 'We understand. We haven't come for trouble. We want you lot to understand a few things, that's all.'

Mr Kern looked towards his staff before he answered. 'All right, slowly and quietly you may enter. Remember, follow the teachers and do as they tell you.'

It would all go smoothly, the headmaster told himself. Many of them were, after all, only young children. Then, his eyes fell upon Jamshid Iqbal. The boy had come, as if from nowhere, to stand in the middle of the front row. He still hadn't lost that impudent look of his. Mr Kern cast his gaze to the houses and the sky beyond the school. He held himself straight. The dizziness was threatening to return.

The playground was filled without incident. Elvira Mason suggested that the children sit down, facing away from the school building. Those who were tired crouched down on the tarmac; others preferred to stand. The banners still loomed above their heads. More teachers had come out. As in morning assembly, they positioned themselves at the front and the sides. The head, his deputy, Mr Busby and Mr Larkins stood facing the crowd.

Suleiman began his speech. 'You might remember me – some of you, anyway. I left last year. I'm not the only one speaking, and we've got a lot to say. Some of it isn't about school, but school has a lot do with that as well.' He had his notes in his pocket; he didn't need them now.

'First, this school is unfair . . .' the crowd cheered in agreement. ' . . . this school is unfair in lots of ways, not just with blacks.' He turned to address those behind him, and then continued. 'It's unfair not just with blacks, but a lot with blacks.'

Mr Busby cleared his throat.

'For example, take caning. It shouldn't be allowed in any case, but in this school it's unfairly done. How come in the last month three Pakistanis, two Indians, and three West Indian boys have been caned? How many whites have you caned in that time?'

Suleiman paused as the others repeated and shouted out his question.

'Last week, two white boys were caned.' But the headmaster's words were lost in the noise. Only Suleiman could hear him.

'We wondered about that, because the racists seemed to be getting away with too much. And when I say racists, I don't mean just the kids!'

The headmaster interrupted him. 'I don't think you have the full facts, but carry on. Finish what you've got to say. We're listening.'

Suleiman wasn't put off. 'Where are these facts? Why haven't you shown them to us?'

There was movement at the back. The crowd pressed forward to hear. 'We don't like the way you dealt with that fight last month – the fight that got Jamshid Iqbal expelled. He should never have been expelled. Either you don't know the full facts, or you are not interested in the full facts. As far as we're concerned, what happened to Jamshid is an obvious racist incident. There's plenty that isn't so obvious, but that'll do for now.'

Suleiman stopped to clear his throat. The others clapped and cheered, thinking he had finished. He waved his arm for more time. 'We want to let you hear some of the facts that you do not know.'

Jamshid stepped forward.

'You kicked him out, but Jamshid Iqbal's back. He'll tell you what this school did to him, what this school kicked him out to, and how in the end it's all the rotten same.'

No one spoke. The teachers looked at one another. Mr Busby and Mr Larkins moved closer to one another. The headmaster ignored the twitching in his right temple.

'Right, I've listened to you. We all have. It's now your turn to listen to me.'

A second year boy called out, 'We haven't finished. Let Jamshid speak!' He blushed at his own daring.

The headmaster spoke again, with heavy emphasis. 'I've listened to you, and it's your turn to listen to me. You don't seem to know what schools are about.'

The talking and shuffling had started.

'I've dealt with the Jam-sheed episode and I've dealt with it fairly – the only way it could have been dealt with. The boy had a knife, and he might have used it. There is absolutely no point in it being brought up again!'

Tahira screamed out, 'Let him speak! We ain't in our classrooms now!'

The headmaster noted who had spoken, and dismissed the girl's outburst. 'I was fair. I looked carefully at both sides. I was fair.'

'There are more sides than both!' Tahira hit back.

'I was fair. Listen to me. Those of you who are sensible and hard-working. Don't let others fool you into doing the wrong things. You don't understand what's happening.'

Fewer and fewer students were trying to listen. Somewhere near the back, the chanting started. Hardly audible at first, it grew louder and clearer: 'PLO! PLO! PLO! PLO! PLO!'

Mr Larkins murmured to Mr Busby, 'What's this obsession with the PLO?'

'Gives it all a bit of drama, doesn't it? Did you see those boys in the leather jackets?'

Their conversation was cut short. The older children at the back seemed to be moving. Busby rushed in their direction.

The drums had joined in with the resolute voices, and a second chant had started: 'Barking Badmaash! Barking Badmaash!' Within seconds, every mouth in the crowd was shouting out the conflation. 'PLO! Barking Badmaash! PLO! Barking Badmaash!'

'Get Mr Aslam,' the headmaster commanded his head of sixth form. 'If he can't get through to them, we'll have to call the police.'

Hamid Aslam faced the crowd. He was out of breath. Behind him stood the senior management of South Park School. Hamid was mindful of his importance.

He had spent the lunch-hour in his tutor room, eating sandwiches and marking books. He had heard of the problem only minutes before Larkins had approached him. He was not prepared for the spectacle that greeted him.

'*Sunho, sunho!*' It was the first time he had used Punjabi at the school.

The chanting subsided.

Hamid continued, in Punjabi. 'Listen, all of you! You've gone far enough. All right you're angry about this and that. All right . . .'

'Hey, Aslam!' a boy shouted, also in Punjabi, 'they can't understand you. You can say what you like. Those kutai can't understand you!'

Laughter spread through the crowd as the exchange between teacher and pupil was repeated. Gita translated for Barry and Ray.

The headmaster smiled at the quietening multitude, and at the maths teacher.

Hamid shuddered with contentment. The line of teachers with whom he stood had need of him. It was indeed rare to stand with the powerful and not be brushed aside.

'Listen!' said Hamid. 'You're angry at this school, you're angry at this country, I know. I understand. But listen, this way of carrying on isn't what your parents want. They want you to work hard at your studies. They want you to work hard and have successful lives. That's their dream, that's what they . . .'

'Yeah, like you're working hard and doing OK!' the same boy interrupted. The irony in the comment inspired some others. '*Chamcha, chamcha, chamcha,*' they called out. And from within the heart of the crowd, the chanting surged again: 'PLO! Barking Badmaash!'

The students at the back started to move again, though Busby was standing near and watching.

Hamid turned to the headmaster. 'I think they're perhaps too lively. We need to be firmer, I think.'

'Yes, you're right,' the headmaster shouted. The wild chanting hammered at his temples. Once more, there was that jumble of thoughts. He stepped in front of Hamid and raised his voice to its loudest. 'If you don't stop this noise and go home, I'll call the police.'

The chanting, and the drum beats, reached new heights of loudness.

Sirens blared two streets away, then one. Nearer and nearer they approached. Their pulsating wail attacked the air. The crowd in the playground would not be intimidated. It was going to stand firm. It had right on its side. It was invincible. Its voice was hoarse but unrelenting. 'PLO! Barking Badmaash!' rang out against the approaching evil.

The sirens stopped. The cars, and the van with its shielded and helmeted force entered the playground. Policemen ran into the crowd. The teachers stood back. The headmaster looked on, stunned. He looked around for journalists and photographers and tried to rehearse explanations for the children's wildness. And God knows what was happening back in the classrooms!

The slogans had faded into silence. The crowd fragmented into smaller groups. Some scattered across the adjoining playing field to escape round the back of the school. Others ran towards the school building.

A boy in a leather jacket shattered a window with a stone. He was the first to be arrested. His pahlvaan friend, huge and angry, was edging towards Busby through the crowd. Amid the noise and confusion, he would get the teacher. He would punch him to the ground and kick him and spit on him and kick him till his brains fell out. A woman police officer, flanked by two policemen, approached him, and told him to empty his pockets. He was arrested for the studs on his wrists. Others were arrested too.

The demonstrators were nudged and prodded along the police-lined routes that took them out of the playground and in three separate directions away from the school.

In the rush to avoid arrest or censure, Tahira, Gita and Suleiman had run across the playing field and sought refuge in the derelict shed. Suleiman and Gita sat on old boxes. Tahira leaned against a wall. The place was filthy. It smelled of urine. The ground was littered with dog ends in one corner, and small white gluey bags in another.

No one spoke. Each was waiting for the security of total silence, when the sounds of the playground would be completely hushed and they could be certain that the danger had passed.

Tahira spoke first. 'Reminds me of the time we was hiding in the loo. Remember? After the fight?' she asked Gita. Gita nodded in answer. Tahira continued, 'Sort of guts you – everything – don't it?'

Suleiman gazed up at the small square window. The glass had long since been smashed out of it.

'What we done was still worth it, though.' Tahira heard herself speak and it was someone else speaking, someone in an heroic tale. 'It was good, all that thinking, all that talking and doing things – you know, the banners and getting out there with all them other kids.'

'Yeah, I know,' said Gita, her voice full.

Tahira remembered her last meeting with Raisa. Yes, she wanted Raisa to see her now; she wanted her, and all those people like her, to know that Tahira Rashid was a fighter, and good. 'All right,' she said, 'so we had some blokes who threw stones and things . . .'

'There was this girl I saw, a fourth year I think, she done it as well,' said Gita.

'All right, so we got some people who didn't do what we said on them leaflets!' Tahira unwound the dupatta from her waist and wound it round her hands. 'So what if them gorrai are strong? Everything helps them, don't it? So bloody what! We'll do it again and again and again, and do it better, and they'll have to listen, at least listen.' There in the shed it all seemed possible.

Suleiman moved over to the window. The light emphasised the shadows under his eyes. His face had a new leanness. His curly hair was dishevelled and falling over his eyes; he ignored it.

Tahira watched him. From somewhere far away came the thought, how could she have ever liked Arif?

Suleiman said, 'They wouldn't let Jamshid speak. They couldn't face it.'

'They thought we were all mad, just out to make trouble 'cos we're like that. That's what they thought.' Gita kicked at the dog ends by her feet. 'And that chamcha Aslam!'

'They couldn't face it,' Suleiman repeated.

'But we showed them, though.' Tahira hid her wet eyes.

They hadn't heard his footsteps. He appeared like a shadow. He asked them who they were, what they were doing in a dirty old shed. He wanted good and quick answers or the van was waiting outside.

His face was so smooth, he could have been a sixth former.

They told him they'd been on the march. They told him they'd hidden in the shed because of the boy with the bottle. He instructed them to stand up, to empty their pockets, all of them. Gita and Tahira didn't have any pockets to empty. He stared at the girls. What were nice Pakistani girls doing talking to boys, sitting alone with them in a shed? What would their fathers say about it? He stood by the door and ordered them to get off home. They were lucky he wasn't putting them in the van.

Eighteen

The supply teacher, an elderly woman with a happy face and protruding teeth, told 5B that their form tutor was absent. She would be taking them for that morning's class period, and she was certain – mature children that they were – they had some work to be getting on with.

She sat at the teacher's desk, wishing that all lessons could be like this, the first of the day, where the classes were thin, and where those present were still too dozy to release their frustrations on each other, or on her. She took out a copy of *History Today* and shuffled through the pages to find the article on Charles II.

'You're supposed to take the register,' a pale, red-haired girl reminded her.

'Yes,' replied the supply teacher, 'you're right. The thing is, my dear, I haven't been given a register to take.'

'Well, loads of the class ain't here.' The girl turned her back on the woman to talk to her friend at the group of desks behind her. The woman strained to remember whether or not she should have collected a class register from the office. She smiled on the class. The children were low-voiced. They were all sitting down. She was happy to leave them chatting quietly. She turned again to her journal.

A boy entered the classroom. 'Who are you?' he asked.

'I'm covering for Miss Beeston, young man,' said the woman, 'I take it you're late?'

'Ain't you too old for teaching?'

One or two students looked up to see what might happen.

'You're a polite young person, aren't you?' the woman said. 'You've reminded me why I took early retirement.'

'Couldn't take it, eh?' he said.

'Would you get to your seat please?' Without the supply work, there'd be no holiday in Normandy. The gangly boy pushed aside the tables and chairs to get to his place at the back of the room.

'Where have you been, David?' asked a girl called Kelly, as the boy passed by her. 'Not doing naughty things I hope?'

'Fuck off,' he replied.

'Fuck off yourself.'

'Ah, little David's been doing naughty things again.' A boy called Simon picked up the teasing.

'All right children, come on now, that's enough,' the supply teacher called out. 'Settle down now.'

'Where's Miss Beeston anyway?' the red-haired girl asked. 'She's never away.'

'She died last night, got run over,' David Birch shouted to the class.

'What?' The news wrenched Nasreen from her book.

'The stupid cow believes me.' The boy's laughter roared across the room.

'Shut up, you berk,' said Brian Harrington, 'you ain't funny!'

David carried on laughing, and then, conscious that no one would join him, he stopped.

Nasreen stole a glance at Brian. Had he defended her, or was it simply that, like the rest of the class, he hated David Birch? The Zahid of dreamland rose like a chimera before her. Of late, that was all he did: surface fleetingly, and then disappear. She could no longer hold on to him, nor the quicksilver world from which he came. The other world had become too pressing – the world of shady streets and bedrooms that were really workrooms, of good girls and bad girls, of fathers over forty, of warring children . . . It was as if her vision and her hearing had been sharpened. She had started to note things. She'd known they were there before now, but it seemed that she hadn't quite focused on them.

There was no comfort, though, in those sharpened perceptions. She saw and heard, and she felt; she wanted all others to do the same.

114

But they didn't, and she could neither catch their ear, nor translate what she knew into the language of argument. Sometimes she fancied she would choke, because the words that wouldn't come out were becoming a congealed mass in her throat.

'Oi, Nasreen!' called Gita, two desks away. She was sitting with a Chilean girl, who had arrived in England two weeks ago. 'Where's Tahira? I thought you and her were seeing that woman today?'

'Not till after break,' said Nasreen. 'I don't know where Tahira is. She'll probably come in later.'

Gita, a Hindu, was more Tahira's friend than Nasreen was. Nasreen thought about Tahira's friends, and all the secrets they shared. She felt the pain of exclusion. The girls spoke with her only briefly; they rarely laughed with her. She had never truanted, nor joined in any of the girlish mischief that all the others semed to be enjoying. She had never really been tempted, not really; and that was as it should be. Still, she should have stood with the others outside the school gates.

The supply teacher surveyed the class; the noise level had risen a little – nothing to be unduly alarmed about though. Over half the pupils had books in front of them; some were in fact reading and discussing their work. The rest, mercifully, were still groggy with sleep.

'What a serious, well-mannered class you are,' said the woman. 'I must commend you to your head of year.'

No one commented. No one seemed to have heard her.

Her attention was soon diverted to the slowly-opening door. Julie Webster, carrying neither bag nor book, walked directly to the desks near the back of the room. There she joined Linda and the taller girl named Kelly. The three of them pulled their chairs closer and began to talk intently.

The teacher left her desk to talk to the new arrival. A 'supply' or not, she couldn't allow students to walk in as they pleased. She braced herself for the girl's response. Bare-legged girls with truculent walks and wispy highlighted hair were a type she knew well.

'Do you normally wander into lessons without explaining your lateness to the teacher?' She leaned over Julie and her friends.

Julie seemed suddenly to notice the teacher. 'Hello Miss, you're new, ain't ya?' She smiled winningly. The small fifth former had the roundness and bloom of a ten-year-old.

'My dear, you should, you know, tell the teacher why you are late.' The woman spoke more gently. 'It's school rules, isn't it, and good manners?'

'Oh, it's all right Miss. Everyone knows why I'm late in the mornings.'

The teacher searched for sarcasm in the girl's words. She found none.

'I take my little sisters to school,' the girl continued, charitably conscious of her advantage. 'It's all right, Miss. My teacher knows and Mr Busby. My mum goes to work early and I have to take my sisters to school. You can ask if you want.'

'Yes, I understand,' said the teacher. 'It's just that, well, I don't know any of this, and a pupil is supposed to explain her lateness to the teacher.'

'Sorry, Miss.'

The teacher urged the girls to continue with their work. She moved on to tour the room, pausing to talk to Brian about the Stephen King thriller he was reading, and to watch the rude boy, who was now leaning back precariously on his chair and blowing raspberries. She ignored him, as did the rest of the class.

Back at her desk, the teacher sighed a little sigh of relief. Everyone was seated and mostly good-humoured. There was no foul language, nor any threatening outbursts. If only all lessons could be as manageable as this!

'Look at the state of it!' said Kelly. 'I mean, look at them teeth.'

'Leave her alone. She's all right,' said Julie. The teacher was too old and past it to be knocked.

Julie looked around the classroom. She saw the new Indian boy. Nasreen caught her eye. 'Ain't that Tahira come in yet?' Julie asked her friends.

'Nah,' said Linda. 'She's probably with the rest of them, swarming outside the school again. Or writing all that Paki shit on the walls.'

'Stupid bitch!' Kelly took off an ear-ring and rubbed her sore ear-lobe.

Nasreen hadn't done with her self-recriminations. She should have been with the others. It didn't matter that the police had been called, or that it was in the papers. How would she explain her absence to the others – and to Raisa? Raisa was bound to talk about it. All sorts of things came out in their meetings. Nasreen would tell her of the pressure from her parents. Maybe she'd try to put into words the other reasons – reasons she had tried to untangle in her head, but never quite to her satisfaction. Maybe she'd try to explain all that to Raisa. Otherwise she'd have to take Raisa's judgment of her – a good little girl without a brain of her own, and without any courage. And there, supporting one another, were the English girls.

'That wanker Jamshid whatever his name is, he don't half reckon himself,' said Kelly. 'Remember him, calling us them names.'

'They all bleeding do,' said Linda. She offered gum to her friends.

'Yeah.' Julie was almost contemplative. ' "Reckon" ain't the word. I ask you, a bunch of Pakis outside the school, trying to scare us!' She carried on. 'I hate that fucking headmaster, and all them teachers. But, you know, when them Pakis swarmed out there, I know whose side I was on.'

'Yeah, but them teachers love 'em really,' said Linda.

'Trying to scare us!' Julie eased her sore foot out of her new courts. 'Take that cow Gita, for instance. Just look at her.'

They turned their eyes on Gita. Gita was no longer helping her new Chilean friend. Instead she was quietly doodling on the cover of an exercise book.

Nasreen wondered whether Gita could hear the English girls: her desk was closer to theirs than Nasreen's.

The teacher left her journal to observe the class. The noise had not risen much at all; everything was perfectly fine. She took a deep breath, stretched her back and would have continued her reading, had one of the Asian girls not come up to her desk.

'Yes, my dear?' asked the teacher. 'What can I do for you?' She saw the girl's flushed face. 'Are you feeling all right?'

'No,' said Gita. 'Can I go to the toilet?'

'Of course. Do you want your friend to go with you?'

'No. I'll be OK.' She left the room.

Julie had raised her head in time to catch Gita's sour expression. 'Fucking bastards, the lot of them,' said Julie, her child's face aged by the sneer.

Nasreen saw their cutting looks. Brian was sitting near them. He must have heard them, and he hadn't said anything. How could Zahid have the face of someone who kept quiet to all that? And without his face Zahid wouldn't be Zahid. She feared losing him forever. She had to let the thought pass. The three girls were talking about her. She concentrated hard, to catch every word.

'It's that wanker Jam-sheed that gets me,' said Kelly, rubbing her ear-lobe again. 'Always did give me the creeps. Know what I mean?'

'Right,' Julie said. 'Like imagine being alone with him.' The three shuddered in unison.

Her head lowered towards her book, her thoughts well hidden, Nasreen took in their venom.

'Tells you about them, though, don't it?' said Julie, 'I mean, you know, how they all stick together like. One of them gets it, and they all gang up together. Makes you sick.'

'Yeah, all of them,' said Kelly. 'Just look at them now. Even that new fat git was with them outside.' With a flick of her head, she indicated the Indian boy who was sitting near to Brian Harrington. 'They was all there. Every fucking one of them. Shouting against us.'

Like a surging pain, Nasreen felt again the shame of her own absence.

Having worked out which lessons he would skip that day, and bored with the tutor period, David Birch caught the tail end of the girls' conversation. 'You talking about that Paki and Terry Ames?' He pulled his chair forward to join them.

'What do you want?' Julie asked, with disgust in her voice.

He repeated, 'You talking about the Paki with the knife?'

'Yeah, that's right.' Julie mellowed a little.

'Pity Ames didn't cut his prick off.'

They all started laughing. David sat more comfortably. The boy who had jeered at Julie's flat tits and Kelly's fat legs was for the moment tolerated.

'I've heard the Pakis are going to get it soon anyway.' In his enthusiasm, David spoke loudly.

'Keep your voice down,' said Julie. 'Miss'll hear.'

'So what if she does?'

'You know the teachers in this bleeding school,' said Julie. 'She'll have a go at us, won't she?'

'Who gives a toss?' he answered. 'That Paki's going to get his head kicked in anyway. Don't matter if he don't come to school no more.' He giggled. 'Ames' dad's going to get him anyway. They'll all get it sooner or later.'

'They should be glad we let 'em in,' said Linda, 'not come all flash.'

They tasted, for a moment, the warmth of solidarity.

'Like that Jacko in Manchester,' began David.

Nasreen lifted her head from her book, and waited.

David looked furtively around him. 'Last September, I think. It weren't really famous or nothing.'

Nasreen fixed her eyes on him, watching his lips so that she would hear every hateful word. She knew what he was talking about. She knew what he would say next. Her face hot, and the congealed mass of unspoken words choking her, she knew.

'You know. The Paki who had a fight with a white boy. In school it was, and he got it, didn't he?'

'What do you mean, he got it?' asked a worried Julie. Her friends echoed her question.

'He got killed, didn't he?' said David.

'Who?'

'The flash Paki, of course.'

The girls seemed to relax.

Nasreen saw their relief. Enough! That was enough! She remembered the Urdu newspaper with the pictures of the boy, thirteen years old. The boy murdered in the school playground. And the picture of his mother – her eyes piercing her with their pain. She remembered all that, and she had seen the relief on the girls' faces. The ball in her throat was growing too big. Her chair fell back. She was standing in front of the four of them. Like the sound of madness, her screaming filled the room.

The teacher dropped her journal, as she rushed to the girl. What on earth had happened to the child? She hadn't even noticed the girl in the room.

'Take the chair from her. Someone get the chair out of her hand.' The teacher aimed her plea at the tall sensible boy. 'Quick, get it out of her hand before she hurts someone.'

Brian Harrington got up, shaken by the bizarre spectacle. He was too slow. Nasreen hurled her flaming meteorite at David Birch, at the burning of pregnant women and their children, at the pains in her mother's body and the dangers around her, at the unimportance of her jobless father, at the stabbing of a thirteen-year-old boy, at the school that couldn't stop it, at the world that silenced her, at herself for taking it all.

No one spoke in the classroom. Brian ran to the deputy head's office. The teacher steered Nasreen, half-protectively, to the classroom door. Would she keep her job, after this?

In the empty corridor, the teacher placed a clumsy arm around the palpitating child. 'There, there, my dear,' she found herself stroking the girl's head. 'It's all right. Everything's all right. We'll find out who did it, and everything will be all right.'

Nineteen

'I don't know what the school must think of her.' Mr Ehsan spoke in English across the centre table.

It felt like late summer, though it was now mid-May. Raisa wanted to take off her pullover, but in the presence of Nasreen's father, she thought better of it.

'I think they must be used to it. The nicest children do occasionally lose their temper.' Raisa, mindful of Mrs Ehsan, answered in Urdu.

'They say she was aiming the chair at the boy's head!' said Mrs Ehsan in her Punjabi, clapping her hand to her cheek.

'Nasreen has never before behaved like this,' said her husband. 'She has always been a polite, respectful student, and now there's this mark against her.'

Rehana came in with the tea.

Mrs Ehsan said, 'Nasreen hasn't been back to school, you know. She's too, too – I don't know – nervous.'

'Ashamed,' said Mr Ehsan.

Rehana joined her mother and Raisa on the sofa. 'Why "ashamed"?' she said. 'She's got nothing to be ashamed of.'

'We are in a country where these things happen,' said her father. 'We have to be careful.'

'She hasn't been back to school,' Mrs Ehsan said, 'but she's feeling better today. She'll be down to meet you.'

Mr Ehsan asked Raisa, 'What do you think, after her O levels, I'll take her away from South Park School and place her in the sixth form of a good school in Romford, all girls?'

Raisa wasn't sure. 'Well,' she said, 'if Nasreen will be happier

121

there, yes, that might be a good idea.'

'It isn't simply a question of her being happier. She must not learn bad ways of behaving,' he said.

His wife added, 'The teachers won't care for her if they think she's bad. This isn't our country – they think we shouldn't be here. We have to work hard and be good.'

Raisa would have debated the point, but the doorbell rang. Rezwan, the youngest child, rushed in, looked at Raisa, and whispered shyly in his mother's ear.

'I have to go to the door for a minute,' said Mrs Ehsan. 'Rehana baitee, check the rice.'

Raisa and Mr Ehsan, now alone in the room, sipped their tea. They could hear indistinctly the words at the door, between Mrs Ehsan and a man.

Mr Ehsan cleared his throat. 'It is unfortunate that your father could not come today. I have heard that he is a clever and good man. I would have liked to have met him.'

His unlined, ruddy complexion made him appear younger than his years. Raisa sensed an avuncular warmth in his manner towards her. She spoke in English, 'Yes, it would've been good to meet, but he hasn't quite shaken off the flu.'

Her father had other engagements.

Mr Ehsan said, 'I was looking forward to meeting him at the milad sharif . . .'

'He would have come,' Raisa answered, 'if he'd been here. He was attending his sister's funeral.' She remembered her Phuppo Razia, elegant and still youthful, before her cancer.

'Of course, of course,' Mr Ehsan replied.

Raisa was distracted by a movement at the window. She turned her head slightly and noted a young man walking away from the house with a pile of clothing.

Mrs Ehsan came back into the room. 'That was our neighbour,' she said. 'Let me see what's happening in the kitchen. You've been here nearly an hour and we've still not eaten!'

She left the room before Raisa could comment on her generosity, and Mr Ehsan had already started to speak.

'If you will excuse me, I'll go up and see if Nasreen is ready.'

Raisa said, 'Please, if she'd rather stay upstairs, let her. If she's not well, she shouldn't come down, really.'

'She herself wanted to come down,' Mr Ehsan replied.

Mr Ehsan had left for the mosque: the Imam was leading a discussion on the importance of Muslim schools.

Rehana and Nasreen were clearing the dishes in the kitchen. Mrs Ehsan and Raisa had returned to the living-room.

Raisa said, 'I hope I'm not keeping you from your work or anything.'

'No, no, no,' she replied. 'I have told you, the work always gets done. Don't worry about such things, baitee.'

Raisa warmed to the affectionate term. She said, 'Machining is hard work, I know it's hard work.' She added, 'Such hard work and so badly paid!'

'Lots of desi women are very lucky to have even this work,' Mrs Ehsan replied. 'Mr Khan has given work to five of my friends. Yes, the work is hard and I know the others don't really like the Khans – it's not easy to like people you have to work for – but if it wasn't for Khan saab, none of us would have jobs. There's a whole queue of women who'd like a job like mine.' She stopped suddenly and swallowed hard, hand on chest. 'Only yesterday, my friend Humaira Iqbal asked me to see Mrs Khan about a job. Poor woman, her life is very sad.'

'Mrs Khan's life?'

'No, no. Humaira's. One son expelled from school. They had such hopes for him, and what's he doing? Working in a factory! Now where's the future in that?'

Raisa said, 'That's the boy from Nasreen's school, isn't it? Jamshid Iqbal?'

'Yes,' Mrs Ehsan replied. 'I think of that family and all their problems, and I thank Allah for what I have – all my children, the future.' She sniffed back the tears and moved to fetch a tissue.

Raisa didn't speak. What recollections, what hopes had stirred that depth of feeling?

Mrs Ehsan walked to the door with her tissue. 'Where are those girls? Nasreen! Rehana!' she called out, and then returned to the sofa. Her weight angled the seats. Raisa sat back.

'Where's Babu?' she sounded worried. She remembered Raisa. 'I don't like him playing outside, not when it's getting to evening time. Did Nasreen tell you about the Angraiz, the National Front

123

who came?'

'Yes. Some of them were school children,' Raisa answered.

'What a land we have come to,' the woman sighed. Turning her body, she moved the curtains to look for her son. 'Hai, when I think of that woman whose son was killed in that school. Rehana!' she shouted. 'Tell Babu to come in now.'

'Amma-jaan,' Rehana called from the kitchen, 'he's upstairs. He came in ten minutes ago.'

Mrs Ehsan relaxed. 'Children!' she said. 'You'll have them one day, don't worry.'

Raisa laughed.

'Come on now, there must be one out of the many clever and handsome men in your baraadri that you and your family like?'

'No, there isn't – not in that sense. Yes, I know it's odd for a woman of twenty-seven,' she reduced her age by four years, 'to be unmarried, but, you know . . .' She hoped Mrs Ehsan would leave the subject.

Mrs Ehsan said, 'Your sister, is she married?'

'No, she's not,' Raisa replied. 'It seems that neither of us has found the right person!' She made light of it.

Mrs Ehsan said, 'You are like my older daughter. I pray you both find good husbands. What's a woman's life without that? I know, now you're young and pretty, you've got your work. But what about when you're older? You can't stay like this. Baitee, a woman's life without a husband and children is very lonely.'

Nasreen came into the room, quietly, and sat on the armchair next to the sofa. There, not having to look directly at anyone, she had some privacy. No one had mentioned the 'incident' in her presence.

'Jaan, why are you hiding over there? Come, sit nearer,' Mrs Ehsan's words, and arms, called out to her daughter. Raisa turned to look at her.

'It's all right, Amma, I'm all right here. I can listen,' Nasreen sounded unwell. 'It's darker here, I don't feel so dizzy.' She spoke to Raisa, 'I'm sorry about this. Can I get you . . . ?'

'Don't be silly, Nasreen!' Raisa answered. 'Just you stay put.' Raisa continued to look at her. Nasreen lowered her head and sank further into the chair.

'It's all right, I'm all right. I'm all right here.' She spoke breathlessly. 'It's darker here. I don't feel dizzy.'

Raisa said, 'You don't sound well. I think you should rest.'

'No!' She checked her abruptness. 'No, I'm all right. Please . . .'
She laid her head on her knees and cried.

Mrs Ehsan ran to her daughter and felt her forehead. 'We'll have
to see Dr Shah if you don't feel better.' She said to Raisa, 'This is the
payment for not being lonely!'

Driving home, Raisa thought of the silent Nasreen, and her
moment of wildness. She thought of Mrs Ehsan and her family, of
Humaira Iqbal and all the others, living and dreaming in Barking.
Where was she, Raisa Ahmed, in all that? She felt a gnawing
dissatisfaction which lay beyond any specific thought, but whose
source included her own life.

Twenty

'Tahira might not be here today,' said Nasreen. She followed Raisa into the English stock-room. 'I haven't seen her recently.'

Raisa placed her cassette recorder on the book-littered table. 'I get the impression she's avoiding me – or is that just paranoia – you know, my thinking she's got it in for me?'

'Yes, I know – paranoia.' Nasreen squinted at the title of a book on the middle shelf.

'Sorry, that's Ms Ahmed the teacher speaking,' Raisa said. 'I should remember you're the bookworm.' She looked at the blob of chewing gum on the seat of the wooden stool. 'I suppose that was put there for me to sit on,' she said.

'You'll spoil your nice clothes.' Nasreen took out a tissue. Raisa watched her pull away at the stretchy pink gum. Her uniform fitted her so neatly. There was a refinement in the way she wore her pale blue shirt, and her navy jumper and trousers.

Nasreen threw the gum into the bin. 'There's still a bit left.'

'Oh, don't worry. I'll put this over it.' Raisa took a piece of sugar paper from the floor and covered the stool. 'It's good to see you. You're looking much better than when I last saw you.'

'We're doing the Surah today, aren't we?'

'At long last.' Raisa had hoped the girl would be less guarded.

Raisa sat on her stool; Nasreen took one of the chairs on the opposite side of the table.

'You know I bumped into Tahira two days ago.' Raisa rewound the cassette. 'She was with her mother, shopping.'

Nasreen was already finding it difficult to concentrate. The first day back had been awful. Things had improved since. Some people still gave her funny looks, and the English must hate her, but no one really talked about it anymore. And now she had the meeting with Raisa.

'It's half-past two,' said Raisa. 'Shall we start?'

'OK.' Nasreen read through her notes.

'Right then.' Raisa spoke deliberately into the microphone. 'I'd asked you to retell in your own words a surah from the Qu'ran – "The Charter of Male/Female Equality", an interpretation in English.'

'Is this a modern translation?' Nasreen managed to ask.

'Quite modern. I used to hear it as a young girl. My father would read out the Arabic and then this English translation. He used to call it an "interpretation" – you know, the word of God is the word of God. Anyway, let's start and see where our talking takes us.'

Nasreen feared the talking. Before she knew it, she'd be asked to explain things she did not want to discuss.

Raisa waited. Nasreen leaned forward. 'The point the passage was trying to make was that Allah regards all men as equal. Oh, before that, I've written . . .' she looked at her book. Just then, as if hurled by the wind, Tahira entered the room.

'Hello.' Her greeting was a public one, the 'h' distinctly pro-nounced. She sat on the empty chair next to Nasreen. 'You got your machine on?'

'*Salaa* . . . hello Tahira.' Raisa smiled at Tahira, willing her to smile back. 'I'm glad you made it. I don't know, I didn't think you'd come, even though I did remind you when we met.' She spoke to Tahira and for the microphone.

'Friday's an all right day for me. Why shouldn't I have come?'

'Oh, just that you looked busy,' said Raisa. 'I know you've been busy with very important things here.'

'Yeah.'

'Yes. Your mother was kind enough to invite me, you know, to make the time for me.' She chose her words carefully. 'Make sure she doesn't do anything special – you know, making a meal or anything like that. I know how my mother used to work whenever guests came over. I wouldn't do it, you make sure your mother doesn't.'

Tahira managed an ambiguous, almost involuntary smile. It was enough to cheer Raisa. Tahira turned to Nasreen. 'You've got your notes?'

Nasreen found it easier to nod her answer.

'You all right?'

'Yes.' Nasreen sat up, eyes wide and awake.

Tahira had heard several versions of Nasreen's outburst. No one had really explained any of it. She was curious and impressed.

'I bet it's horrible coming back to school.'

'No. Why should it be?'

'Right,' Raisa intervened. 'Let's start on the Surah. OK?'

'I ain't got any notes,' said Tahira.

'Did you manage to read the stuff? We can easily read it now.'

'I did read it. I read it ages ago.'

'Great. Come on then.' Raisa pointed to the microphone.

Tahira moved her chair closer to the table. 'Nasreen can go first,' she said. 'Can't think at the moment.'

Nasreen's face was turned away. In profile, she looked older than fifteen.

'The point that the passage was trying to make,' she began again, 'is that Allah regards all men and women as equal. I've written, "Allah will greatly reward the men and women who have abided in this world according to Islam, and it is for these that Allah is ever-rewarding." '

'Did you get that bit from another translation perhaps?' asked Raisa.

'No, not really.' Nasreen looked up. 'It came to my mind when I was reading the piece you gave us.'

'You think like a book then,' said Tahira.

'I've read it in a book and it's stayed in my mind.'

'Carry on.' Raisa noticed a purple swelling on Nasreen's lower lip.

'Allah regards all men and women as equal,' Nasreen read from her notes and then expanded on them. 'You know, even though they have different roles to play, He still regards both as being equal and does not see one superior to the other, and He will give both His full protection, and give to both equal unmatchable rewards, you know, as no other can.'

'God!' Tahira breathed out loudly. 'She does sound just like a book and she ain't even reading.'

Raisa said, 'When you say that they are equal but they have different roles, what do you mean?'

'Like, in the eyes of Allah, He sees both men and women as equal. I mean, if man does good, He won't think it's better than if the woman did good. He rewards equal rewards to both.'

'What about these different roles? Does this text tell you what the roles of a woman are?'

'No, but it's sort of,' Nasreen was struggling for clarity, 'you know the woman, she brings up the children, and she looks after the house, she cooks the dinner, and she washes her husband's clothes. Everything like that, and the man's a sort of breadwinner. He earns for them.'

'Is that written here? Where does it tell you that?'

'It implies it.' Nasreen looked at the table-top.

'Perhaps you're bringing the idea from somewhere else. Perhaps you read it somewhere else. Maybe in your particular translation of the Qu'ran.'

Neither of the girls spoke.

Tahira was restless. 'It's a translation, right, but I still don't understand it.'

'Yes, the words are a bit unfamiliar,' said Raisa.

'It isn't just that,' said Nasreen. 'You have to think about it. Maybe have it explained.'

'Well let's try and see what we can make of it as it is.' Raisa was disheartened.

'Well,' Nasreen began eventually, 'it says "men sincerely obeying the behest of Allah" and women doing the same . . .'

Tahira asked Raisa, 'What's "behest"?'

'Command, wish, order.'

'Yeah. OK.'

'It says, "men truthfully fulfilling their natural covenant to Allah" and women doing the same.' Nasreen looked up from her reading. 'Well, Allah's behest is that even though we're equal, we have different roles in life. You know, it's natural for a woman to have children and look after them and so on.'

'Yeah, you know, the women have to stay home and look after the kids,' Tahira now joined in. 'It ain't exactly they have to, but that's what it's like. There's nobody I can say in my family or relatives who's not done it. It's funny, but in a way I think it is natural for women to stay at home if they've got kids and for men to go out and earn money. In a way I agree with all that.'

'Does your mother go out to work?'

'Yeah, she has to, don't she? She had to when we were little babies.'

'And she does the other things as well, doesn't she?' asked Nasreen. 'When I do my homework, all I think about is my mother doing all this work. It's really up to me and my sisters to help her.'

Tahira said, 'I help my mum, but so do my brothers. Don't seem right though, does it?'

Nasreen said, 'My brother's only little and my father helps when he can.'

'But listen, your mothers have their outside work, and their "natural" inside work! That's double the work!'

'You're making it sound like men have it really easy,' said Nasreen. 'But my father works very hard. He's worked hard all his life.'

'Right,' said Tahira, 'and he's gonna lose his job soon, ain't he?'

Nasreen kept quiet.

'Yeah,' Tahira went on, 'I bet most of the people who're gonna lose their jobs with your dad, I bet most of them ain't gorrai.'

'Some are. Quite a few are.' Nasreen looked thoughtful. 'You said gorrai. Pakistanis suffer because of other Pakistanis as well.'

'Yeah,' said Tahira. 'But the government let it happen, don't they?'

Raisa browsed through her interview notes. Their conversation was moving all over the place. She tried to make some order of it.

'There's so much in what you're saying,' said Raisa. 'You've both raised some incredibly important points. Can we get back to the Surah now?'

Tahira said she didn't mind.

'You brought up the question, Nasreen, of what the natural woman is. Is that what a woman is, then, in her natural state? Someone who gives birth and looks after the family? Is that what the Surah tells you? This surah doesn't actually say it.'

'It must mean it because everything tells you that. Only women have children; women are supposed to have children and most women in the world – not just eastern women – do look after them and do the house things. So it must be natural.' She added, 'But that isn't the only thing women do. Women can be lots of other things

– doctors, lawyers – but having children is a very important thing. That's what makes them women.'

Tahira said, 'I ain't wild about having kids. I don't want to cook and clean for them and I don't want to go out to work. Not just 'cos it'll mean double the work, but 'cos the work I'll end up doing won't be worth it.' She picked at her nail polish. 'I'll have to work though, won't I?'

Raisa asked Tahira, 'You still think having children and the rest of it is what's natural for a woman?'

'Yeah.'

'Then why don't you want to do all that?'

For a second too long, Tahira's eyes did not leave Raisa's.

' 'Cos there are women who don't. They're happy and free and don't take rubbish from no one. And they've got friends who are probably like them and don't think they're weird. Some of them are Muslims as well, sort of.'

Nasreen shelved her fears and spoke. 'People might want, might want to be like all sorts of things . . .'

'Not just want to . . .' said Tahira. 'People could be all them things at the same time. I mean like, I agree with everything my mum says to me and a lot of the time I do try and live like that, but I also agree with things that are like the complete opposite. And I think and do things that ain't exactly the opposite, but just sort of different.'

Raisa attended to every word.

'So what you're saying is, a woman isn't just one nature, there isn't just one of you. If that's . . .'

'But I ain't saying that I'm Asian at home and English at school. That's what I said to my teacher once. But it ain't like that. It's much more than just that.'

'Even if a person might be all sorts of different people,' said Nasreen, 'they've still got a real self, someone that's really them, for example when they're at home with their family and they're being good.'

'Is that your real self, then?' asked Raisa. 'Then what are you when you're with your friends? Listen, when I had my sixteen-year-old friends, we used to hang around together at school and we used to go out to places. They used to support my lies – I used to lie to my father – I'd say I'm going on a school trip, whereas in fact we were at a friend's house, you know, pretending we were grown up and cooking food, having a nice time. I don't think I did anything bad. Of course, mixing with boys – there were boys around – was considered bad. Just to mix with them was bad. The thing is, I wanted to be with my friends; I thought it was good and important, nothing wrong. I also understood what my parents believed and wanted me to be like. I thought they were right. The lying – I felt so bad.'

Her words tumbled out. She had not thought like this before. Tahira felt that it was to her that Raisa was talking. She wanted to hear more about her badness.

Nasreen said, 'You felt bad, you felt bad because . . .'

'I felt bad, I felt like, why should I need my friends when what my parents tell me is right? What I was with my parents was important, it was me – my religious values – '

Nasreen carried on, 'You felt bad because you were guilty. You weren't being who you were.'

'Yes, I was guilty. The point is, what I was with my friends was me as well. It was an important part of me.'

'It must have been a bad part. . .' Nasreen corrected her disrespectful tone, ' . . . you must have thought it was a bad part because why else would you feel the guilt?'

Tahira said, 'I take what you're saying but it ain't just that. You feel bad 'cos the pressure is on you – you know, you're hurting your mum, or she won't love you, or your relatives will think your family's bad and keep away. It's the same with the other things. If you don't go round with your friends, you're going to be out of it when the others are all together. You won't get no chance to meet new people – girls or boys. That's important as well, 'cos you think you're missing out on all that stuff you hear about.'

'Going against your parents *is* bad,' Nasreen insisted. 'It isn't bad just because if you don't obey they'll be upset or not love you or all those other things you said. Some things are just wrong and you believe they're wrong and they are. That's why I'd feel guilty.'

'I ain't saying you don't believe they're wrong or right. Anyway, you got lots of views, views on all sorts of things.' Tahira wanted to leave the argument.

'Say more.' Raisa slid the recorder nearer to Tahira.

'Well, like wanting to be like the posh, rich Pakistanis and thinking the uneducated ones – the poor ones – are cheap and lazy and,' she broke eye-contact with Raisa, 'and hating the posh Pakis as well, 'cos you know they're the ones who're greedy and cheap, not half as good as you.'

Raisa kept her smile and nodded for her to continue.

'Or like wanting to be white – I said that to Miss Beeston last year and in a stupid way you could say I still do.'

'That's interesting.' Raisa placed an elbow on the table.

'Yeah, but being proud of who you are as well. Really proud!'

'Who are you when you're proud?'

'Last month we all knew exactly who we were.' She started to plait her ponytail.

Nasreen kept very still. The tightness in her jaws spread down her shoulders. This was it. She would have to explain. She managed to keep the tremor out of her voice. 'Shall we carry on with the Surah?'

Tahira saw the bulky notes in front of Nasreen. She stifled a yawn. 'We are doing the Surah. You know, we was saying it was natural for women to be this and that, and now we're saying it ain't just that.'

Raisa had seen the yawn, but she was impressed by the girl's easy alertness. 'We seem to be going way beyond your first statement about the nature of women. It's interesting how you immediately read into . . .' she searched for the line, ' "Women fulfilling their natural covenant with Allah", the bit about having children and looking after the house.'

'That is what most women do.' Nasreen sought to pull their talk back into safer areas.

'Yeah, yeah,' Tahira was impatient to move on. 'Last month, when we was outside this school, we knew exactly who we were. All them girls out there, they weren't exactly looking like they'd be satisfied having babies and all that.'

'They don't have to do just one thing. They . . .' Nasreen stopped in mid-sentence, fearful that her contribution might return them to the multitude that had gathered without her.

'But we never said that, not first thing,' answered Tahira, 'and that's funny really, seeing as Hadrat Ayesha never had no kids and she used to ride next to Prophet Muhammed, didn't she?'

Raisa added, 'And Nasreen's grandmother fought with all those other women in Pakistan, against the Raj.'

'Funny, ain't it, how you forget them sort of things? I reckon it suits blokes that we forget all that. I mean, I know my dad worked

133

hard – lots of men do – but, when you come to think of it, women do work harder. When we was little and my dad was round, he worked hard at his work, but my mum did that and she done all the house things as well.'

'Women shouldn't do all that – my father helps as well – but it is really for the woman to do. It is really.' Nasreen held on to the self-evident.

'Only 'cos a lot of women have been doing that for ages. Come to think of it, it does make you sick!' Tahira began to unplait her ponytail. Her face was slightly flushed. 'You don't have to do all that.' She addressed Raisa, 'I bet your mum never.'

Raisa looked down at her notes. 'I have to work. I think I work hard. Teaching, or studying, isn't really easy work.'

'In them days, when my dad was there, when we was kids, my mum used to make plugs in some factory.' Tahira's chin was high as Raisa continued to shuffle through her papers. 'She never come home till late, and she was always hurting somewhere – in her eyes, or her shoulder, or her back.'

Raisa didn't ask what her mother was doing now.

'Teaching ain't nothing like that. None of your family do them sort of jobs.'

Raisa didn't answer. Even if she had said that her family had worked slavishly hard, the words would have been feeble. The girl saw what she saw, and it made the girl sick. Tahira left her chair to stretch her legs. Raisa pointed to the recorder and pressed a forefinger to her closed lips. Tahira leaned against a dusty shelf.

'You know, it makes me sick how you do things – you know, important things – that you can't not do, and then you get a load of rubbish for it!'

'What do you mean?' asked Raisa.

'Well, all them things we had to do to get that march together.'

'Ah, you're talking about your demonstration outside the school.' Raisa arched her stiffening back. 'I was hoping to focus on that at our next meeting.'

Nasreen held her breath; she concentrated on the table-top graffiti.

'But you keep coming back to it. Do carry on.' Raisa glanced at her watch and caught Tahira looking at her. She added, 'It'll soon be next lesson. I wish we had more time.'

134

'I weren't doing nothing bad – well, I suppose I was in a way – you know, bunking lessons and all that.' Tahira sat down again. 'What we was doing was important though. We had to do it – meetings at the college or Suleiman's house or at the Wimpy. My brother was there as well, but not all the time. We never told our mum what we was up to. She'd only have got worried and all that. But when my uncle or some nosy friends saw me with all them boys, they'd slow-poison my mum, saying I was getting bad.'

'Yes, I know,' said Raisa.

'What I was doing was right. Deep down my mum would agree with me, I know she would. But she has her *izzat* as well, don't she?'

'You knew that and you carried on with the meetings?'

'I had to. We all had to. Just like Nasreen's grandmother, right?' Tahira felt the rush of adrenalin as, once more, seemingly disparate ideas joined into a new sense. 'It's the same thing, ain't it – old ideas that might not stop you from doing things, but still make you suffer? I bet,' she turned to Nasreen, 'your nani had to put up with a lot of rubbish from your relatives.'

Nasreen cleared her throat. 'Lots of people were glad that even the women were fighting the English.'

'Lots weren't glad, I bet.' She chased another idea. 'That's what I don't understand. We're girls, but what we was doing was helping all of us, the blokes and everyone, but they still don't let us. I mean, I understand them teachers not wanting us to get together like that . . .' She remembered the policeman who had caught them hiding in the school shed.

'Go on,' said Raisa.

'You know this policeman come up to us after the march. He sort of knew about Muslim girls, you know, how they're supposed to behave. He comes up to me and Gita – she's Hindu, but we ain't that different – he comes up to us and sort of tries to scare us and shame us up. "What'll your families think, you shoving around with boys and that?" '

'He was using his muti-cultural training to control you.' Raisa thought aloud.

'That's right. That's what he was doing. Just like what my mum's manager at the plug factory – he was a gorra – just like what he done with the Indian and the Pakistani women there. They were gonna strike or something – something to do with money and the way they

135

had to work – and the gorra manager said what would their dads and husbands think. See, that gorra was doing the same as that policeman.'

'Yes. You were saying, you can understand . . .'

'Yeah, I can understand them wanting to keep us down, but not your own people, not when what you're doing is for their good as well.'

Nasreen said, 'Maybe they don't agree with that way of doing things. They may not think that's the best way of getting things sorted out.'

'Or maybe they think the girls will get out of hand and won't do what they're told in other things!'

'But it isn't just the girls.' Nasreen held on.

'No, but it is the girls they're really worried about. It's worse if they don't do what they're told. You can't say I'm wrong there.'

Nasreen went back into her silence.

'Nah,' Tahira defended her actions, 'what we done was right. It was right for us, girls and all, to march out there and shout against all that rubbish. We was all out there, all of us.'

She turned and caught Nasreen's eye. She stopped speaking. For what seemed a long time, no one else spoke either.

'Right!' said Raisa. 'We've come a long way from where we started off. Shall we return to the written word?'

'I went to my lessons. I didn't go on the march,' said Nasreen. It could no longer be avoided. 'You were all friends together,' she said to Tahira. 'You were all in it from the beginning. I don't know your friends. I don't go out.'

'There were loads of kids there who didn't know our friends,' Tahira answered. 'We gave out leaflets and explained everything. You must have got one, or heard about it.'

'I had to go to my lessons. That's what I've always done. I'm not saying you're bad or anything like that, but I've never missed lessons.' Nasreen despaired at the lameness of her defence. What must Raisa think of her?

She looked at the topmost bookshelf.

'I should have been with the others, I know I should have. I saw you all out there. There were so many of you and I wasn't there. I was on the wrong side.'

No one spoke.

136

Suddenly, without reserve, she opened up. 'I knew my parents would be happy that I had gone to my lessons and hadn't put myself in any danger. But what about everyone else? What about Raisa? What would she think? I was so ashamed. I still am.'

'I understand why you didn't leave your lessons,' said Raisa.

'But you admire Tahira. It's obvious.'

'Yes, I do admire her – you're right.' Was she being responsible, Raisa wondered? 'I also understand why you stayed away. You don't have to feel ashamed.'

Nasreen wanted to cry. She swallowed her tears.

'There's another reason why I didn't go with you,' she said to Tahira. 'But I can't put it into words.'

'Go on,' said Tahira.

'It wasn't just my parents and missing classes . . . It was like, if I'd gone with you, I'd have had to have been ready to argue with the teachers and the English children. It wasn't that I was scared – not really. It was to do with how could I explain – no, how could I explain and prove what I knew inside me. There are too many things about the school and about the rest of it – difficult things that I can't put into words. And I couldn't go on the march unless I could argue.'

Raisa thought of her own study, and her struggles to express the complexity of things.

'We did argue with them. We worked out our arguments at our meetings,' said Tahira. 'We would have argued more. We weren't allowed!'

'That day in the classroom, I heard and saw things – all around me they were.' Nasreen's voice became quieter. 'I threw the chair because I couldn't not throw it.'

'You should have come with us,' said Tahira. 'You should have come to our meetings.'

'I couldn't.'

'You should have come. We was all out there. Those teachers, they was scared, you could see they was scared.'

'But they called the police and stopped you, didn't they?' Raisa threw in the question.

'They was still scared. We found out we could scare them and, do you know, Miss Beeston and some other teachers, they're really gonna try and get the school to stop caning kids. They're writing to the council and the education people and everything. It ain't much, but it's something, ain't it?' She placed one foot on her chair and hugged her knee to her chin. 'That march was good. It's like, you don't have to take no rubbish from no one.' She thought of Arif. 'You know, like you don't have to be scared of anyone. You can sort them out.' She was euphoric. Raisa did not question her.

'My goodness, look at the time. We'd better start packing up.' Raisa switched off the recorder. 'I'll transcribe this as soon as I can and I'll send you the copies.'

'God!' said Tahira. 'We've ended up talking about everything!'

'Yes,' said Raisa, 'it's all very complex.'

'What we first said about women when we read that bit of the Surah ain't all there is.' Tahira walked about the little room.

'Some of the things are bad. That's what Islam teaches us.' Nasreen spoke fervently.

'Yeah, but people can call things good or bad for all sorts of reasons, and it don't have to be what God really said, you know.' She stood in front of Raisa. 'It's like you got to fight over what things mean, you know, good and bad.'

'Yes,' said Raisa.

The buzzer went. Nasreen collected her notes. Tahira straightened her school trousers and cardigan.

'I'll try to arrange another meeting for next week and let you know,' said Raisa as the three walked out into the corridor, now filling with students.

They had reached the door of the staffroom. 'OK you two, *khuda hafiz*. I have to go in here. I'm meeting Miss Beeston. Nasreen, give my salaams to your parents.'

'*Khuda hafiz*,' said Nasreen.

'I'm looking forward to meeting your mother tomorrow, Tahira.'

'Yeah.'

Raisa entered the staffroom.

Twenty-one

She knocked for the second time, embarrassed by whisperings and scurrying on the other side. Someone rushed upstairs, and the door opened. A youth stood before her. He looked at her, quietly, unblinking; there was no insolence in his gaze. Raisa took in the startling contrast of his pale skin and his jet-black hair.

He said, 'Are you Tahira's . . . ?' He was lost for a description. Raisa answered quickly, 'Yes, I'm working with her. I mean, she's helping me with my work.'

His eyes wandered to one side of her.

Raisa continued, 'I'm from the university.' Her words seemed to compound the distance between them; she understood this even as she spoke. She smiled, '*Asalaam-alaikum*. I'm Raisa Ahmed.'

'Yeah, come in. I'm Tahira's brother.' He moved to let her pass.

'Your mother's expecting me,' said Raisa. 'I spoke to her yesterday, on the phone. We arranged it for this afternoon. I hope I'm not early.' Raisa did not mention that his mother had invited her for lunch.

The dark, narrow hallway was soundless. Yesterday's cooking smells, of coriander and spices, still lingered in the air.

Raisa waited at the foot of the stairs, expecting to be shown into the room on the right of her, or past the staircase to what must be the kitchen. The youth moved ahead to open the door of the front room.

'Hello,' Tahira called from the landing. She came down. Raisa was surprised to see her made-up face and her 'designer' jeans with the rips at the knees. Tahira's words in the interviews had suggested a different home scene.

'My mum ain't in,' Tahira said, and then, as if to qualify her abruptness, she explained, 'she had to go out for a minute. She'll be back soon. We thought you'd come later – I mean, she thought she'd be back before you got here.'

'Oh God, I'm early, aren't I?' Raisa was still standing in the hallway.

'No, it ain't that,' replied Tahira. 'My mum had to go out for a minute, that's all.'

Her brother opened the door to the room. Once again, Raisa became conscious of his gaze; its directness startled her. He looked at his watch. 'I got to go and meet a friend,' he said. 'Bye.' He walked away.

'That's Hussain, my brother,' Tahira said.

There was a clinking of keys outside the front door. 'That'll be my mum.' Tahira ran to the door. Raisa remained in the hallway.

The woman was out of breath. Her hair, tightly pulled back into a ponytail, was windswept. Her dupatta had slipped down to her neck. She was perspiring uncomfortably, even though the day was cold and she was wearing a thin mac and the flimsy-thin shalwaar khameez that Raisa had come to view as an emblem of exile and poverty. The woman was taken by surprise. She put down the Gateway bag of shopping. Her hand brushed back loose strands of hair.

'*Salaam alaikum.*' She smiled at her guest. Tahira spoke to her mother in Punjabi. Then she lifted the bag of shopping. A packet of custard creams fell to the ground. Raisa picked it up and placed it back in the bag.

Tahira took the shopping to the kitchen. Her mother led the way to the front room. 'I'm sorry, please, please sit down!' The woman pointed to the sofa. 'God, I didn't think I'd be so late!' Mrs Rashid's English had taken on some London features.

Raisa replied, 'Oh, don't worry. I've only just arrived, only minutes before you.'

'Give me your jacket,' Mrs Rashid said. 'Make yourself at home, please. I'll be back in a minute.'

Tahira's mother was younger than Raisa had imagined. She had expected her to be a contemporary of Mrs Ehsan's. The two women had joined their husbands within weeks of each other, and had been friends.

Raisa looked around her. The room had recently been tidied. The gold-embroidered cushions from a Punjabi bazaar were neatly positioned on the sofa, and though the carpet was patterned, the trail marks of the hoover were freshly visible. The furniture was too large for the room; and it couldn't hide the damp and peeling wallpaper.

Mrs Rashid sat on the armchair, opposite Raisa. Tall, like her daughter, and straight-backed, there was an elegance in her movement.

'It's kind of you to make time for me,' said Raisa. She recalled the chance meeting with Tahira and her mother in Barking town centre.

'What's this "make time"? Tahira talks about you so much, and she's been to your house so many times!' Only once, thought Raisa.

'I've told Tahira lots of times – ask your friend to come here and see us.'

But Tahira had not asked. Raisa understood. The girl had wanted to keep her out, out of her home.

'My friend – she met you at the Khan's milad sharif – told me you go to Bulquis Ehsan's house,' said Nargis. 'I thought maybe you weren't interested in us, and you maybe wanted to only meet educated people.' She laughed, and Raisa again flinched. She had to defend herself, even if that meant compromising Tahira.

'But I've said to Tahira – God knows how many times – that I'd love to meet you. I've told her so many times! You were busy, and once you were ill.'

'Ill? It's not true. Why is she saying that?'

'I was busy as well, some of the time, and I'm sure Tahira was thinking of you – you know, the strain of having guests.'

Nargis seemed not to have heard. 'Yes, I'm busy. I go to work and don't get home till late, sometimes not before nine. I get tired, but I haven't been ill.'

'Well, that must be it,' Raisa said. 'Tahira's been worried about you.'

'I don't understand,' said Nargis. 'Maybe she told you secrets that she's scared you might tell me.' Suddenly, there was a lightness in her voice. 'You know how children have secrets from parents! I know her secrets – she isn't too clever for me. I know she's naughty at school, and she thinks I don't know what she's getting up to.'

Raisa thought of the dusty stock-cupboard.

Tahira joined them, standing in the doorway. 'What're you

talking about?' she asked her mother.

'Don't you mind!' Nargis answered.

Tahira's voice quivered with sudden anger. ' "Never you mind"! It's "never you mind", not "don't"!'

Raisa looked away.

'Listen to her manners,' said her mother, 'and she hasn't even brought the tea. Her older sisters were never like this.'

'The tea's brewing.' Tahira sat down on the sofa, a seat away from Raisa. Then, on second thoughts, and without a word, she got up and left the room.

'Anyway,' continued Nargis, 'you've come to my house. You're here now. You want to ask me some questions, yes?'

'You make it sound so businesslike. I feel greedy and embarrassed, as if I've come here to take things from you,' said Raisa, pleased that she was at least being open with her host. She did not dwell on the acquisitive side of that openness.

'Oh don't be silly!' said Nargis. 'You're one of us. I must help you if I can.' She rubbed her eyes and yawned. 'That's how tired I get sometimes – I forget my manners.'

'Goodness, don't worry about it.' Raisa reassured her, and felt more relaxed.

'What is this work you're doing? What's it about?' asked Nargis.

A simple question, but whenever Raisa was asked to answer it – especially by those outside the university – she had to pause and think, and re-invent. She tried her best. She said, 'I want to understand identity. I mean, I'm trying to understand who we are, we – Pakistani girls and women in England.'

'Who we are?' Nargis' expression was one of acute concentration.

'Yes, who we are – how we live, what we think is important, what we suffer, how we fight back.' Raisa was not sure whether it was the effort of simplification that made her words seem so facile, or whether there was some wider, uncrossable gap between the ideas she deployed with such deft enthusiasm, and what must be the dense, complex circumstances of Nargis' life. She continued, 'I want to understand who we are, and how we have become who we are.'

'How we live, what we think's important,' repeated Nargis. 'They do these things in England, in the university?' She paused for a moment and then asked, 'Why?'

142

'I'm in the education department, you know, where teachers study,' said Raisa. 'They think it's important that teachers understand the lives of the children they teach, to make them better teachers. Of course, there's more to it . . .'

'You are Pakistani. You have to study this?'

'It's because I'm Pakistani that I want to think about these things,' said Raisa. 'I want to inspect . . .' She started again, 'I want to look at what I think I know. I want to look at what has already been written and spoken about us.'

'Who we are?' Nargis' question was more a statement. Both women turned to the door as Tahira walked in, carefully balancing a cup of tea in either hand. Placing one cup by Raisa and one by her mother, she left again. Then she returned with her own cup, and a plate of custard cream biscuits.

Her mother, dropping her voice and speaking to her in Punjabi, asked her to come closer, to lower her head to her. Nargis whispered some words, a prayer, and blew three times on her daughter's head.

'She's had some bad dream about me,' said Tahira. 'It's daft, ain't it? Later, she'll take some meat and wave it above my head and throw it in the river.'

Nargis recited a verse from the Qu'ran and told her daughter to show more respect.

'They do these funny things, the people in her village,' said Tahira. 'That ain't being Muslim, is it?'

'Close that nonsense!' Nargis shouted at her daughter in Punjabi.

Raisa looked to the window, and then to the flaking ceiling, and the widening stain of damp. Tahira's eyes followed Raisa's. She said, 'We're thinking of moving soon, to a really big house.'

Nargis said, 'Buy a big house? In my dreams, I think!'

'What do you mean?' Tahira snapped at her mother. Unconsciously, she dug her foot into the carpet. Raisa nodded with interest, but said nothing. No words that she might utter would appease the girl's anger. Nargis said, 'If both my sons got proper jobs, and Tahira, and if my married daughters and their husbands help us, maybe we can buy a big house.'

'Yes, houses are so impossibly expensive, aren't they,' Raisa answered, in spite of herself.

'You've got a big place, all to yourself,' Tahira challenged her.

'It's a two-bedroomed flat. It only looks bigger because of the way

I've decorated it.'

'But you've got it all to yourself. No husband or children or nothing. Just living on your own, doing what you like, no one to stop you.' She would not let go.

Raisa said lightly, 'It's the family's flat. I don't really live on my own.' She turned to Nargis and smiled. She did not want Tahira to see her unease.

Nargis said, 'Tahira, bring me more tea. Bring the pot.'

Tahira left the room. And now, with particular force, Raisa understood her anger – understood that she, Raisa Ahmed, must also be its target. She said to Nargis, 'I can understand Punjabi, you know. If I'm relaxed and not bothered about making mistakes, I can speak it as well.'

'Tahira said to me you speak English, mostly,' Nargis replied. 'I'm happy you speak your language, but it really doesn't matter, if you know who you are. Unless,' she joked, 'you don't understand my English!'

'God, no, I mean yes. Your English is really good. Did you study in England?'

Nargis laughed, 'Oh no! I haven't studied nothing since I was eight or nine in Haila, my village. Do you know Jhelum District?'

'Of course. North-west Pakistan, near Islamabad. I've been there, and I've heard a lot about it.' She had driven through it in 1979 and knew where it was on the map.

Nargis said, 'You don't know my village. Haila is a simple village. No,' she continued, 'I learned English in England from people at my work – in my past jobs, not where I work now.'

'How clever!'

'I want my children to study, to pass exams and learn things, but they have other ideas,' said Nargis. 'My eldest son left school with only a few qualifications. My other son, and Tahira, are doing the same. Their minds are somewhere else.'

'I suppose there are lots of distractions,' said Raisa. 'Lots of children switch off in school, are bored.' She thought of South Park School, and of her own, and added, 'It doesn't really have much to do with the important things in their lives. But then, a lot of learning happens outside school.'

Nargis bit on a custard cream and moved the plate towards Raisa. She said, 'I don't know what my children are learning out of school.

144

Tahira hasn't been going to school, lots of days every week – the school has written me a letter. What is she doing? Where does she go?'

'Lots of children stay away from school, especially those who are Tahira's age – fourth- and fifth-year children.'

Nargis continued, as if to herself, 'She and Hussain, they're doing something, I know. Hussain's friends, some of them are gundais – not the Iqbal boy, but the others – they're gundais. They're doing something.' She looked directly at Raisa. 'Do you know what Tahira's doing? What she's learning out of school?'

Was the woman accusing her, or was she asking for assistance? Raisa said, 'I know what Tahira tells me. We haven't really talked about her staying away from school. We've talked about the school and Barking, and the conflicts between English ways and Mashriqi ways, things like that.'

'The food's on the gas. Hussain's done it all.' Tahira put down the pot of tea. She sat on the floor, leaning her back against her mother's legs. 'You talking about me?' She prodded Nargis' foot.

'Yes, you – a headache!' answered Nargis. 'How will they get nice jobs without exams and qualifications?' She turned again to Raisa.

'She ain't on about that, is she?' said Tahira. 'My older sister left school with five O levels, and she's only working as a cashier!' She added, 'Mind you, there ain't nothing wrong with that – someone's got to do it, ain't they?' Then she said, 'What lipstick do you use? What colour?'

'Oh,' said Raisa, surprised, 'it's some cheap make – "Truly Plum".' She turned from Tahira's inspection.

Nargis said, 'I don't want my children to work in the places I have to work. I want them to have a better life.' She had started to stroke her daughter's head.

Raisa warmed to the scene, though it excluded her. She wondered at Nargis' troubles with her husband and his family, her 'hard time' as Mrs Ehsan had put it. She asked, 'Do you work near here?'

'Not very far, one bus ride, on the industrial estate,' she replied. 'A mile from here.'

'It ain't the sort of work you or anyone in your family does,' said Tahira. 'I've been to my mum's work and helped out, and I can tell you, you wouldn't know nothing about that sort of work.'

Nargis said, 'I sew clothes. Bulquis Ehsan does it at home. I do it in the factory – there's more money.'

Tahira said, 'I got nothing against Nasreen. She's all right – and her sister, but her family reckons they're better than us. Their mum still does the same work as my mum. Just 'cos she don't go out and get seen doing it!' She looked through the Indian movie magazines on the table. She returned to the sofa with the latest *Stardust*.

Raisa asked, 'Is this Mr Khan's factory?'

'Yes, "K & K Fashions".' Nargis turned reflective. 'I think some-one's told him why I left my last job. He has another reason to dislike me.' She sighed. 'Word gets round very quickly!'

'I reckon it's Nasreen's mum what told him,' said Tahira. 'She's all friendly with his wife, ain't she? You can't trust no one.'

Raisa was struggling to understand.

Nargis elaborated. 'In my other jobs, I spoke too much, asked for too many things.'

'Yeah, like proper money and safety while you're working!' Tahira joined in.

Nargis said, 'Not that I've been any trouble for Mr Khan. No, I'm too tired now. The time comes when you're too tired.' She changed the subject. 'Your family are big and educated?'

'Some people in my family are considered to be big and educated,' answered Raisa.

'Your father, mother and sister are barristers and big people,' said Nargis. 'Bulquis Ehsan told everyone after you went to her house.'

Raisa said, 'My mother's dead.' The stark words that she had so often avoided had now the effect of distancing her from the event.

'*Bismillah! Maeri jaan . . .*'

Tahira moved a seat closer to Raisa and poured her a fresh cup of tea. Raisa noted the warmth of her gesture. Why had she told them? Just to stir sympathy? She had cheated.

'I ain't gonna stay on at school,' said Tahira, 'but I'll do my CSEs and get an office job. That's better than doing what my mum's doing.' She addressed her mother, 'But I'm telling you, I ain't gonna stay on at school. Anyway, we need the money.'

'She does this every time,' Nargis spoke to Raisa. 'She knows what I think. She knows I want her to stay at school, and do better and better and definitely get a good job – who knows, one day in Pakistan.'

'You must be bloody joking!' answered her daughter.

146

Nargis sniffed at the air, at the strong, aromatic scent of cooking. She said, 'Look at this clever girl. She has started the cooking, and she is letting it burn!'

Raisa said, 'What's that beautiful smell? It's making my mouth water.'

Nargis laughed. 'It's karelai and roti.'

Tahira said, 'I hope you like it, 'cos it's Hussain doing the food, and it'll be hot!'

'For your information,' answered Raisa, 'I eat chillies like sweets, and if it's karelai, well then!'

'Bittu's cooking?' Nargis spoke Punjabi to her daughter. 'Bittu's going out with Ijaz and Jamshid this afternoon.'

Tahira answered, also in Punjabi. 'They're all meeting later. Jamshid's lost his job – they don't need him no more. They're going out tonight 'cos he won't be working.'

'They're going out at night? Where?' Nargis was alarmed. 'They must be careful not to carry on like gundai.'

Tahira, in English now, said, 'Bittu ain't a little kid, you know. He can't stay in all the time, just 'cos you're worried!' She explained to Raisa, 'Bittu's our pet name for Hussain.'

'Yes, I know,' said Raisa. 'I've got one as well – "Mastani".' Everyone laughed.

'You know what that means, don't you?' asked Tahira.

'Yes, yes I do. It means "mad"!' She added, 'I'm not English you know.' The laughter subsided.

Nargis said, 'I better go and see about the dinner.' Before she could leave her chair, Tahira jumped up. 'Amma sit down. It's all right, Bittu's looking after it.'

Nargis relaxed. 'They're good children,' she said, 'but difficult to control.'

'Yes,' said Raisa.

'All of them except for Ashraf – he is my oldest son – all of them were born here. They don't understand the dangers in this country, and they don't care that people talk and their name becomes bad. When I have enough money to buy my land in Haila, how will they live there if they have a bad name?'

Tahira said, 'If you got money, it don't matter if you have a bad name!'

Raisa said, 'I think a lot of young Pakistanis do understand about reputation and good name. It's just that, perhaps, they're developing their own way of living in England – a way that you couldn't really call "English".'

Nargis rubbed her eyes and tightened her ponytail. 'I know that,' she said, 'but how will they live when we go back to Pakistan?'

'Maybe they don't believe they'll ever go back to stay. Some don't want to.'

'That's right,' said Tahira. 'What would we go back to?'

'Does that mean when I go back, my children will stay here?' Nargis slowly shook her head, incredulous. 'I send money, whenever I can, to my mother, but it's not much. I haven't got a husband.'

Raisa nodded to her to continue. '*Inshallah*, my mother will live with me and my family on my land, in my house. My children know all this. They know their mother's dream.' Then, her tone denoting both anger and suffering, she said, 'Do you know, after a life of working, my mother has to live in one small room, a rented room, with my younger brothers, and both grown men!'

Neither woman had noted that Tahira had moved to the window and, pensive and still, was gazing out through the greying net curtains. She turned round, suddenly, and said, 'I'm going out to the shops.'

Her mother looked at her and said nothing.

'I'm going out to the shops,' repeated Tahira. 'I'm calling for Tanni, then we're going round the shops. She's looking for a bag. I said I'd go with her.'

Nargis spoke Punjabi to her daughter's English. 'When are you going?'

'Not till two. Tanni won't even be up yet,' answered Tahira, straightening her blouse and avoiding her mother's eyes.

'When will you be back?' The tension grew.

'Around six or seven. Don't know.' Tahira adjusted her ear-rings.

'The shops Tanni goes to close at five-thirty.'

'It takes time to get there and back. We're . . .'

'It takes you five hours to buy a bag.'

'We're shopping in Southall.'

Nargis looked intently at her daughter. Raisa had picked up the copy of *Stardust*. She saw the sex-kitten gaze of the Indian starlet on the front page of the magazine. She heard Nargis' fears for her daughter.

Hussain appeared at the door. 'Food's ready,' he told his mother, acknowledging neither his sister, nor their guest.

Nargis left her chair. 'Come on, everybody, let's go to the kitchen.'

'I'm not hungry. I'll eat later,' said Hussain. He left the room.

Tahira tutted at him. 'I tell you, that boy's weird,' she said.

Nargis waited for Raisa to walk before her. She took her arm as they entered the narrow, smoky kitchen.

Twenty-two

She had wanted Tahira to wear desi dress; Tahira had
worn her jeans. Nargis watched her daughter and, for that moment,
was impressed by her separateness, her otherness in the world.

There was no traffic on Rosaville Road. A suburban silence hung
over it, though it lay within minutes of Fulham Broadway.

'What's your hurry? We're here now!' Nargis' Punjabi rang out.

Tahira waited for her mother to catch up. Rosaville Court – the
grand stone steps and gateway, its lofty entrance – stood before her.

'What're you shouting for?' Tahira looked around. Her gaze
settled on her mother's sandals. 'Why're you wearing socks with
them shoes? You're supposed to wear tights or pop socks. Your socks
ain't even the right colour!'

'That's right, speak in English, so everyone can hear you insult
your mother!' said Nargis. 'There's nothing wrong with my socks,
it's your empty head that's wrong – empty except for the nonsense
that's in it!'

Tahira didn't answer. She sighed noisily and tapped her foot.
'You rush me with "we'll be late, we'll be late", and now we're going
to stand out here and admire the building?' She looked at the ground.
'I can't stay long, you know. The play starts at five.'

The mother nudged her daughter jocularly. She wanted her in
better mood. They had come out for the afternoon – Ashraf would
come later to pick them up. It was almost a family outing, so why
spoil it with arguments and bad temper? 'You're a strange girl,' said
Nargis. 'Here we are, outside your friend's house.'

'She ain't exactly a friend, is she?' snapped Tahira, still using
English to her mother's Punjabi.

150

'Your friend, your teacher, your teacher's friend, whatever she is!' answered Nargis. 'We're going to stand out here all night, are we, like two lufungian?'

'Bloody shut up, will you!'

'Yes, this country's taught you a lot,' answered Nargis. 'Raisa Ahmed would never have told her mother to shut up. I hope you'll show better manners in front of her.'

'What's lufungian got to do with standing outside someone's house!' She was irritated, but she kept her voice low. 'Anyway,' she continued, 'Raisa Ahmed can take me as I bloody am!'

Nargis saw herself in her daughter – her daughter who was also so mysterious and distinct. Love surged in her. She prayed for her daughter's safety. She thought of her secretiveness and she prayed that no one should take advantage of her, or harm her in any way. She took hold of Tahira's chin and blew the breath of prayer and protection over her face.

'Oh, bloody hell, Amma,' said Tahira, sobered nonetheless. 'What're people gonna think?'

Tahira followed her mother into the foyer. Nargis walked through the entrance and paused. She had a feeling that someone would stop them and ask questions. Who could they be visiting there? She pulled at her mac, smoothing the creases and conscious of the tea-stain by the collar that the dry-cleaning hadn't removed.

Her back extra-straight, Nargis walked to the stairway. 'Go on then, hurry up!' Tahira came up behind her, forcing her to move further in. There was a stillness about the place – the red carpets, the gleaming windows, the polished wood and the palm plants could all have come from a poster on the wall of the art room at South Park School.

The porter's desk was unattended. 'Can we go straight to her flat, or do we have to ring for someone?' asked Nargis.

'Course we don't have to call no one. She lives on the second floor. We can take the lifts through that door.'

Nargis took pleasure in her daughter's confidence. 'One minute, one minute!' She fumbled through her tote bag and followed Tahira. 'Let me get her present, you.'

Tahira pressed the button for the lift. 'It's a daft present,' she said. 'What'd she want with a silly wooden boat anyway? It won't even go with her other things. Could've bought chocolates or something.'

'Shut up,' Nargis answered. 'What do you know? It's a boat from Pind and Raisa will like it because of that. She'll like it because it's from Pind and it's made by hand.'

Tahira rolled her eyes and tutted. 'You're mad!' she said.

The lift doors opened at the second floor. '*Asalaam alaikum!*' Raisa was there to greet them. 'I'm sorry, I'd have met you at the station, or even collected you from Barking, but my car's being serviced.'

'Oh, don't you mind!' said Nargis. Tahira sighed and looked away. Nargis carried on speaking. 'We had a nice walk to here. You live in a nice area.'

'Yes,' said Raisa. 'Our flat's to the right, here.' She walked ahead. 'How are you, Tahira? Last week you entertained me, this week I'm entertaining you!'

'All right,' and almost as an afterthought, 'thanks.'

Raisa opened the windows to the balcony.

'The meal was great,' said Nargis. 'Nice desi food. Your mother taught you well.'

'Would you like some chai, or coffee?' Raisa asked in Urdu.

Nargis, continuing to speak in English, answered, 'Now stop thinking about our stomachs. Come and sit down, and let's talk.' Invitingly, she patted the seat next to her on the long, black sofa. Raisa joined her.

Meanwhile Tahira browsed around the room, pausing at the books on the shelves, moving on to the balcony and the view of a well-kept garden. She thought of her own bedroom.

'How's your college work?' asked Nargis. 'Your mother would have been proud of you. Your father must be too.'

'I suppose so,' said Raisa. 'Education is a big thing with all of us, isn't it?'

'Yes,' Nargis sat back, 'and the poorer you are, the more important it is really.' She added, 'But very few poor people have good education.' She returned to the subject of Raisa's mother. 'Did your mother like it in England?'

Raisa became thoughtful. She said, 'I don't think so but then, I'm not really sure. She always wanted to go back, to stay. I think that's right.' Raisa cleared her throat. A strong breeze entered the room. 'Is it too draughty, shall I shut the window?'

'No, no it's fine.' Both women looked to the balcony and the curtains billowing dramatically.

'Tahira!' Nargis called out in Punjabi. 'What're you doing there?'

Tahira was standing by the mantlepiece. She had in her hands a pale, glazed vase, round and heavy. 'Just looking around, that's all!' answered Tahira.

'Feel free to look around or whatever!' said Raisa. Indicating the vase, she added, 'I put flowers in that sometimes, huge purple and pink ones!'

'Where'd you get it?' asked Tahira.

'From a place in Wales, from the potteries.'

'Where's the boat from Pakistan gonna go?'

'I'll have to think about that . . .'

'It won't go in here. It don't go with none of them things.'

'Oh I don't know. It's a beautiful boat. The other things will have to make room for it!'

Tahira looked at her watch. Nargis looked at Tahira. Raisa sensed the tension between the two. Nargis said, an exaggerated lightness in her voice, 'She's looking at the time. She's going with the school tonight.'

'Yeah, that's right,' said Tahira. 'We're going to see some play at the Royal Court. That's a theatre near here, ain't it? Sloane Square.'

If she was telling a story, Raisa thought, she's prepared it well.

'It's her CSE exam,' said Nargis. 'When she can go out away from the house, her examinations become very important!'

'Come on, Tahira,' coaxed Raisa. 'Come on, sit here with us. Come on now.'

Tahira sat on the armchair facing the two women. She had sat there the last time, when she had come with Nasreen.

The bastard had had the nerve to come up to her school, to ask around for her; and yesterday he had phoned Tanni about her. She'd thought it was all over and done with. She would have to do something. He must not start all that again. He couldn't. She wouldn't let him. She'd show him; he could never scare her again. She had to think about it; she had to work things out. Mumtaz would help her. There was no one else she could talk to. She looked again at her watch.

Nargis stood up. 'Where's the bathroom, please?' Raisa led her to it.

Nargis noticed the urn of water on the floor by the commode. She hadn't expected it. She had been prepared to use a water-soaked tissue instead, as she did at work. The bathroom, like the rest of the flat, was wide, airy and spotlessly clean. Nargis wondered whether Raisa paid someone to clean it. She sat there quietly and thought. How much difference was there, she asked herself, between Nargis Rashid giving up her time to clean Raisa Ahmed's house, and Nargis Rashid giving up her time to talk about the lives of Pakistani women? Hadn't Raisa's people always used people like her? Was it for Raisa that she had pretended to be unwell, to avoid working that Saturday? Was it for Raisa that she had lost the money and tempted fate? She knew she felt resentment, which at another time would be stronger than now, but Raisa Ahmed really was open and grateful and eager to please. Nargis had become curious about her research, and about her.

She washed her hands and rinsed her mouth. The face in the mirror didn't have the usual dark shadows under the eyes and around the mouth. It looked rested, unharassed. The light must be flattering, Nargis decided – it wasn't as if her life had changed.

Nargis returned to the living room. Raisa and Tahira had brought in the tea and fruit juices. 'Do you want to ask me the questions now?' she enquired.

'What?' Raisa was startled. She had said nothing about questions, but Nargis was right.

'Do you want to ask me the questions now?' the older woman repeated. 'You know, your studies, what you're doing?'

'Oh, there's no hurry about that,' Raisa stammered. 'I'm learning a lot without the questions.'

Nargis' confidence grew. Raisa had sought her company. 'Tell me again about what you're studying.' Her eyes narrowed in concentration. 'Tell me again. I'm not sure I understood everything the last time you told me.'

'I'm not sure if I understand it myself, to tell you the truth!' answered Raisa. 'I'm still working at it, though. It's funny how the topic's sort of changing before me.'

'Oh?' Nargis didn't follow her now.

Raisa became anxious. Her ideas were on trial. She said, 'I want to show how the official and well-known descriptions of eastern women, of Pakistani women's lives, don't really describe or explain those lives.'

Nargis listened. Tahira helped herself to the juice. Raisa continued, 'I suppose I think it's important to explain our lives more adequately, better.'

'Why? For who?' asked Nargis. Then, trying to lighten her critical tone, she smiled. She was, after all, a guest, and Raisa was well-meaning enough.

Raisa was relieved by her guest's smile. 'In the first instance,' she said, 'I suppose I'm doing the research, the study, for the university, to get the MA. Yes, in the first instance, it is for the MA.' She was in a corner. 'But it's for us as well, for me. I mean,' she said, the words an incantation, almost, 'unless we understand who we are – how we live, what we suffer, what we admire, what we hate, what we put up with, what we fight for – and how we have become who we are . . .' she paused to breathe – 'unless we understand all that, how will we ever change the things that hold us down?'

Tahira said, 'I know what I'd change.'

Nargis looked at her daughter.

'You're looking at Pakistani women, their lives. Let me tell you about my mother,' said Nargis. 'For years, she worked on a little piece of land my father rented.'

'Who from?' asked Raisa, promptly becoming the interviewer.

'From a family who were given lots and lots of land from the British, a long time ago. The grandfather or great-grandfather was in the army, and the British gave them the land as a present for helping them. So many zamindars, you know, landowners, got their land like that.'

Tahira said, 'It never belonged to them gorras in the first place. They just took it.'

Nargis returned to her mother. 'For years she worked on a little piece of land my father rented, in Haila, our village. She worked in the fields, she made the flour, and she worked in the house.'

'Loads of women do that in Pakistan,' said Tahira. 'It ain't nothing special, is it?'

'And yet they're always saying how women in Pakistan don't really do that sort of work, you know, producing things,' said Raisa. 'I read somewhere that Pakistan's own official documents say only one hundred and forty-eight women work on farms and things.'

Nargis spoke on. 'She didn't get paid for the work. She was

working for the family. Then . . .' she paused, 'then my father died – yes, in 1974 that was – and my brothers got jobs. One went to Jehlum and worked at the mill where they use machines to make the flour. The money wasn't much and the mill didn't give jobs to the women.'

Raisa absently slipped off her shoes and curled up into the sofa. 'Was your family still living on the rented land?'

'No, they had moved in with my aunt's family. After my father's death, my mother couldn't keep renting the land – it was in my father's name.'

'They manage to ignore women's property rights.'

'She had no rights to it,' she answered. 'The zamindar increased the rent, so even my brothers couldn't keep the land.'

Raisa poured fresh tea into Nargis' cup.

Nargis continued, 'Some years ago, yes in 1978 or 1979, my mother and brothers went to my older brother and his family in Jehlum. My brothers work in a packaging factory. My mother – she's sixty now – still works, but for money now.' She passed both hands over her head, pushing back loose wisps of hair. 'She's a cook for a big family. They're well off.'

Tahira shifted uncomfortably in the armchair. She said, 'She's their cook 'cos they're lazy pigs and think it's big having servants.'

Raisa said, 'When I went to Pakistan and saw all that I felt sick. I saw an old man, a servant, opening doors and fetching things.'

Nargis said, 'A cook's job isn't as nice as some other jobs in the house, like an ayah, but a cook gets more money.'

Tahira pulled at a loose thread on her blouse. 'You're supposed to be ashamed of being a cook even if it pays you more than some of the other jobs. They sort of try to make you pay for getting more money, ain't it? But if you need the money, who cares?'

Nargis seemed to be concluding the story of her mother and brothers. She said, 'Now my mother lives in one room with my two younger brothers.' She added, 'They're not married yet. She's looking for good matches.'

Raisa said, 'And you're here, all these thousands of miles away, working and looking after your family.'

'I have one brother here, and his wife. Ashraf, my son, works for him now and then – Abbas doesn't have children of his own. My husband's sister and her family are here too. I'm not . . .'

'My dad's dead an' all, just like my grandad,' said Tahira.

Nargis said, quite simply, 'My husband didn't die; I divorced him. We agreed on a divorce. He's dead now – he died three years ago – but we were divorced.'

Tahira was watching Raisa. 'You're shocked, ain't ya?' she asked.

'I'm surprised,' said Raisa. 'I thought Pakistani women would rather die than get divorced.'

Nargis said, 'Yes, there are people who think I'm bad. Bulquis said something to you. Yes?'

'Mrs Ehsan?' said Raisa. 'No – nothing in any detail.'

Nargis let it pass. 'I've worried about it. It doesn't look good for my daughters. The arguments were too much. He did too many things that weren't right. He . . .' Nargis stopped for a second. 'My mother, my brothers, even my husband's sister understand me and don't think I was wrong having a divorce.' She breathed deeply. 'My family aren't against me. I can work and look after my children. Two daughters are already married and divorce isn't bad when two people can't live together.'

Tahira said, 'There are still loads of people who try and make you feel like you're dirt and like you're not as good as them.'

Raisa was drawn to the woman and the girl; she was being pulled into their lives. Her eyes met Tahira's.

Tahira said, 'I'll have to go in a minute.'

Raisa stood up. 'Shall I make some more tea?'

Tahira, looking neither at her mother nor at Raisa, said, 'I got to meet my teacher in about one and a half hours.' She turned to her mother. 'You might as well ring Ashraf and tell him to meet us at Sloane Square Station in an hour. It's stupid him coming all this way. You can go home with him and I'll wait for my school lot.'

Nargis thought of her daughter, of leaving her at the station to wait alone. She shuddered.

'Can I use your telephone?' she asked Raisa.

They left the flat. In the foyer they met the gardener.

'Excuse me, can I help you?' he asked. 'You don't live here do you?' His words were a little too loud, a little too much space between them.

Tahira said, 'We ain't lost and we don't live here.'

Nargis and her daughter left the building.

Twenty-three

Nargis Rashid ignored the itch in her left eye. Like a ghost, she leaned against the bus shelter. The Friday morning queue was getting bigger. She pulled herself out of her daze and moved along.

Her eyes skimmed above the heads of the people: a mother and child; two young men, lost in their own thoughts; Abid Saab taking his after-prayer walk along Ilford Lane. Nargis raised her dupatta to her head. The old man stood peering into the window of the newsagents. Nargis averted her eyes and waited for him to walk on. Men like him judged her, and her children, in a way that she understood very well. She allowed her shame and guilt and anger to be repressed by the anxieties of the morning. What time was it? She had forgotten to check it all the while that she was waking and urging the others to school or job centre. She had followed her inner clock, the movement of time within her regular chores. She mustn't be late for work, not again. Mr Khan wouldn't accept her fourth lateness that week. She stood up straight and alert. Her dupatta slipped down to her neck. Abid Saab was forgotten, though still just yards away. She thought now only of the 169. Why hadn't it arrived? Why didn't it ever come on time?

A bus turned a distant corner. She prayed it was hers. Seconds passed; the distance decreased. The 169 moved slowly towards her. Her deep sigh spoke of relief, of quiet satisfaction. She took her usual seat at the very front of the bus, with the driver's seat ahead to the right, and a clear view of the road before her. Again she wondered about the time. It couldn't be late; the roads were still clear. She sat back and tried to relax.

It was at the corner of her vision, and if it had not been for the familiar swing of the girl's pony-tail, Nargis wouldn't have turned to look. The girl had her back to her. Her pose was unmistakable – one hand in the side pocket of her jeans, the other holding on to the strap of her shoulder bag. The girl turned just as a grey car stopped next to her, and just as the bus gathered speed. Nargis strained to see more, oblivious to the stares of the other passengers. What was her daughter doing in Barking? She should be at home, getting ready for school. She couldn't be waiting there for Mumtaz or her school friends – Ilford Lane was out of their way – unless they weren't going to school at all.

Had the grey car stopped for Tahira? Nargis rubbed her eyes. More and more her life had become an endless chaos of worries. As soon as one was temporarily put to rest, another came forward to drain her energy and to deny her peace of mind. All she had were little respites: pauses, where hope, or anger, or simple forgetfulness offered her some rest. And now, again, there was her daughter. What was she doing? What secrets was she keeping?

The bus moved into the right-hand lane before it stopped at the traffic lights. Alongside the bus, below her window, was a grey car, its engine noisy, and its exhaust spouting huge bursts of fumes. The car zoomed ahead as the lights turned to amber; other cars sounded their horns. Nargis had caught the briefest glimpse of driver and passenger: a man, and a girl with long black hair. She fled, terrified, from the deep and entangled fears that threatened to rise up and form into thought. She paused to catch her breath.

The clock in the window of the undertakers that usually triggered such profound, ominous meanings told her simply that it was 7.40 a.m. and that, once again, she was late for work. Nargis hurried her step.

The three-storey pebble-dashed building, with its ground-level extension, lay on a turning off the main road. It was detached, but stood among smaller terraced houses. From the outside it would have passed as a family house, except for the name boards on its front. 'Satellite Shoe Manufacturers' had leased the ground and first floors; 'K & K Fashions' ran the length of the second. The gleaming brass letter-boxes on the two newly painted doors, and the hanging plants on either side of them, bore little resemblance to the sweatshops of East London.

Nargis entered the door on the right and, two steps in each stride, rushed up the stairs. She wiped the dots of perspiration from her face before walking into the small, makeshift reception area.

'*Slaan Laikum*,' out of breath, she addressed Mrs Khan. The women spoke Punjabi.

'*Slaan Laikum*, Nargis,' answered the owner's wife. She held a large pile of nearly finished garments, collected that morning from a homeworker. 'Take these to Zaibie,' she said, 'tell her I'll be checking her buttonholes like an eagle today. So no mistakes.'

Her coat still on, bag still in hand, Nargis took the dresses. Mrs Khan went over to sort the other piles that together formed a huge mound in the corner of reception. Nargis squeezed her way through a narrow door. Where once there had been two bedrooms, there was now a rectangular work floor. Alongside two of the walls, the pattern making, the material cutting and the pressing machines lay tightly positioned. In the centre, and spilling outwards, the room was crammed with islands of sewing machines. The windows, already fitted with opaque glass, were hidden by bulging clothes stands, some carrying the finished garments, others with those waiting to be checked, tagged and bagged.

Work had its own rules of courtesy. No one greeted Nargis as she entered the room, garment-laden. Mr Khan was talking to his three male employees – the cutters and the presser. And amid the whirring and hissing of the machinery, the eight seamstresses were lost in their own silent efforts.

'Mrs Rashid.' Mr Khan left the men to their work. He looked at his watch. 'I must have a word with you about your lateness.' His Punjabi was icily formal.

Nargis said, 'The bus is always late. The driver takes too long collecting the money, and the traffic . . .'

Mr Khan spoke quickly, 'We'll talk later. Please start your work. I'll see you during morning break.'

Nargis thought, *My tea-break is my time. See me after my tea-break, in your time.* She said nothing; she dropped the bundle of blouses and massaged her arm.

'Start your work.' Mr Khan didn't like the divorced woman's manner. She was beautiful, but there was nothing gentle or sweet about her. 'You can work at your machine after break. Before that, check those two racks. Balbir isn't here. The second rack has Mrs

160

Hanif's buttonholing. Make a special check of that and tell me if there are any mistakes.'

Nargis looked at the man's shoulders, stiff with the padding of his dark suit, and speckled with dandruff. There he was, the villain, setting one worker against another. She knew of the craftiness of owners, but it still amazed her that an old woman with failing sight inspired no pity in him.

'Mrs Hanif isn't working as she used to,' he went on. 'My business can't put up with sloppy work.' Then he added, 'Remember, all your jobs depend upon me staying in business.'

Nargis would have worried about Zaibie's future at the factory, but she had her own problems, so many of them, and anyway, what was the point? Zaibie, along with four other women, wasn't even working with a national insurance number. In secret conversations, Nargis had tried to make the women understand how they were only helping Mr Khan, not themselves; how they had to be registered because without that they couldn't claim any benefits – sickness, unemployment, whatever. Didn't they realise that without registering they couldn't even begin to argue with Mr Khan? He could pay them as little as he wanted; he could make them work for however many hours he wished; he could fire them for nothing. The women hadn't been persuaded. They'd be the first to fight Khan Saab, but the difficulties were too many. They were nervous of the penalties for not registering and, who could tell, if they made themselves known to the authorities, they might be deported – they didn't know what was what with all those new immigration laws – and anyway, who else would give them a job? And Nargis herself, they told her, might pay her national insurance, but she still couldn't argue with Khan Saab; he could fire her tomorrow, and find someone else in the same second.

Nargis had faced her own impotence. She had, of course, known it all the while that she was hectoring the others. But she couldn't just stand and accept things that weren't right – she hadn't in her marriage and she shouldn't in her work.

Mr Khan continued. 'When you finish with the racks, you can carry on with your skirts. My wife will tell you about the sample that we have to finish by this evening. I've already seen Haroun and the others. You're in charge of the sewing.'

'I'll start the work,' she said.

'I'll see you at ten o'clock,' he replied. She watched him walk to his 'office', a box-room just off the work floor.

Nargis dropped the pile of garments on the floor by Zaibie's machine. Zaibie Hanif, a woman in her late fifties, was too busy to have noticed either Nargis or the clothes. She had found a rhythm of work, and thought only of completing the targets she had set herself – four more blouses by nine o'clock, nine more by ten, thirty-five in all by lunchtime. At the start of the day it was almost a game, to beat the target. Later, as her eyes and neck and bottom felt the strain, it was simply the promise of money that kept her going – forty pence a whole blouse, one pence a buttonhole.

Nargis moved deftly through the tiny pockets of space to the other side of the room. The air, especially around Haroun's cutting machine, was filled with minute fibres of material. Someone sneezed. Others coughed. She took off her mac and placed it on the chair in the corner with the other coats and cardigans. Mrs Khan, pushing a trolley of skirts towards the press, still managed to glance up at the clock just as Nargis placed her bag under a stool and set to work. White neon lights, one of them flickering, glared down at the workers and cast a staleness and a pallor over them and the room they worked in. On the wall between the two windows ahead of her, and barely visible, were two yellowing posters. Nargis had pushed through the hanging garments once to read what they said. Her English wasn't good, but she had followed the gist. 'Factories Act . . .' 'Health', 'Safety', 'Welfare', 'Employment of women and young persons'. Words, all words. Nargis looked around her.

She thought of England and of her time at the plug factory, and made a cynical noise: Raisa had asked her for details of her present job, and Raisa would speak and write still more words. She was educated and she might write about all this, but what did she know? Nargis pulled out an unchecked dress. Chic and expensive; she could imagine Raisa wearing it. Bulquis Ehsan had spread the word that her grandfather was rich in Pakistan and owned carpet factories. Nargis passed the dress. The girl could not be blamed for her grandfather's factories. You could see she was trying to do the right things. Nargis snipped at loose threads and fixed on the designer tags. She moved to the second rack. She had meant to look at the clock but instead saw a stranger, an older woman, working at Balbir's machine. She waited for Mrs Khan to leave the room. 'Zaibie!'

Nargis called her friend. The old woman looked up from her sewing, as if woken from sleep.

'*Salaama laikum, paihn.*' She smiled, revealing one gold tooth. 'All right?'

'Where's Balbir?'

'What can I tell you?' started Zaibie. 'She came to work this morning, and that dog,' she tilted her head towards Khan's office, 'he told her she wasn't needed any more. That turd told her he couldn't afford to keep her any more – that's why he's got someone else in her place!'

Nargis' eyes flitted cautiously across the room.

'Balbir's worked in this hole for nearly, yes, for nearly two years – before I started here – and that's how he pays her,' continued Zaibie.

'It's because of the two years, and because she paid her tax that he's sacked her,' said Nargis. 'He doesn't want to take any chances. After two years of working, the law says we can fight "unfair dismissal". That's what they call it here – "unfair dismissal".' She laughed. Mrs Khan entered the room with another trolley of skirts. Nargis pretended to be checking Zaibie's sewing.

'As if Balbir, or any of us, would ever manage to take him to court!' Nargis continued.

Zaibie leaned forward with hunched shoulders and started her machining. Nargis thought of the Khans' dissatisfaction with Zaibie's buttonholes. She realised the woman must be nearing the two-year mark herself. She saw the thin machinist with the black creases in her small brown face and imagined the matriarch at home with her sons and her daughters-in-law.

The fibres from the cut material and the steam from the press had started to collect in the air. Zaibie coughed – deep, chesty coughs. 'Look,' she spoke through her coughing, 'that pig can't even allow us windows you can open.' Every expletive was emphasised by the waving of a stretched hand. 'That greedy dog says he's fixed the ventilation, but has he? The dog!' She stopped to clear the phlegm in her throat. 'You know what I dreamt last week?'

'What?' asked Nargis. Dreams had meanings; sometimes they were premonitions. Mrs Khan had her back to them. She was busy giving instructions to Anwar, the presser.

'It's in the morning, very early, before anyone's here. I walk up the stairs, like I'm gliding on air. The door falls down before me; I don't have to open it. All this time, there's no sound, not a single sound. I carry a flaming torch in one hand, an axe in the other. Then, suddenly, I can hear the noise of the machines and smell the sweat and the dust, and there I am, burning all the filthy dresses and all the filthy material. I break all the machines, smash them so easily, I have the strength of a thousand men . . .' The coughing returned. Zaibie remembered her work targets. 'That's what I dreamt,' she said.

Nargis relaxed her jaw. She had been following Zaibie's dream with her teeth clamped tightly.

'Zaibie! Got no work, hanh?' Haroun dropped a wad of freshly cut material into the basket beside her machine.

'What're you doing, you stupid boy?' shouted Zaibie. 'Don't mix them with the blouses.'

'You better start working, you two. Here comes the wife.' He gave the warning and walked back to his area of the room.

Nargis left Zaibie to her battle against the hours and went back to the clothes racks – the sooner she finished the dresses, the sooner she could carry on with her piecework.

The bell sounded for morning break. Nargis was mid-way through the cuff of a blouse. She'd stay and finish it, she thought. Mr Khan was supposed to be seeing her – she might as well wait until he called.

Anwar the presser was still working. He was barely older than her elder son. He earned more than she did. Pressers and cutters always earned more than the machinists. Just then, he was moving the hand-iron over the shoulders of a dress. She could iron as well as that, she thought, and the pressing machine wasn't hard to operate. But, so far as she knew, pressers were never women.

Anwar's movements and his concentration were mesmerising. Holding the garment, he pressed lightly in one place, shot bursts of steam in another. He took pride in his work. Partly to stretch her legs, partly to break the monotony, Nargis left her stool to chat with him.

'Still working, hanh?' she asked.

'Got a lot to get through.' He carried on with the ironing.

'Has he increased your pay yet?' Nargis leaned against a trolley. 'His cousin used to work slower than you, but he got paid more!'

'That's the way it goes, isn't it?' Anwar seemed unmoved.

'He still worked him hard, his own cousin.'

'Khan's a pig,' said Anwar. 'But he got where he is through hard work. You've got to respect that.'

'You respect him, do you?' Nargis moved away from the trolley.

'No, I hate him,' Anwar answered. 'As his worker, I hate him. But what is a man to do?' He paused in his ironing. 'One day, I'll have a factory. Bigger and better than this one.'

'Achcha!' Nargis returned to her stool.

She watched Anwar. One day she might be working for this boy. Anwar put down the iron and hung up the dress. Nargis continued to watch him. On a hook behind him was his jacket. With his back to Nargis, he searched a pocket for cigarettes. His thick dark hair touched the collar of his shirt. She remembered again the man in the car, and the girl sitting beside him. The injustices and indignities of work were suddenly eclipsed. She had tried all morning to smother her anguish, but in that second she lost control, and the anguish turned on her.

Tahira was a child, only a girl, not much older than Munty. An obscene image forced itself into her mind. Nargis closed tight her inner eye and ran from it. But the image wouldn't go. Just as she thought she had escaped, up it leaped. Her daughter couldn't be doing that, couldn't be with a man, doing that. Her heart beat faster and a coldness swept over her as she looked on. No, she challenged, it couldn't be Tahira. Tahira would never do that.

Yet daughters did sometimes meet men, in secret. She had heard they did. She looked again at the hair that curled over Anwar's collar. No! Tahira could never behave like the girl she had imagined. She might have been in that grey car. She might even be meeting a boy. Yes, it was bad and dangerous, and she must be stopped, but at worst Tahira could never go beyond flirting with the forbidden.

Nargis managed to quell the tormenting image and find an uneasy peace. Her thoughts became less unbearably vivid. At last she was able to think, without her panic taking over. What could a mother do if a daughter had a mind to start something and to break the rules? Was it really so bad, in itself, so long as no one knew? Nargis recognised the words of the devil, and flinched at her own shameful thoughts. She prayed that the girl in the car wasn't Tahira, nor, God forbid, anyone else's defenceless daughter.

'Begum Rashid.' Mr Khan stood at the door of his office. 'Come in please.' He spoke in English. Wearily, Nargis left her machine and entered. 'Sit down there please.' He pointed to an old office chair opposite his desk.

He switched to Punjabi. 'You've been late four times this week, four times,' he said.

'Yes, I told you, the bus . . .'

He cut her short. 'Many people use the bus and they arrive on time, Begum Rashid.' Absently, his eyes wandered to the hollow of her throat, then quickly moved on. 'I know we have relatives in common. I know that.' He cleared his throat. 'But I have a business to run and I have to run it properly. You must think about my position.'

She thought about it. Was he simply displaying his power, or was he about to sack her? She was, after all, connected only distantly to his wife's family. And anyway, it had become quite honourable to fire even your own brother in the name of business. 'I'm sorry,' she said. 'I'll try to be on time.'

He modified her words. 'You must be on time. I pay you more than the other women, more per garment.' Mr Khan reminded her. 'I pay you more because you're reliable, and because we're related.'

You pay me a little more than the other women, thought Nargis, and the other women hate me a little for it; you pay the men a little more still, and we hate the men a little. Your generosity keeps us apart.

Mr Khan looked at the Rolex on his wrist. 'Yes,' he said, 'Kurshid must be cutting the sample now – it's a pure silk dress. You can start on it as soon as he finishes.'

Nargis stood up to leave. Perhaps she would have time for a quick cup of tea. Mr Khan had more to say. 'This factory,' he said, 'is better than many. You have your breaks, a reasonable room to work in, fair wages . . . I've achieved all this through hard, honest work, not through running from debts and cheating the taxman. We all have to work hard, Begum Rashid.'

'Yes,' said Nargis, looking at his gleaming watch. Then he added, 'Perhaps your daughter could come in again, to help you with your other sewing. Every penny helps, I know.'

The bell for the end of break sounded loudly. Mr Khan shuffled through the letters on his desk; their conversation had come to an end. Nargis went back to her work. She would lose herself in it, in case the goblins in her head woke up.

166

Twenty-four

The Datsun stopped outside the 'Nan-Kebab House'. Tahira slammed the passenger door behind her, and without pausing or looking around, entered the café. Arif locked the car doors and checked them before he followed her in.

Two youths – one desi, one West Indian – waited at the counter for their take-away teas: the queue outside the social security would be long and slow moving. A bearded old man sat at the table by the window. The owner of the place wasn't there. Jaswinder Singh, his old helper, was serving alone.

Tahira left it to Arif to order the teas. She made straight for the table in the furthermost corner, away from the counter, the window and the customers.

'Tahira yaar, what's all this, hey?' Arif sat opposite her.

'What's all what?' She narrowed her eyes in contempt.

He was alarmed by her manner. What was up, he wondered? She'd been angry with him before, but this, he was sure, was different.

She ignored the censorious glances of the old man. He didn't know who she was; he could go on looking and think what he liked. 'I can't stay long,' she said.

'Hey, come on – you always say that.' Arif stretched his legs and leaned back in his chair. 'Remember, *you* called me. After all this time.'

Tahira pulled her pony-tail forward over her shoulder. Her fingers wove irritably through the long strands of hair.

'You said you had to see me. What was so urgent?' He sat upright. 'Hey, come on. Relax.'

167

Both elbows on the table and chin resting on her hands, Tahira studied his face: the droop of his eyes, the yellow-tinted skin, the hairs in his ears. She saw his over-confident pose; she remembered his bragging talk.

Arif cleared his throat. She was looking at him so strangely. She was nothing like the girl he knew. He coughed nervously. And then things started to make sense. He'd handle it, he told himself. He hadn't spoken of that one time with anyone who knew her, or her family. Thank God, their families didn't know each other. He said, 'It'll be easy. It ain't like the old movies. You don't have to pay, nothing like that. The doctors'll do it for free. No one will know.'

Had she understood him correctly? Was this how he understood her? The stupid prick. Her fury was too intense to be spoken. Arif moved back as Jaswinder Singh placed the tea on the table. Arif switched to Punjabi, 'Everything all right?' Jaswinder waved his arm across the little café and shrugged. Tahira smiled at him respectfully. He returned to the counter.

'Yeah, that's better,' said Arif. 'It's nicer when you're like this.' Under the table, his leg sought hers. She jerked away. He laughed and offered her a cigarette. Tahira ignored him. He lit one for himself and inhaled slowly. 'Come on yaar, it's no big problem.'

Tahira watched the movement of his mouth. From a distance, she heard him.

'Yeah.' He tilted back his head and blew smoke at the ceiling. 'It's no big problem, don't worry – I'll tell you what to do.'

'You think I'm pregnant? You think I called you 'cos I'm pregnant?' Barely above a whisper, she spat the words at him. 'Listen you, I did nothing with you – it was nothing. Like you, it was nothing!' Her speech gathered momentum. 'How could I get pregnant when it was nothing? I had a bath and scrubbed and scrubbed myself and nothing happened.'

Arif felt the waves of her disgust. He lit another cigarette, very calmly. He concentrated on staying calm. 'You're not pregnant,' he said, trying to conceal his relief. 'Why did you call me?' He turned towards the voice of a woman customer. She was fat and dowdy; he said, 'You know, I was worried for a minute. But, you know, we didn't do it properly.' She was looking at him in that strange way again. He found himself grinning at her and saying, 'You want to start meeting again?'

A hateful unreality surrounded Tahira. She recalled a car parked on a lonely road. Degradation. 'I've hated you,' she said. She hadn't said, 'I hate you', but watching him there, grinning, she loathed him.

'Why did you try to see me again?' She spoke flatly. 'You came to my school. Why?'

'Hey, that was two weeks ago! I was just passing, seeing how you were. What's wrong with that?'

'You came up to my school to start your rubbish again. You phoned Tanni. The past week, I've been thinking.'

'What are you talking about?' He tapped his foot. He saw the expression on her face. 'Look, I know you're not interested, right. So let's leave it.'

'I ain't scared of you. You can't bloody touch me. You can't do nothing.'

She despised herself for letting him disrupt her life and loathed him because he hadn't been worth it. She was wretched. She couldn't feel the righteousness of the innocent and she loathed him for that too. Anger, and shame.

She hates me, he thought. Is she going to pull out a knife or what? 'You called me to tell me that?' he asked. He felt like an injured little boy. He swallowed the lump in his throat.

'I called you to tell you . . .' she paused a moment, 'to tell you what you did to me. You said you'd tell my brothers if I didn't carry on seeing you. You threatened me and you followed me about. I was scared. I was worried sick my uncles would hear, and my mum . . .'

Arif looked away at the window. The old man was still there, lost in his meditations.

'Hey, come on, I was only joking!' He had to make light of it. 'You don't really think I'll go to your brothers and tell them I've done it with you?'

'Once, only once, and it was nothing.' Her whispers shot out.

'OK, OK yaar, it was nothing. Can we leave now?' She was mad: it wasn't as if he'd forced her or anything. He wanted to get into his car and drive away.

'You knew I had more to lose than you, and you threatened me. I was scared and sick. You did that to me.'

'I told you, I was only joking . . .'

'You started turning up outside school, following me.'

'I was joking,' he said, shifting restlessly. 'I came after you 'cos I liked you. I wanted you to know – like sending you flowers.'

Why hadn't she noticed the lump on his nose before now? Had this boy really been the hero of her conversations, night and day? Tahira marvelled at her blindness. It wasn't him she had liked at all. The realisation was liberating, and poignant – heroes lived only in the mind.

She pushed back her pony-tail. 'That's right. You scared me. But that was then.'

'Yeah,' he came in quickly. 'That was way back. I haven't seen you since then. I haven't told anyone. What's the big problem?'

Tahira carried on. 'I understand things better now. You can't touch me 'cos I won't let you. You don't know me. You weren't really interested in me.'

'What is this, yaar?' He dropped his arms to the sides of his chair. 'You're making out like I'm a real bastard.' He stubbed out his cigarette. 'I didn't say anything to your friends.'

'So what if you had said anything?' She paused to watch the old man leave the café. 'I'd have denied it. I'd have said I never saw you alone. My brothers know I go places where there are boys. So what? If my mum or anyone had heard your shit, I'd have just denied it. All the time girls get things said about them . . .'

'Oi yaar, I've heard you, OK!' Arif thought of leaving her and driving away.

Tahira carried on. 'My mum or chacha would've had a go at me, maybe kept me in for a bit. But I'd have gone on denying it. They'd believe me in the end, and they'd back me up to everyone.' Her speech rolled out easily. Arif fidgeted with his car keys. 'They'd believe me; I mean, how could her daughter be a slag? They'd want to believe me. And everyone else would have to believe it if they wanted to stay friends with us. And not forgetting my brothers,' she added, ' they'd want to sort out the bloke who was spreading all them lies and upsetting our family.'

Arif put the car keys on the table. He didn't have to listen to this. Who did she think she was anyway? His scene with her had been a bad waste of time. He didn't owe her anything – he hadn't forced her.

He stood up. 'I'm going, yaar.'

'You sit down! I haven't finished.' There was a tremor in her voice. Then she smiled. 'There again, I might just have told my lot that you forced me – you know, like raped me, and I was too scared to say before, but now that you was blackmailing me and all I . . .'

He sat down again. 'Why are you telling me all this? You hate me, OK. I thought we'd already finished anyway. I won't bother you, and that's the end, right?' She was looking at him in that strange way again.

'I wanted to tell you what you put me through,' she said. 'I wanted to tell you you can never do that again.'

'You told me and I heard you,' he replied. He took a deep breath – he'd change the subject. 'How's your friend?'

'Who?'

'Mumtaz.'

'She's my cousin. You don't remember that?'

'I meant your cousin. Course I remember. Want more tea? Something to eat?'

'No, I ain't got enough money.'

'I never let girls pay. You know that.' He ran his hand down his cheek.

'I ain't thirsty or hungry.'

He carried on stroking his cheek. The gesture irritated her.

'We can leave it now, right? It's all finished with.'

'Nothing's finished 'cos nothing started,' she said.

He glanced at his watch.

'Do you ever think about anything?' said Tahira. 'Do you think about what you do and why you do it?'

What was she talking about? He heard her derisive laugh.

'You don't think much, do you?' she continued. 'It's all big talk with you, ain't it? You know, "I'm gonna buy a gold watch" or "I'm gonna take over my dad's business and make it really big".' She mimicked him.

'What d'you mean?' Arif sat up.

'You're full of thick talk, that's what I mean.' She wouldn't stop. 'I mean, your dad's bakery's not much more than a bread stall, is it? You ain't got no gold watch. Just a broken-down old car, that's all.'

'Bitch,' she heard him say.

She could taste blood now. 'That's all you can really do ain't it – talk big? Do you know last week when you phoned up Tanni to chat her up – I reckon you've always fancied her, I mean her dad's rich, ain't he? – when you phoned her up,' she continued, improvising, hardly pausing for breath, 'I was there. Do you know, we both

171

listened to your chat-up, and didn't we have a laugh afterwards! I mean, you don't know nothing.'

'You're a bitch,' he said. 'You're all bitches.' He swallowed his bitter saliva.

Tahira barely heard him. 'I mean, what are you really? Just a poor little Paki who helps his dad on his little stall shop. You don't know nothing about how the big people live.' She laughed again. 'Ha, you wouldn't even know how to sit with them.'

She saw his intense, unblinking gaze. Suddenly, amid the frenzy of attack, she tasted fear. What if, angry beyond words, he made her pay? She wasn't as brave as her words. If he were to defame her, would she really be able to challenge him? She thought to appease his anger, but she didn't know how.

'You and your friend sat and laughed at my call,' he said, as Tahira paused, 'and I'm a poor little Paki, am I? You went out with me, remember? No one forced you to do nothing. What do you know about my dad's bakery? What do you know about anything?' His hurt and his aggression garbled out. 'You and that Tanni – you think you're something, hanh?' He shrugged an exaggerated contempt. 'I know lots of girls – more special than you or any of your friends.'

She was a bitch, and mad. He wanted nothing to do with her. But there she was, still speaking. 'You wouldn't like no one treating your sister like that, would ya? You wouldn't want no bloke to be with your sister as you was with me, would ya? Answer me that?'

'You leave my sister out of it!' He raised his voice.

'Yeah but you wouldn't want no bloke to treat her like that.' She persisted.

He stood up, opened his mouth to speak, but said nothing. He went up to the counter and paid the old Sikh. Then he walked out of the café.

The train sped towards Paddington. Tahira caught her reflection in the window: huge, dark eyes in a pale, transparent face. She looked like a spectre; she felt insubstantial and unreal. She pulled forward her pony-tail and rested her head against the metal bar above her seat. The English boy opposite her smiled. She was too exhausted to notice. She wished she could sleep.

She had seen him, and she had had her say. She didn't feel elated, as she had thought she would. She had hit back. It had been self-defence, but what had been her weapons? The shame of poverty, and the shame of the Paki. The very things which she would fight against, she herself had just used. She felt shabby.

And she feared the anger she must have caused. She had told him she would fight him. But the fear of what men, angry men, might do was still there. Grimly she told herself, she wouldn't be the victim.

She might as well go in for afternoon school. She turned her mind to the note she would forge explaining her morning's absence, and to her mother's daily query: 'How was school today?'

Twenty-five

It was the first hot day of summer. The corridor was lit grey-yellow from the afternoon sunlight falling on the walls. An end-of-term stillness hung over the place. Tomorrow, the fifth formers would begin their examination study leave; most, already, were staying at home. They would never reassemble as a year again.

Tahira stood outside the English stock-room. She was early, but she had half expected the others to be there before her. Now she waited, scanning the car park through the window. *Was this the last time?* she thought. Raisa's car wasn't there. She turned away. They had spoken, once, on the phone, but she had not seen her since that dinner nearly two months ago.

The heat had taken everyone by surprise. Tahira rolled up the sleeves of her baggy blue jumper. From her trouser pocket, she took out her 'Truly Plum' lipstick. Looking at her reflection in the glass panel of the stock-room door, she painted her mouth a deep, purply red.

The sound of footsteps made her turn her head.

'You're early an' all then?' She put away the lipstick.

'It's all revision now. I can do it at home,' answered Nasreen.

'You know, I can't get used to your new hairstyle and that.'

Nasreen's shorter cut and shaped eyebrows had transformed her appearance. She even carried herself differently.

'It looks nice. But it's so . . . don't your mum and dad mind?'

'Why should they mind? I'm not doing anything bad.'

Tahira flinched. Stuck-up little cow. To think she'd ever felt kind towards her, after her turn. But that was to do with other things anyway. She changed the subject. 'I told Miss Beeston it was at three o'clock.'

'I told Mr Crawley the same.'

'I thought you were a nice sharif girl.'

'Raisa should be coming soon,' said Nasreen.

'I suppose you'll miss her.'

'You're making it sound like it's the last time.' Nasreen leaned back against the window. If it was the last time – the thought was strangely painful – they should be nicer to each other. 'We're bound to all get together again. She said she'd get in touch as soon as she writes up her thing.'

Tahira picked up warmer signals. 'Well, you and me ain't really likely to see each other after we've left here, are we?' She remembered Bulquis Ehsan rushing into Gateway rather than meeting her mother. 'You definitely going to that college?'

'Yes.'

'Is that 'cos of what happened, you know?'

'Partly.' Nasreen looked away. 'I don't really want to go over all that.'

A car door slammed shut. Both girls turned to look. Raisa was hurrying towards the door of their building. She looked flushed from the heat and driving. Three fifth-year boys passed by her and then stopped. She walked back in their direction. Now she was talking to them.

'Why do you think she's chatting to them gorrai?' Tahira looked at her watch.

'She's probably telling them off for being cheeky.'

'They wouldn't go "cor" if she told them she was a Paki.' Tahira inspected Raisa's slim figure and trendy jeans. 'Do you think she's a flirt?'

'No,' answered Nasreen. 'She's just friendly. You know, like some grown-ups, or teachers, people like that.'

'You mean like educated, upper-class sort of people who dress nice and wear make-up and are nice to you?'

Raisa left the boys and soon moved out of view. The boys laughed among themselves as they made their way to the main building.

Nasreen said, 'Do you like her? I mean, after all these months? I know you weren't really keen on her at the beginning.'

Tahira didn't answer the question. She couldn't, and Raisa was now walking along the corridor, smiling broadly at them.

'Look at you two! Already here and waiting. I'm impressed. And Nasreen, what a lovely hair-style!'

She was pleased to see them. Tahira could tell.

'We saw you from the window,' she said.

'What, you were spying on me, were you?'

'We were wondering what you was doing with them boys.'

'Well, if you really want to know, I was telling them off.' Raisa went forward to open the door of the stock-room. 'It's nice of the department to give us this room.'

No one entered. The room was shabbier than ever. A broken desk had been placed in the tiny space. It was balanced against the table. There were piles of books everywhere. The cardboard boxes and old folders seemed to have multiplied.

'It ain't exactly a room, is it?' said Tahira.

'It never was.'

Nasreen said, 'I think they're counting the books.'

They gazed at the room that had heard all those thousands of words, some of them so private and dangerous; the room in which they had made their eager, flailing efforts to connect experiences, to make sense.

Raisa mostly asked the questions, thought Tahira.

Raisa shut the door. Her final visit would not be marred. 'Let's go and sit outside. I'm sure no one will disturb us.'

'We could sit on the grass by the playground,' said Nasreen.

'Yeah, come on,' said Tahira. 'They can all watch us from the classrooms.'

They found a shaded spot on the uneven grass. The three sat in a semi-circle with the playground to one side and the main building behind them. Ahead, in the distance, lay the playing field and the road beyond.

Tahira lay on her back, her eyes closed to the bright, cloudless sky. Raisa watched her. Her hair was spread out; her face looked like a child's. Raisa thought of heartless, predatory men. A rush of concern came over her. Did the girl know how to look after herself? She was fiery and she could argue. Could she cope by herself? Then there was Nasreen. What did the future – that impersonal unknown – hold for her? Raisa took out a hankie. Her throat felt tight.

Tahira raised herself on to her side. 'That's where we was when the police rushed us.' She pointed to the playground. 'We'd come to tell them, but they stopped us.'

'Now we're here in this same place. We can say what we couldn't before, and they're not here to listen,' said Nasreen.

'We still made them shit themselves. There was so many of us.' Tahira was reliving that afternoon. As time passed, it acquired wondrous qualities.

Raisa thought of herself, a schoolgirl in the sixties, when Grosvenor Square was raging, and the Springbok tour was being blocked. She saw the empty playground and filled it with a ghostly mass of children. 'It's weird, you know, to see a place after you've heard so much about it.'

Nasreen said, 'All the older pupils will be gone for good after the exams. We're most of us leaving.'

Nothing stirred. The green field, the playground, the school building – all could have been a picture, a thought, isolated and picked out for all time. Raisa swallowed the tightness in her throat. How could her concern for the girls be anything more than an indulgence? After all, it was unlikely that she would meet the girls again. And did she care enough to alter that?

Nasreen let her cardigan drop down her shoulders.

Tahira asked, 'Why did you tell them boys off, in the car park?'

'One of them made a stupid comment – a real badtameez comment.'

'What?'

'He said "sexy".' She was surprised at her own embarrassment. 'They said they were being nice. I told them I could do without that kind of niceness.'

'I don't suppose they understood what you were talking about,' said Nasreen.

Raisa laughed. 'I'm sure they hate me for snubbing them.'

'Paki blokes ain't no better,' said Tahira. And then, returning to Raisa, she said, 'Them gorrai can probably see us now, from one of them rooms.'

The three looked at the inscrutable walls and windows.

'You know what this reminds me of?' Raisa grasped her knees and rocked lightly. 'The grass, and us sitting out here?'

The girls listened.

'When I was sixteen, me and my friend Helen bunked off some

177

lesson or other. It must have been maths. I used to hate maths.' Raisa
smiled at the past. The girls watched her. 'We'd gone to sit in the
middle of the grass – just like in the film we'd seen at the time, *Women
in Love*. There we were, talking about this and that, when down came
the headmistress. She was horrified, so she said, that two fifth formers
had the audacity to be truanting in the middle of the school field. She
asked us why we weren't in our lessons. I had my leather-bound
Works of Keats in my hand. I'd bought it in a secondhand shop. I used
to love Keats. I told her we were reading 'Ode to a Nightingale'. She
couldn't really tell us off after that. She told us to go to our lessons
but you could see she was impressed – two young girls reading poetry
on the grass.'

'Who's Kates?' asked Tahira.

'Keats. He was a poet. He died over a hundred years ago, very
young. He's famous. My father introduced me to him when I was
eleven or so.'

Tahira had turned away. She was busily pulling out grass and
making a small mound of it by her side.

'There's no reason why you should have heard of him.'

Nasreen said, 'He's like Shakespeare and Jane Austen – people like
that?'

'Well, yes – he is your "English Literature".'

'You haven't brought your recorder along,' said Nasreen.

'No, today's a chatting day. I've got as many tapes as I can handle,
thank you very much.'

'Do you like living on your own?' Tahira flattened the mound of
grass. 'Don't no one say nothing funny to you?'

Raisa said, 'The relatives who might think it's bad don't know for
sure that I live away from my father's house. We've never really met
our relatives, not often, and the ones we do meet from time to time
aren't shocked. I am twenty-seven, grown-up you know, and I have
my work and I need the space and quiet.'

'Ain't you never gonna get married? What about kids?'

'You don't look your age,' said Nasreen. 'My mother was surprised when you told her.'

'Anyway, you're rich – you are really – and you've got your
friends, right?'

Raisa wanted the conversation to move on. Today of all days,
they should be dwelling on points at which their lives met, not

differences. But the differences were there and the sadness of things passing filled the hot afternoon. It would be a day of farewells.

'Come on, you two, let's talk about . . . I don't know . . . You think of something, Nasreen.'

Tahira stood up and stretched. Looking down on them, a near-silhouette against the sky, she said, 'I know – I'll tell you more about Solly, when we just started going out there. I ain't told you that before.' For the first time since the trouble with Arif, she felt able to remember Southall, as it used to be, before it was tainted. She wouldn't go back there for a while yet, but she could think about the old days.

'This'll shock Nasreen, I reckon,' she said.

Nasreen protested.

'I ain't being funny. It just ain't your sort of thing.'

'Come on then, start talking,' said Raisa.

Tahira sat down, this time facing Raisa, Nasreen and the school building. 'Believe it or not, we'd never have gone to Solly on our own if it wasn't for Mr McCormack. We'd been there once or twice with our mums and dads, never on our own. McCormack told us we could do a project on the "Asian shop community". We told him we wanted to do it in Southall. We never done it, though. It was too hard. What we did was,' she laughed, 'we started bunking off once a week and going to Solly.'

'What on earth were you doing there all that time?' asked Raisa. 'As if I can't guess!'

'The very first time, you should have seen the day we picked.' She spoke almost feverishly. 'We had these really high winds. It was a Tuesday. The winds had died down but it rained a lot. We had a great time, me and Gita and Mumtaz.'

A bee moved in and out of the grass nearby. Raisa watched its heavy body, as the past lingered about her. Sunday afternoon. She and Helen were walking across Putney Bridge, past the yellow stone church to the station. Fairport Convention were playing at the Roundhouse. Amie was in Lahore. Nana Abu was dying.

'I'm talking too much, ain't I?'

'No, no!' Nasreen's vehemence surprised everyone.

'You're reminding me of things,' said Raisa. 'Carry on, we both want to hear.' She sat up straight.

'Well then, there were these blokes in the shop. I dunno what was

179

so special about us except that we was all soaked. Most of the people in the shops started to notice us.'

Raisa interrupted. 'I see, just like the Indian movies. You know, the beautiful woman getting soaked in the rain, to the skin!'

'In Solly we did some really stupid, I mean *stupid* things that we'd never dream of doing in Barking. You could do anything down there, you sort of felt free.'

'What sort of things?' Nasreen leaned forward.

'Like when I stood in the middle of the road, the traffic lights had just turned green, and I stuck my fingers up at these blokes in a shop.'

Nasreen saw that Raisa wasn't at all perturbed; her expression of shock was too comically drawn.

'There's a story behind all that, mind. We was walking up and down the Broadway – that's the name of the street – '

'Yes, I know,' said Raisa.

'Yeah, we was walking up and down there, and these guys that worked in Burtons whistled at us and kept staring. So Gita dares me to go in there and Mumtaz nearly dies of shame.' Her words were spilling out. 'It looked really funny – going into a blokes' shop after being whistled and shouted at. We all went in. We went to where the suits were and we were surrounded by four of the most ugliest looking idiots you could find. On a scale of one to ten, they were minus a hundred! We didn't know whether to take it as a compliment or die of shame!'

All three shrieked with laughter.

She continued. 'They started saying things about the way we was dressed. They said we had winter clothes on, and they reckoned it was summer. We just said sarcastic things back, and we walked out. We got outside and we had a right laugh.'

Those days in Solly had been mad and innocent, blissfully untouched. She wanted Raisa and Nasreen to know about them, before they parted.

'Were all these boys desi?' asked Raisa.

'Yeah, Indians, Pakistanis, East Africans,' said Tahira, her legs now stretched out before her. 'There was this other guy who worked in this little mall. 'Cos we were soaked, we went in there and looked in a mirror inside one of the shops. This bloke came up to us and started talking. He was a right pervert – he told us to come next door and he'd blow-dry our hair.'

Raisa fanned herself with the hem of her blouse. 'Was Solly really about the girl–boy thing then? You know, meeting *the* guy?'

'It weren't just that. It was the place – the shops, the music and everything and, you know, no one knowing you. But it was a lot to do with the boy–girl thing as well. We never done nothing bad though.'

Her eyes met Raisa's. She rushed back to her 'Solly'.

'Talking about men, I reckon most of the girls are picked up by men in cars. We had so many cars that stopped and asked us to go with them.'

The grey Datsun. She fought back the image. Solly must not lose its magic. The meeting and talking with Raisa would come to an end, and she had to hold on. She continued, 'One car wouldn't leave us alone, till they saw someone they knew and went off.'

Nasreen heard the tremble in her voice. 'Are you all right?'

'Yes, you do look pale.' Raisa reached out to feel Tahira's jumper. 'You're too warmly dressed for a day like this.'

Tahira said, 'I'm all right. It's just that it's the last day and – well, you know.'

'I know,' Raisa moved closer. 'School might be boring, but when you leave it, it's still sad. The end of childhood. The end of a period. It's like a death, isn't it?'

'Yeah.' Tahira avoided Raisa's eyes.

'Who were you in Solly?' asked Raisa.

Tahira remembered their earliest conversations in the poky stockroom. Now, in the sunshine, she sighed as the seconds passed by.

'Who were you?' Raisa repeated. 'I can imagine some of the English girls carrying on like that.'

Tahira wondered if she was being criticised. 'I was myself. Not English or Pakistani or that. What we done in Solly we done 'cos of what we wanted and what we knew. Can't really explain. I mean, what we done in Solly, we could only have done there. You know, like no one knew us there and there were other girls there like us – worse than us – and we sort of grew there, something new. And it weren't bad. My friends and their friends don't think it's bad. But then, like we said the other time, you ain't just one thing anyway. It all depends, don't it?'

'Yes,' answered Raisa. Her voice came from a distance of years.

She thought again of the Roundhouse, and the parties.

'It's all weird and bad to you, ain't it?' Tahira asked Nasreen.

'It's different from what I do.'

'What do you do? I mean, after you've done your school and house stuff?' Tahira was fascinated, perversely. She wanted to be friends, but she also sought to expose the tedium of Nasreen's life.

'I read, for pleasure.' Nasreen was nervous, alone. She looked to Raisa, whose smile urged her on. But her feeling of isolation remained. 'I read for pleasure. I go out to weddings and family things. I go visiting with my mother. My cousins stay with us; I stay with them. That's what I do, that kind of thing.'

'Well, I think that's more than enough, don't you?' Raisa's levity was wasted.

Tahira had another question for Nasreen. 'What about boys? Do you think about them, about meeting them?'

'I think about all sorts of things, like . . .'

'Do you mean daydreaming?' Raisa's eagerness made her seem younger. 'I used to daydream – just sit there thinking, not wanting to be disturbed. I'd actually look forward to the times I'd be alone.'

Nasreen listened, apprehensive and quite amazed. The three of them were sitting more closely now, a tight triangle.

'You ain't gonna say what you daydreamed, right?'

'Are you challenging me?' Raisa met Tahira's gaze.

'You ain't gonna say!'

'Not everything – it's too private!' She laughed.

The girls joined in the laughter; and then Nasreen remembered Mr Rodriguez in the dark-room, and looked away.

'I'll tell you one of my daydreams. I still remember it.'

Nasreen sat still. The heat, the grass, the school were forgotten.

'I couldn't have been more than twelve or thirteen when I used to think about this. Let's see. I'd be Rusty, the beautiful young woman living in New York in the spacious penthouse apartment that I shared with a girlfriend. I'd be the twelve-year old Raisa, sometime in the future. It would be like a film, one of those late fifties American romantic comedies I used to watch on television, Sunday afternoons. I'm driving my sleek Cadillac into a parking space and – wait for it – like the cute, beautiful, dotty young woman I am, I knock into the car behind me. Of course, the car belongs to Jeffrey Hunter – a famous actor, better looking than Mel Gibson. He comes out, we argue and argue – he's very handsome . . .'

'Yeah, I know,' said Tahira, 'and in the end you get off with him.'

'I can't remember if I ever got to that part. I know I used to keep playing that scene over and over again. That's why I remember it probably.'

'It's the best bit really. Everything just starting off. Looking forward to all sorts of things, you know. It's the best bit.' Tahira wiped the perspiration from the back of her neck.

Nasreen said, 'I daydream a lot – well, I used to, until recently.'

'Did you ever talk about them, to your friends or cousins?' asked Tahira.

'No!' The idea was incredible.

'I tell Mumtaz everything. Well, near enough. Daft, ain't it – dreaming and all that, and, you know, wanting things? It's sad. I mean, wanting is one thing and getting is another.'

Tahira lifted her face to the sky. Nasreen's 'Everyone dreams' died on her lips, and Raisa fell into silence. The moment lengthened.

Tahira straightened up suddenly and spoke. 'It's funny, you know, about that daydream of yours. You being stupid and thick with the car.'

'Stupid and cute!' Raisa showed mock-indignation.

'It's not that,' said Nasreen. 'It's wanting the man to be stronger and cleverer than yourself.'

'I don't think I want a man to be cleverer than me.' Raisa was serious. 'Clever and interesting will do.' Then she laughed, and continued, 'And good-looking, and rich, and totally fascinated by me . . .'

'And nice,' said Tahira. She was not laughing. They might never again talk like this. 'You won't tell,' she spoke to Nasreen, 'you won't say nothing to no one will you?'

'There was this bloke I used to see – just see, mind. Nothing funny.' Her gaze wavered slightly as she addressed Nasreen. 'You probably saw him outside school – everyone else did!'

Raisa had not missed her tell-tale clumsiness. She thought of Nargis with her dreams of going back. Maternal feelings surged in her. 'I hope you've got everything under control. He's not still bothering you, is he?'

'No, he ain't bothering me.' She paused. 'You know, if he'd been nice, and important, and if he'd loved me and all that, well, I'd have gone off with him. I'd have taken the rubbish.'

Nasreen was astounded. 'You'd have gone with him and left your family!'

'Might have done.' Tahira blew the grass off her trousers. 'I'd have gone on seeing him, anyway. But he was thick, and he was nothing. The last time I saw him, I felt sorry for him.'

Nasreen blushed. 'I can't imagine someone I actually know doing that.'

'You don't know what goes on. You're a sharif girl. How would you feel, say, if a fifteen-year-old girl weren't a virgin?' Her eyes flicked at Raisa.

'Do you know a Pakistani girl of fifteen who's not?' asked Raisa.

'Yeah, I know a fifteen-year-old girl who ain't . . .'

Raisa thought, does Nargis suspect? She said, 'Do her parents know?'

'No.'

'Why do you think she did it, and not you? What's the difference?'

Tahira thought of Tanni. 'Because she's spoiled. Her parents have given her too much freedom. She goes round with an English bloke she met in her dad's restaurant.'

'What do you mean, too much freedom?'

'Not freedom, like to go out with boys and that. I mean she doesn't have to go places with her brother or cousins looking after her. She can go out, and even if she's got her cousins with her, it doesn't matter 'cos they don't care. They're just like her. I mean her mum and dad let her have parties with boys there.'

'Does this girl live in Barking?' Nasreen was gripped by an appalling fascination.

'No, you don't know them.' She carried on. 'She don't tell her mum and dad she goes out on her own. Her brother knows. She don't listen to him. He's worse than her, but then, he's a boy ain't he?'

'She has an English boyfriend, you said?' asked Raisa.

'Yeah, she goes out with a gorra. She don't just have Pakistani friends, anyway. Her cousins go to art college and they all go round together with lots of different countries' people.'

'You sound as if you don't approve of her going out with an English boy.'

Nasreen listened.

'In class last week I heard a gorri say to this gorra – who would you like to go out with, a Paki girl, a girl with Aids or a dead girl? Do you know what he said? He said, the Aids girl *and* the dead girl. They all thought it was funny.'

'Not all of them thought it was funny.' Nasreen had been there.

'Yeah, but I didn't see no gorrai telling them off.'

'Brian didn't think it was funny.'

'Oh him!' Tahira raised her eyes. 'No, it ain't right with gorrai. It don't even look right. You sort of wonder why the girl's with the gorra, or why he's with her. It ain't right. I wouldn't fancy them.'

'Does your friend's brother know that she carries on with English boys?' asked Raisa. She saw that Nasreen was sitting further away, at the lengthened end of the triangle.

'If he knew, she'd be dead,' Tahira replied. 'Well, maybe not dead, but you don't really want to think about it.'

Nasreen spoke again, as if from a distance. 'It could be lies. Couldn't it be lies?'

Tahira was lost in her own ideas. 'If the people around you – girls – go out with boys and do things, and you see them taking risks and God ain't striking them dead, well, one day you might go and do it as well. You don't feel right, not really, but if you like the bloke, it would feel good, wouldn't it? So you do it, and as time goes by, and the people around you, and you, carry on like that, well, it becomes like normal, you know, like a habit. Even if you still worry about it sometimes.'

Raisa said, 'You tell yourself you're right even if, as you say, a part of you doesn't agree.' She tried to make connections. 'You work out arguments to back yourself up. Remember when we were discussing those stories of good and bad women, and the Surah? Well, OK, you step outside a way of thinking and behaving and all sorts of things make that possible – different stories, all sorts of things. Those stories, you use them to justify what you're doing. Don't you think?'

Nasreen raised herself on to her knees. 'To justify bad things?'

'You might do, but I don't think it's as simple as that.' The conversation had taken a chaotic turn, and Raisa was thirsty. She'd think about it later.

'That's wrong.' Nasreen put her doubts aside and defended truth. 'It can't be right. You can't change the truth and do bad things.'

'All right, what about my mum?' Tahira faced Nasreen. 'If you're good, you don't get divorced, right? Lots of Pakistanis think that's the truth, right? In their book, my mum's bad. I mean, your mum don't talk to her no more. I ain't getting at you, but all them people who don't mix with us, they ain't bothered with why she got divorced. I reckon they're the bad ones – doing bad things and backing it up with what they reckon's the truth.'

Nasreen did not aswer.

'We keep coming back to the same things, don't we?' said Raisa. 'And I'm getting thirsty.'

Nasreen moved back to her spot on the grass. Tahira saw the distance stretched out between them.

'My friend carries on with blokes, but other girls might have done it just once.'

'If you come from a true Muslim home, you'd never do it – even if the people around you were bad. You'd fight it with what you know is right. You wouldn't mix with those people.'

'Some girls might have done it just once,' Tahira repeated. 'You know, a part of them is caught up in all that stuff.' She looked at Raisa. 'But other things tell them it isn't worth it.'

'I don't know how a Muslim girl could do it,' said Nasreen. 'The boy will think she's bad. If she wanted him to respect her, she'd never do that.'

'Not all Pakistani boys think that way, though.' Tahira ran her palms across the grass backwards and forwards. 'Mind you, I reckon they do deep down, and I suppose in a way a girl does put herself down by acting cheap. There again, it ain't fair, 'cos it's different for blokes, ain't it?'

'Not if they're Muslim. A Muslim boy has to be the same.'

'That ain't real life though,' answered Tahira. 'It's the same with gorrai. No gorri wants to be called a slag, and it's only girls who can really be called that, right? I know you could turn to a bloke and call him a slag but it don't hurt him.'

'Jamshid called the English girl a prostitute, didn't he?'

'Yeah. It was the worst way he could hurt her.' She laughed. 'She couldn't turn round and call him that back, could she?'

'They said worse things to him than prostitute.' Nasreen looked up at the school building and remembered that afternoon.

'Oh yeah!' Tahira laughed again. 'About the size of his you know

186

what. Oh yeah! I know it ain't funny but . . .'

'But you're having hysterics anyway,' said Raisa.

'No, it ain't funny.' She stopped laughing. 'You know, it really makes you think. Of all the bad things a girl can do, stealing or fighting, murdering – of all them things, the worst is sex. It does make you think.' She paused. 'Do you know what the sex thing does do? It stops you from doing things.'

'Lots of things stop people from . . .' Nasreen was the first to hear the chattering and laughter. A group of English girls and boys were coming out of the building. Tahira stood up in time to be level with the group as it passed. She yawned and met the silent glare of one of the girls. The group walked on; one or two looked back.

She knelt down. 'That was Julie Webster. They've only come in 'cos it's the last day. I used to be friends with her in the first year.'

Another bee came back, flitting over the blades of grass. It settled on Nasreen's shoulder. She kept very still. Tahira waved it away. It hovered around Raisa's head. She screamed and covered her face. It touched her wrist.

'Don't move,' said Nasreen. 'It's attracted to your watch, the shiny bit.'

Tahira flicked at it. The bee moved on.

'You're just like a kid.' Tahira smiled.

'Sorry about that.' Raisa looked at her watch.

'It'll be the end of the lesson soon, and that'll be it.' Tahira's voice was strangely thin. 'You've told us some things about yourself, but you ain't really said a lot.'

'I hope we're not strangers though.'

Nasreen's arm brushed against Raisa's as she moved in closer. 'What were you like when you were our age?'

'What did you and your mates get up to?'

Raisa blinked under their gaze. 'How strange! I honestly don't know what to tell you.' What did each want to hear? 'Every Sunday for a while, I used to get off at Chalk Farm with my friends and go to a place called the Roundhouse. I loved going there.'

'What was the Roundhouse?' Nasreen asked. 'What did you do there?'

Raisa was conscious of the stillness aound Tahira.

'I used to love dancing there, and you met all sorts of people there. My parents didn't know anything about it. Sometimes I didn't get

187

home till eleven or twelve. I always had a good excuse.'

'What sort of dancing?' asked Tahira.

Nasreen inspected her hands.

'Not close-up dancing with men. Nothing like that. It was that wriggly, hippy dancing – you must have seen it in films. I used to love it.'

'Did you have boyfriends?' Tahira again. Nasreen shrugged in embarrassment.

'I had friends who were boys – one or two – not "boyfriends".' She glanced at Nasreen's lowered head. 'We didn't do anything bad. You know, sipping coca-cola, talking. My friends were mostly girls from school.'

They might never again meet like this. Was that the impetus for her desire to be a Tahira for Tahira, a Nasreen for Nasreen – a parting present?

'What are your plans, Tahira? Have you sorted out your job yet?'

'I ain't heard from the bank. I probably won't get my CSEs anyway.'

'You never know.' Slowly, she started to collect her bag and papers. Tahira watched her every move. 'And what about you, Nasreen? Is it definite about the college?'

'Oh yes, I've got a place in Havering. Their A level results are very good.'

Tahira wrenched out handfuls of grass. 'I don't wanna work in a boring bank for the rest of my life. It might be better than my mum's place, but it's still boring ain't it?' She forced a smile. 'I'll take my exams again. Evening classes, maybe. And this time, I'll work really hard. I ain't thick, you know.'

'Anyone who thinks as you do could never be called thick, Tahira.'

Nasreen asked, 'What will you do after your research?'

'I haven't really thought about it. I haven't had time. Believe it or not, the research has become important to me for reasons other than career development. But I suppose I will try to use it to get promotion.'

Suddenly, Tahira said, 'We won't see each other again, not now we've left school.'

'Of course we will,' said Raisa, because that was the only thing she could say. 'I'll definitely get in touch with both of you after I've

188

finished writing up the research. I want you to read it. Bits of it you'll find interesting, I think. It will use words like "culture" and "identity", but it's really about who we are and how we live here. I, as well as you.'

'You'll see us to give us the stuff.' Tahira spoke in a monotone. Her heart was heavy. She watched the woman who had come into her home, who had sat and laughed with her mother, who had made her want something else. Who she was and the way she lived could be the sky and stars above Tahira's bedroom when she lay there at night. And in ten minutes she'd be gone.

Raisa was speaking. 'After the holidays, definitely before Christmas, I'll contact you.'

Nasreen buttoned up her cardigan. 'I'd like to read what you write. My father and mother would like to as well.' Then she said, 'I'll write to you.'

'Yes, both of you must write.'

The end-of-day bell echoed across the school grounds. They stood up, stretching their legs and straightening their clothes. Children rushed out of the building. Raisa brushed the grass off her jeans.

'Tahira, you must thank your mother for that information about the factory. It was very useful. I tried to phone her, but I couldn't get through.'

'The phone ain't working.'

Raisa started to walk. Nasreen followed her, but Tahira had not moved. She said, 'We might all be girls and we might all be Pakistanis and all that, but we're different, you know. You're even more different than me and Nasreen. You ain't even lived like us. You've never worried about half the things we worry about. Where you live, the people you meet, it's all different. I bet your mum never had to wear no dupatta or work for no pig. I ain't being rude, but it's true, ain't it?'

'Not entirely.' She tried to relax. They must not part on such a note. 'After the holidays, definitely before Christmas, I'll contact both of you. We'll meet then.' She looked at her watch. 'I think I'll go to the staffroom for a drink. Don't forget,' she took Tahira's arm, and Nasreen's, 'we must write to each other.'

Raisa walked off to the staffroom. Nasreen left to meet her younger sister. Tahira saw Gita in the distance and ran towards her.

Twenty-six

Nasreen and Tahira,

I promised I'd give you copies of my dissertation. But before that, I'm sending you this letter.

I've been thinking about your lives and now I'm considering mine; and in that movement, I've arrived at understandings. Yes, the differences are there, unmistakably, but so are the points of meeting. None of us can overlook either if we are to stand together against the injustices of our pasts and presents.

The hour is late and I fear that I'm being poetic. All the same, I have thought and I have written. Before I sleep, and before my reserve gets the better of me, I will post my words to you.

I have thought hard, I have searched my mind; I have spoken to my father and sister; I have read history and juxtaposed the details of our lives – but where do I start?

I came to London in the September of 1961. My tears and screams had not helped me stay behind with my Nani Amma and Nana Abu. It was a sad and powerless seven-year-old who stepped off the plane to a cold, wet London night. I knew then I would never again see my grandparents.

We had left Lahore to join my father. He had been away for most of my life, and had only returned once, for a two-week visit. I barely remembered him. He was a barrister now, from Lincolns Inn – the same Inn as Mohammed Ali Jinnah's.

The stories I'd heard about my father had always placed him at a distance. My youngest uncle used to tell me how strict and fierce he was. My grandmother used to tell me how clever and wise he was. My mother used to tell me how tall and handsome he was. I saw him as all these things. His gaze frightened and fascinated me.

I think of those early months in London, and the memories and images leap out: my grey school blazer and striped tie, the short trousers of school boys, the flame-coloured flowers that bordered so many neat gardens in our road in Fulham, my mother taking her daughter through laburnum tree-lined streets to Burntwood Primary school, sparkling dewy mornings, the attention of teachers and pupils who wanted to know real people from those far-off, mysterious lands. I must have been happy, though the memories are tinged with a melancholy, an *udasi*.

I was scared, too. I had always dreaded the night. In the London darkness I heard the djinns with their horrible whisperings; I dreamt of witches. Naughty children had to be punished and I feared that my own mother would let the demons take me.

We were sitting in the living-room – my mother, little sister and I – watching the Sunday matinée on BBC One. My father was working in his study. The phone rang. I got up to answer it. I remember looking at my mother amid the large quilted cushions she'd recently bought. I remember looking down on her chestnut hair and fiery green eyes, and thinking how beautiful she was, how relaxed. The last letter from Pakistan had spoken of an improvement in my grandfather's health, and her brothers seemed to have stopped bickering over their father's property.

The call was from her sister in Lahore. My mother ran to the phone. Pallor spread across her face. Her father had been taken into hospital.

She left early the next day. Once a year, as she had vowed, she returned to her father's house. That annual return was now rudely brought forward. I hugged her and then I left for school; and during morning lessons, whenever a plane flew overhead, I prayed for her again and again.

We awaited her news. Two days later she phoned. My grandfather's condition was stable; he would soon be out of hospital, thanks be to God.

The days after her leaving were quiet. I thought of her constantly. Was she happy with us? Would she rather leave her daughters and husband, and stay with her older family in Lahore? But how could

191

that be? Her brothers were callous. Their father was ill, and they were already planning to write their sisters and mother out of their share of the property. Was she happy with us?

I remember thinking all this, and other things. Her brothers were mean; my father, though a barrister, wasn't making the money that barristers in London were reputed to earn. She didn't take money from my father and she didn't have a private income, so where did she find the money to pay for her visits, to buy presents for us and for the house? My father would joke that she had a secret job. It seemed the only explanation. Her daily trips to the 'shops' or to the houses of friends took on a new meaning, as did her regular visits to Leyton to see her Kasuri relatives. My grandfather's daughter must have been working in some shabby, dreary office. My anger turned against my father. He should have provided for us sufficiently, he with his education and status.

Thoughts such as these – painful and humiliating – were soon put away as I was swept into the whirl of adolescence.

I bled for the Palestinians. No one spoke of them in those days. At home, I heard of the Deir Yessein massacre and of the thousands and thousands of refugees. I was horrified by the silence that surrounded them: their voice wasn't heard; they were not seen. They may as well not have existed. I attended the Young Communist League meetings because the YCL supported them. I remember my outrage at the atrocities against blacks in South Africa. It was with a sense of retributive purpose that I joined the demonstrations against the Springbok rugby tour. The war in Vietnam was a reality for me. I remember hating the American government, hating it with such intensity when I saw a photograph of a group of soldiers from the Green Berets proudly holding aloft the decapitated heads of Vietnamese men and women. The student riots of 1968 lit my imagination. Danny the Red, Rudi Dutschke and the students in the streets of Paris weren't that much older than I; they were fighting, and they were being taken seriously. I was moved by the drama and the power of slogans: workers of the world unite.

Then, of course, there were the Beatles, John and Yoko and transcendental meditation. Things Indian – Maharishi Mahesh Yogi, incense, flowing Kashmiri dresses, hashish, sitar music – acquired mystery and glamour. The message was, 'Love is all you need', 'Make Love not War', 'Peace, Brother'.

I've recently learned that the term 'Paki' was in fact current in my early teens. Why didn't I hear it? Or have I forgotten? Perhaps there was a deafness on my part.

In 1969 I was in the fourth year, in the A stream, of a large girls' comprehensive in South London. All my friends were English. I'm not sure who gave us the name, but we were known as the 'Arty Lot'. Between us, we loved Keats, Impressionism, Surrealism, Schubert, Mozart, Rachmaninov, Bob Dylan, Leonard Cohen, Captain Beefheart, the Beatles, Santana, Pink Floyd, Michaelangelo's David, antiques, off-beat clothes, walking barefoot . . .

The world of the Sarah Lintons of Putney and the Horatia Greys of Knightsbridge was, in the main, a middle-class world. As far as I can recall, what I experienced there was openness and interest. I rarely felt that I was an outsider, and when I did, I would simply project myself as a mystery, an enigma. After all, we were living in the decade of the overland trails to Afghanistan, Pakistan and India. At the least, it was stylish and 'in' to be eastern.

Two events stand out in a sea of forgetfulness.

In the second year at Ashley School, during the lunch hour, I clenched my teeth and hammered my fist into Judy Butlin's face. I can't remember how the argument started. What stays in my mind are the words she had used: 'You fucking half-breed, go back to your mud hut!' I remember a wave of heat passing over my face. I wanted to kill her; I wanted her to die.

That night I asked my father the meaning of 'half-breed'. The other words I understood. When he told me that it was originally a white American term of abuse for people who were half-white and half-red Indian, and that it also referred to the breeding of horses, I knew it didn't apply to me and that Judy Butlin was an ignorant girl. I thought of poor Judy with her scruffy clothes and free dinners. I felt sorry for her; I reminded myself of my glorious past – of the Mughals and Ottomans. In the mirror I pointed to my arms and boasted, 'The blood of Tamberlaine runs through these veins.'

I didn't notice Pakistanis at Ashley School. Some were there, however. In retrospect I can see them.

In the autumn of 1967, Rezwana Shah joined 2H, my tutor group. She was a tall, olive-skinned girl, from Sind. She didn't say much in class. I don't remember having conversations with her, though we did look at one another.

Lee Rollings, a sharp, foul-mouthed bully, often entertained herself and her circle by abusing Rezwana. She used to ridicule the chooridar shalwaar Rezwana wore under her school skirt, and insist she bathed in curry. The class was amused. I didn't join in the 'fun' but neither did I defend Rezwana. I think she must have left Ashley School by the end of the third year. I can't remember her in the fourth and fifth years. Perhaps I stopped looking at her. I feel ashamed.

My family did not belong to an 'Asian' community. We didn't really participate in the Eid festivities; we didn't attend weddings or funerals; there were few meetings with fellow 'Asians'. The links only appeared when we were hosts to visiting relatives. Family friends were a cosmopolitan set – from Pakistan, Afghanistan, Egypt, the States, France, Iran, Germany, England. My friends, some of them close, were all English. They had more in common with me than with girls like Judy Butlin; I had more in common with them than with girls like Rezwana Shah.

I asked my sister, Atiyya, how she remembers me:

1969. Let me see. You were fifteen, I was eight or nine. I remember you were always dyeing your clothes. Burgundy colour wasn't it, at one time? You didn't like neat, stiff clothes. Your style was hippyish, not quite hippy. I think you wanted to be original. You didn't want to belong to any conventional group. You know, your own style and all that.

What else?

You had to be responsible for me because you were older. You used to take me to school. I knew I couldn't go on my own. You knew, in relation to me, you had to be grown up. When we got to school, you'd do this amazing, confident act in front of my teachers to explain why I was late.

I was obviously not that responsible if I made you late.

I loved the stories you used to tell me about flying away in those beautiful dresses. I loved those stories. I really believed them, you know. I think you did as well, while you were telling them.

Mmm. What do you think was happening? I did enjoy them. I wasn't playing games. I mean, I wasn't entertaining you. I was entertaining myself – if 'entertaining' is the right word.

While you were telling them it was like you actually believed them – getting on a magic carpet with silken cushions and quilts, flying away, and deciding what kind of dresses we'd wear. You'd always wear the green chiffon one.

Oh yes. Green, because the flag of Pakistan was green.

Do you remember your obsession with mirrors? It was like a compulsive thing you had. Looking just right. Mirrors. You were obsessed with mirrors. The other thing was, everytime we passed a shop window, we'd have to slow down so you could see your reflection. That went on for years. You always picked the mirror you knew you looked all right in.

Oh yes! And Amie taking the mickey out of me.

Also Amie going on about it – how you were so self-conscious and everyone wasn't like that, there was something wrong with you (laughing), you were more interested in yourself than in other people . . .

You say, or Amie said, it was vanity. I'd say it was insecurity on my part. It wasn't that I thought I was wonderful. When I looked in mirrors it was a frustrating experience. I used to get the mirgee. Is that vanity?

I must have been responding to the call of the 'beautiful heroine'. I heard it in the looks and words of the people around me. I heard it in the films I saw and the books I read. The attention to clothes and the preoccupation with the mirror must denote the extent to which I identified with that call. It told me there were some women, the select, who were beautiful and therefore destined for beautiful, womanly things: captivating the hearts of heroes, inspiring desire and admiration in all, and envy in other females. It told me it was good to be such a female, for such females were powerful – the heroes they enslaved could be princes or powerful presidents or great revolution-aries. It told me it was possible that I might become such a woman. It unleashed desires and fears.

Could such a call rest with some of the others to which I turned? How could I reconcile it with Judy Butlin's words or Rezwana

Shah's humiliation? Though I'd resisted with whatever means I could find, those incidents touched me. How did 'beautiful heroine' sit with 'half-breed' or with the 'clever woman' who is interested in books and politics – in getting things done? I recognised, or wanted to recognise, a self in that, too, but the intelligent, liberated woman of the sixties had very different lifestyles and many were shunning make-up and things that 'beautified'. Their rise to fame and influence, when it was accomplished, seemed dowdy.

As an adolescent, I never spoke of my interest in mirrors. I just continued looking in them. The calls that I heard were indeed various and conflicting.

I know what I looked like on a particular day in the summer of 1969 because I spent a long time examining my reflection in the full-length bedroom mirror. It was a hot Sunday in May. My mother had been in Pakistan now for two months. I was dressed in black – long black skirt, black blouse, black jacket, black tights and almost black hair.

Looking was accompanied by frustration. The girl in the mirror did not resemble the 'beautiful Raisa' in my mind. My dissatisfaction must have been made worse by the feeling that that day would open up a world of secrets from my father and mother.

My father was away. I thought of my mother's last letter – her father's condition had worsened; she believed he was dying. My Nana Abu was dying.

I felt nervous and sick. I also anticipated a good time with the girls from school. For weeks they had been asking me to go with them to the Roundhouse, in Chalk Farm. Helen Simpson, my 'best friend' had told me of the 'fantastic' and 'alive' atmosphere. I was tantalised by the description, and I wanted to 'belong' to my group of school friends. There was also the uneasiness. Some of the girls had relationships with boys. I knew my parents would not want me to keep company with such girls. How had I accepted the arrangement that Alex Brown, Sheila's brother, should call at my home and accompany me to Chalk Farm?

I was looking in the mirror, and the doorbell rang. A terrifying thought entered my mind – what if Abu came back now? Atiyya ran into the room to tell me about the boy at the door. She looked alarmed. I emphasised how innocent everything was, but told her not to tell Abu because he would be sure to misunderstand.

I went to the front door and smiled politely at the burly boy with the yellow hair.

I felt embarrassed, ashamed even, walking with him towards Parsons Green tube. I didn't like his attention. I didn't want anyone to think he was my boyfriend. For one thing, he was nothing like the friend of my imagination.

Helen, Horatia, Sarah and Sheila were already at the station. They had two boys with them. One of them was Philip Lindley. I'd heard about him from Helen. I can see him now – he was drinking Cocoa-Cola from a bottle. I thought he was mean and ill-mannered: he didn't think to offer the bottle to the others, or to drink it when alone.

I had never before travelled such a distance on the tube without a member of my family.

Chalk Farm was busy with street vendors, pedestrians and little cafés. On a wall, in bold white paint, someone had written HO CHI MINH, and further along VIVA CHE! In discussions at home we had approved of the men – freedom-fighters against western imperialism. I felt proud to be walking past the graffiti.

The Roundhouse wasn't far from the station. The eight of us mounted the open-air stairs leading up to the huge, circular building. I remember how I kept edging forward in the queue, away from Alex and his attentions.

At the door, a long-haired man in a colourful robe was marking people's wrists as they paid and entered. Inside it was dark and full of noisy activity. Psychodelic lights were flashing everywhere. I could smell incense, and something else. Hippies in a circle were smiling and passing round a large, clumsily made cigarette. Helen was keen to show me everything; she wanted me to 'get the feel of the place'. We moved in further.

Different events were happening simultaneously in the many corners and on the various levels. Men and women – older and younger – were freaking out to impossibly loud music. A drama workshop was in progress; some of the actors were completely naked. A Marx Brothers' film was being shown. Ethnic clothes and jewellery were on sale. A group seated in the lotus position was chanting 'Om, Om'. I found myself talking easily to my new acquaintances.

There were many more trips to the Roundhouse. It became a weekly ritual, a necessity even. As I look back on this period of my life, one point begs particular attention – how was I able to mix and talk so easily with boys?

I went to an all-girls' school. The only males I knew were my father, and my uncles and cousins – when they visited London. Just a year before, I was the girl who, rather than go to the boy greengrocer to buy fruit for my mother, waited petrified a full half-hour outside the house. The impossibility of explaining my 'problem' to my mother finally forced me to mumble the order to the boy and rush out with the bananas. I suffered. How I remember my inability to talk to males outside the family without perspiring and panicking!

It occurs to me that these ways of behaving are in me still, under certain conditions. Two years ago, a fourth-year pupil was amazed and entertained by Ms Ahmed who crossed over the road to avoid passing a group of men.

In the summer of 1969, while my mother was away and my father was busy with his work, the Roundhouse and my group of friends were important to me. I would lie, or withhold the precise truth both from my father, who was in charge of his daughters, and from Atiyya, for whom I was responsible.

In time the lies became less frequent and gave way to semi-truths: I revealed where I was going, but I presented the Roundhouse as a respectable theatre. How could I have possibly told my father that the Roundhouse was the place where one of my acquaintances, a boy, smoked pot, drank alcohol, took off all his clothes and danced naked for all to see?

A month ago, I spoke to my my father about this period of my life.

I would say this – when you were fifteen or sixteen, nearing your O levels, you did have certain friends with you – girls – who, like some other English girls of the time, were experimenting with ways of behaviour.

Are you talking about boys?

Boys, drugs, things like that.

You thought I had friends who were living such lives?

Yes. And so it was likely that the company of those girls might have influenced you in certain direct or indirect ways which led to your becoming, for instance, vegetarian, or associating with drop-outs and hippies. But they were not doctrinaire drop-outs in my opinion. There were four or five boys who (once or twice) used to come to the door . . .

Oh yes, Philip Lindley and . . .

Who had beards, and looked drugged, whom I wouldn't tolerate within a mile.

My father knew about my friends – some of them. They were good friends, but the silences were still there. Most of those girls smoked pot, drank alcohol, sometimes took LSD, and had sexual relationships. I did none of those things. There was indeed a distance between us: Horatia's mother knew that she was taking the pill and Sarah had actually discussed with her parents the type of contraceptive she should use. Yet they, and not Rezwana Shah, were the girls with whom I spent my time; we had things to say to each other. Sarah, in fact, was the one member of the group who, along with me, took more than a passing interest in Vietnam, South Africa and the student risings.

Helen, my closest friend, did not take drugs, and for the greater part of our friendship, while we were good friends, did not have sexual relationships.

Two months had passed since I'd hugged my mother goodbye. Sometimes, and suddenly, I'd remember her smile or her perfume – Madame Rochas, it was – or something she had said; and then, quietly, I'd miss her. Thankfully, for much of the time I had plenty to distract me.

The June evening had turned chilly. I paid the taxi man; Helen held the five – five was a lucky number – cartons of orange juice. I never took wine. How could I offer to others that which was bad for myself? Helen went along with my moral logic, and anyway, she didn't like the taste of wine.

Sarah's house overlooked Putney Heath. A tall gate and a long footpath separated it from the road. All was quiet, except for the muted sounds coming from within. We paused at the door and shook our hair to dramatise our appearance. I placed an extra coat of 'Biba Plum' on my lips. We laughed at each other. We were dressed alike. Our dresses were flowing and black; we had stars on our foreheads and stars in our hair. We entered the house together.

Pink Floyd music blared at us. The lights were dim. The house was bursting with people. Incense, hashish, sweat and alcohol. Entwined pairs were swaying in the centre of the room. Others were kissing intimately. A boy and a girl, arm in arm, walked upstairs. Knowing looks passed between those who'd seen them. Sarah's parents were away for the night.

Someone tapped my shoulder. I turned to find a smiling Philip Lindley. I smiled back, politely, and asked him how things were. We started talking about the evils of drugs and alcohol. He was sipping from a can of Double Diamond. I asked him if he and his friends were demonstrating on Saturday against the continued American presence in Vietnam. He shrugged his shoulders; he hadn't seen any of the leaflets. I stressed the importance of action. He asked if I'd like a coke. I laughed and said yes, and thought it was all fine, as far as it went.

Alex Brown was waving at me from the far side of the room. He started to walk over, but the music changed suddenly to the drum beats of Santana. Helen and I shrieked at each other. Leaving everything, we ran to the dimly-lit dance area.

The highlight of the Roundhouse was the dance floor, and I loved parties because of the dancing. I came for the dancing. I dressed and made myself up for it; I practised it for hours in front of my bedroom mirror. I knew I was good. I sought admiration. I entered make-believe.

The space cleared around us. Dark and dreamlike it was. Our movements were clever; they were hip-centred and sexy. They gave a pleasure, of the forbidden – to me who was both the owner and the observer of my dancing body, and to the audience beyond me. There in that beyond, as always, was the man I had never met, and he was watching me. It was my body, but I was the black-eyed gipsy, the temptress of folklore, or the dancing Pakeezah of the haunting love-tale. I wanted him to want me; I wanted him. In the snatches of light – near the lampshade, by the door – I saw myself as he saw me: desirable, beautiful, sensual.

The music faded. The dancing stopped. Helen, with her smudged mascara and ghostly white face, came into focus, then the others in the room. I felt clumsy. The 'waking up' was always a little clumsy.

I laughed loudly; so did Helen. We displayed our laughter. Then, theatrically, we hugged each other. The gesture had many meanings. In it we covered our clumsiness. Through it, we flirted with an alternative way of carrying on. It allowed us to demonstrate how we didn't especially need or want male attention. It spoke of uniqueness and confidence.

A slow record followed Santana's Latin beat. Couples came back to the dancing floor. Helen went off to the kitchen. In the darkness a boy – a stranger – approached me. I had my ready, oft-used answer: 'No thank you. I don't do close dancing.'

Sarah appeared before me with a plate of food. She wanted me to meet some friends. I felt energised. I wanted to check my appearance, and put on fresh lipstick. I wanted to see what 'he' might see. Answering party chatter along the way, I made my way to the bathroom.

I saw him before he saw me. He was standing with a man and a woman, outside the dance-room. He had his back resting against the wall. He was half-listening to his friends and half somewhere else. He was taller than the others. His hair was fair but his skin looked naturally dark, not orange like blonds in the sun. He must have been in his twenties. I had to pass him to reach the bathroom. I became horribly self-conscious. I entered his view; his gaze touched my skin, I felt it like a touch. I looked up and met his eyes. Blue, deep eyes. He smiled; I looked away, as they do in stories.

Sarah asked me what I thought of the Danish man. I watched her slippery golden tresses that wouldn't stay clipped back. I knew who she meant but I pretended not to know. She told me about him. His name was Eric. He was in London for the summer. He had come to the party with her cousin Jeremy. Jeremy had met him at a concert in Hyde Park.

It was late. Helen said her farewells. I said mine. We turned to the door, and there in front of us stood Eric. He was smiling. 'Bye,' he said, 'how come you dance so good?' He spoke with an American accent. 'We'll meet again, yeah?' I was breathless. I hoped he was speaking to me, exclusively to me.

In the days that followed, at home or at school, even on the street, I would find quiet moments to think about 'the gaze'. I would speak out, 'Bye', 'How come you dance so good?', 'We'll meet again, yeah?' I would imagine all sorts of futures.

In a secret book I wrote down everything I could remember – from the most significant to the most trivial detail. I wrote it like a story so that no one would find out. I called it 'The Gaze'.

One day that same June, I was alone in the house. Atiyya and my father had gone shopping. I think I was reading 'The Gaze' when I heard the postman. The letter came from Lahore, from my mother. It was heavy with paper and perhaps also photographs. It was addressed to all of us. I opened it. My mother had written in Urdu. I looked for an English word, any at all, so that I could make some sense of it. The photograph fell on to the floor. A black and white photo, a close-up of an old man sleeping in white sheets. His face yearned skywards; white stubble covered his cheeks; his mouth seemed to be breathing a gentle 'aaah'. Who would take a picture of a sick old man? Photos from home to exile, or from exile to home depicted other things, not sickness and age. Then I saw the thin and yellowing newspaper cutting. It showed an open coffin being carried through the street, above the heads of the procession. I read the English. Muzaffer Ali Khan was dead. Nana Abu was dead. I was stunned, but not with a sense of loss. I didn't cry. As a child I would have died for him. I remembered that. Miles and years away, I shed no tears and I didn't feel the loss. I couldn't cry, so I wailed instead, one long wail in a silent house in Fulham. Nana Abu, Nani Amma . . . I thought of the past, and then my tears came . . .

When I was sixteen, the past meant essentially 'family history'. There were many things I didn't know then. At thirty-one, I think I know more.

The old man whose final photograph lay before me had been rich. He owned many factories; he employed hundreds; he gave much to charity. When he died, crowds filled the streets through which his body was carried.

He had not always been wealthy. His father inherited a couple of hundred acres in Kasur. Like many peasants, he dreamed of owning more, but for all his labour, the money he hoped to put aside was eaten up by wages, by taxes, by the sheer costs of living. When land did come on the market, it was bought by the big landowners.

Muzaffer listened to his father's hopes, and observed their slow extinction. He hated the big landowners; he wanted to be as rich and as powerful as them. In 1923, he moved to Lahore. Lahore was the great marketplace of the Punjab, and a capital of the Raj. The colonials were there, and it was to them that my grandfather turned. With borrowed money, he bought curios and carpets from the local artisans and sold them at the gates of the English houses. The crafts of the east filled the homes of the English, and Muzaffer was glad to provide them. And that, two generations before me, was the origin of my family's wealth.

Muzaffer expanded his business, diversified. He traded in carpets, buying cheap in Persia, selling less cheaply in Lahore. His goods had a reputation for quality; his profits were large. He married. Shahnawaz, a woman of his baraadri, came from a family of hakims who owned shops in the bazaars. I know little else about her.

Some years passed. Muzaffer, now with three young children – a daughter and two sons – and a pregnant wife, sought new markets. He sold his shops in Lahore and in 1937 he took his family to Missourie, a hill station in the United Provinces of India. High up on a ridge of the outer Himalayas, it was cool and leisured: the most popular resort of the British in northern India. He prospered and, ever-vigilant, he considered his future.

He listened intently to the voices around him: a good businessman must now attend to politics. As a devout Muslim, he shared in the urge to create a separate nation of the pure and godly. As a trader, he estimated the uncertainties of business. He had heard the campaigners of the Pakistan Movement speak of full compensation for those who left their interests in India and settled in the new state. He transferred his savings to Lahore. A year later, in the riots of 1947, Muzaffer, his wife and his children – five by now – with their jewellery hidden about them, arrived in Pakistan.

For many – as you know, Tahira and Nasreen – partition brought hard times and great suffering. My grandfather knew that too, and helped his poorer relatives on the land. He also planned his own future.

He had the showroom on the Mall that had been given to him as compensation for his imagined losses. He had his money; he had an expert's knowledge of carpets and carpet making. He decided to go into production. His workers, cheaply recruited in the economy of those times, made carpets that matched the classic Persians in design and quality, but cost far less. The artisans' fingers nimbly and without visible tiredness produced the carpets and my grandfather controlled their sale. He had a specialised luxury market which was not affected by the hard times. His customers were the indigenous rich, the lingering British, and the increasing numbers of Americans. As for exports – licences were quite easy to come by, provided the right people were paid.

Muzaffer's wealth increased. It was sumptuous, I know: the great house in Lahore; the summer dwelling in Murree; the hired trains; the aeroplane. Few people lived like that in Pakistan. Yet I know now, the wealth had no deep roots. The old man established no great dynasty.

What, in those golden years, was my grandmother thinking? I know she rarely left the house, except under the watchful and protective eyes of sons or husband as eager to protect their reputation as their own. Though Muzaffer planned the best of modern education for his sons, his wife did not ape western ways. Those who saw her veiled form rarely and briefly step from house to car were quick to recognise her moral worth. I know that she tried to live by the book. But what was she thinking?

Perhaps there was an anger that stirred inside her. Her sharp complaints about the laziness of servants, or the slyness of jewellers, may have arisen from a deeper dissatisfaction. She may have felt despair as her sons moved almost beyond the reach of her loving influence. But I don't know.

I can piece together a purpose, a sense of will that drove my grandfather through the accumulations of his life. But what ideas, hopes, longings, dissatisfactions filled my grandmother's mind? I – her daughter's daughter, blood of her blood, a woman, a Muslim – cannot imagine. I have not even a photograph.

I had barely returned home when Atiyya rushed at me. Feverishly she repeated her news. Amie was coming back, she'd be back by the end of the week, and I wouldn't have to collect her every day from school anymore. I put down my school bag. My father read us the letter. She was returning to London but so much was being left unsettled in Lahore. The brothers were united against the sisters over their father's property. They wanted their sisters to accept a single payment as their share of the inheritance. Azra Khala was already toying with the idea – her brothers' greed, and their arguments, were becoming unbearable. My mother needed Azra to hold her ground. They had no right to deprive daughters of their rightful share. My mother wouldn't accept anything less than her rightful share of her father's property, but for now, she was returning to her daughters and her husband. She had been away long enough.

I became anxious for her. I was angry. The Islamic law of inheritance was equitable, it liberated women. That's what I'd always heard. My father approved of my outrage – I could see that; I knew that. My outrage became more articulate. Were my uncles seeking to override Islamic law? My father explained. We, his daughters, listened. Countries may call themselves Islamic but Islamic law was rarely practised. Women rarely inherited what was due to them in money, still less in land. I went to my room. I had my homework to do. I lay on the quilt that my mother had bought for my room, and thought about her. Brothers were supposed to love their sisters. They did love her. So why the arguments over money and land? From under my mattress I took out 'The Gaze', now a strange and incomplete story.

You're too thin – what have you been doing to yourself? Tie back your hair – it's looking wild. So my mother greeted me on her return. She spoke to us in Urdu, never English. She looked happy. The sun had taken away her pallor. She'd been away nearly three months and now once again her voice filled the house. She hugged Atiyya, then she hugged me. She smiled at my father. I shuddered with contentment. There before me sat my mother, father and little sister, safe and together. We did not speak of Nana Abu, not then. Nor did we mention the wranglings between brothers and sisters. My mother asked me about my school work, and what else I'd been doing with my time – I hadn't been neglecting Atiyya, had I?

My mother was not pleased with the changes she saw in me. Why did I need to visit my friend's house every other day? It didn't matter that it was only for an hour or so after school. Helen was a nice girl. Perhaps she could come more often to us? All this avaaragardi, this gallivanting about, was unbecoming. She liked my Sunday excursions even less, even though now I left the Roundhouse well before dark. What manner of a theatre was it that I had to go there every week? 'Look at the way you're neglecting your younger sister.' She thought I had become distracted. 'What's in that head of yours? What're you dreaming about?' I told her she was mad.

The summer holidays had started. I did meet Eric again, at the Roundhouse, four weeks after the first meeting. Helen and I danced

205

and laughed around him. He looked. He laughed. He was a student in Denmark. I asked him if he had any contact with the students in Paris. We discussed sports and apartheid. I wanted him to think I was brilliant. He said that I had lovely hair. I was happy. He asked me where I was from. I told him I was Persian. Persia connoted splendour in the way that Pakistan did not. He said he had to leave, but he might be back. The rest of that afternoon, and evening, was spent in anticipation. He might be back. But he hadn't come by nine-thirty and at ten, with still no sign of him, we left.

Helen stayed at my house that night. My mother said nothing about my lateness. I knew she wouldn't, not in front of my friend. My father called me to his study and looked at me with a new sternness. He wanted an explanation. My mother must have spoken to him. My anger turned against her. She was stirring things up, that's what she was doing. I wove my lies and left the study. In my room, into the dawn, Helen and I relived that day: what Eric said, what he did, what he thought. We contemplated the hour that he would leave for Denmark. We imagined his return. I spoke of his eyes and how they were all I could remember of his face whenever I thought of him. Helen said nothing; she had fallen asleep.

A day or so later, my mother's fears and anger found expression. We were in the kitchen. The doors to the garden were open to the evening sun. She had been out all day, working. She worked full-time now. We still didn't talk about the details of her work. She wasn't trained for anything 'professional' – her education didn't count in this country – but we all knew that she worked full-time. I was washing the dishes and preparing the evening meal, and hoping she had forgotten.

'What's happened to you? How are you any different from those cousins of yours?' She raised her voice – how was I any different from Soraya and the rest of them? I slammed the dishes in answer. Two girls, wandering the streets at night. I smarted at the innuendo. I shouted back – we weren't wandering and it wasn't late! She looked tired, but her eyes flared with anger – it was dangerous, it was unbecoming, I had no regard for my family. What wonderful things living in England had taught me! She wouldn't leave things alone. I ran to my room and drowned the image of her tired face with my thoughts about Eric.

This is what my sister has to say.

Do you remember Helen? She used to spend nights at our house, quite often she did that. Of course, for me to do the same was out of the question!

Well, it's the same for me now. I don't stay out nights, and even for you, it hasn't really changed, has it? Abu phones you most nights and you're always in.

Just to go out, I had to explain where I was going, with whom, when I'd be back. That's reasonable of course – parents have a right to know. The thing is, I always felt that I shouldn't be interested in my friends. The boys – forget it! I'm talking about girls, even.

Yeah, I know what you mean – your family's the important thing and that should be enough.

I couldn't do what the English girls did – go to late parties, hang around with boys and the rest.

Yeah, I know!

The funny thing is, it wasn't exactly spelt out. It just went along with everything else. Abu and Amie hardly ever discussed it with me – the boy thing. I just knew.

Well, it's not very eastern to talk about these things.

Not in our family, anyway. I can't remember Abu, or Amie, saying – 'don't you ever' you know 'mix with boys'. It must rarely have been spelt out – if it was at all. And if it was, and I can't remember it, well, that's interesting as well.

Not talking about a thing can underline its badness, can't it? You know – the taboo.

Yes. If you don't, and can't even mention it, how could you possibly face your mother and father if you did do the wrong thing?

You'd lie.

All sorts of things control your behaviour, all sorts of things.

On the subject of love, I recall 1966. I was twelve at the time. I have a snapshot of those days – my cousin Soraya and I are standing on either side of my mother. We're in our sunny garden sipping lime juice. My mother looks so young there; her hair is flaming in the sunlight. That year Soraya was in England. She was studying for her A levels at a boarding college in Sussex.

Most of her weekends and holidays were spent with us in Fulham. My parents were her guardians here. Regularly, they spoke and wrote to Phuppo Razia and soothed away the worries she may have had about her daughter. Everything was fine until Soraya met Mustafa.

She made furtive phone calls from her bedroom in our house; she spent weekends away from us, 'staying at school'. My father wasn't alert to these signs. Discreet enquiries soon told my mother that Soraya had started something with a man. If that wasn't enough, the man was Mustafa Mobin; his people knew my mother's people.

One night Soraya came to my room and told me about Mustafa. I was intrigued, though too many details were beyond my comprehension. He was handsome and besotted. OK, he owned a chain of shops, but he knew the top fashionable clubs. She had no intention of letting it last; it wasn't anything serious, on her part. She was just having a good time. Her friends in Islamabad got up to worse; her mother knew about them. The guy and his circle weren't a threat; they weren't important. There wasn't any harm in a girl having some fun.

My mother knew that Soraya told me things. After dinner, at the dinner table, while my father was out and I was in the next room, she spoke to my cousin. She chose her argument: the madness of the match, a mere shopkeeper; she, the daughter of a diplomat. She was seventeen years old – not a child; she couldn't be so irresponsible. Did she want her mother to find out?

Soraya listened to her mumani, and denied everything. It was all a misundersanding. And she carried on. My mother informed my father. Her relations in Leyton – she had taken to visiting them regularly – could so easily find out. Poor and simple they might be, but they were baraadri and she was Muzaffer Ali Khan's daughter. In front of me, my mother shouted at my father. For all their education and travelling about the world, that's what his sister's brood had learned. Their father had been a Rhodes scholar, their mother was fashionable and educated, and the children had no regard for izzat. I heard her shouting. I think it was during those months that my mother, in the privacy of her home – always in the privacy of her home – took to shouting her anger. While Soraya was away, she reminded him of his own young daughters and of what they might be learning. She spoke the father's words to my father. If anything went wrong, it wouldn't be because she had forgotten to speak them.

I wished my mother would stop complaining. There were days when it seemed that was all she did. But I could see that it was important to her. Izzat mattered. And so I hated Soraya for being wilful; and I hated my father for being too busy in his legal world of conferences and bar dinners to put anything right.

He came to me, some days later. He said I was an intelligent, analytical girl; books and discussion were my interest, not boys and romance. He urged me to talk sense to my cousin. I was not to allow her to forget her Islamic background. I was to describe to her the purity of the truly Islamic woman. I was inspired. Five years younger than Soraya, I went in to her with my wisdom. I became my father's agent; I said what I knew he would say. Eloquently, I spoke his words and grasped at their meaning. Little consciousness did I have then of the desires and values that might have led me – or even a small part of me – to question my father.

I wonder when and why Soraya finished with Mustafa. She never did mention him to me again.

Here's another conversation with Atiyya.

I'll never forget that night – I was in the fourth year, wasn't I? No – it was in the fifth year, I was fifteen. You went wild because I'd lied to you about that party.

Yes, I remember. I collected you from the station and those friends of yours – Hannah and I forget the other one – they didn't seem to know anything about the play you were supposed to have seen.

You might as well have been Abu when you found out. Only he wouldn't have been so noisy!

It rained hard that night. There was a black-out for nearly an hour.

If I'd had a younger sister, I'd have behaved the same with her. That's why I lied to you in the first place.

And might still, eh?'

Wouldn't you like to know?

What you mean is, in our 'responsible' roles we all follow the same law within the family.

Well, when you know you've got to be responsible, you act it.

It isn't simply 'got to be'. I was worried about you and everything and – all right – angry. I was angry at your deceit. You know, how dare you plot with your friends and treat me, your own sister, like an idiot!

August moved towards September. I spent my secret hours re-reading 'The Gaze'. Eric had still not returned. The Roundhouse became more enticing. Eric would be there. Maybe, next time, he'd be there.

I told my parents that Helen and I were going to the Queen Elizabeth Hall for a Schubert recital. My father believed me; he liked Schubert. My mother was indifferent; she was concerned about my wandering. She suspected my deceit. She could easily stop me. I feared the words she could speak to my father. I feared and hated them for their power to work on him. I prayed that she would let it pass, just this once. Eric was bound to be at the Roundhouse that day. He was bound to be, and I couldn't not be there. The thought was unbearable: missed chances; ill-fated timing. She came into my bedroom, watched me moving backwards and forwards in front of the mirror. There was the hint of a smile on her face, almost as if she was taking pleasure in my dressing up. I ignored her. I had decided to play the injured party – she'd feel guilty and let me enjoy my youth. She questioned me. What exactly was being played at the Queen Elizabeth Hall? Who had the tickets? How would we get there, and home again? Why did I go out so often? She was suspicious. I was nervous, I stammered my lies. She left my room. I heard her voice outside, loud and insistent. I heard her argument. I wished she would shut her hateful noise. She was a spiteful, ageing woman who couldn't bear to see a young girl enjoying herself. Just because her family in Lahore was giving her trouble she was taking it out on me. She was talking still and my father, the silent fool, was listening.

'What are your daughters learning in this country? They're learning to be English. You're teaching them to be English. What else are you doing when you encourage their mother to wear skirts, to wear skirts to her work and pass for English? The shame!'

She was stopping me. Oh God, she couldn't stop me, not today. Please God! I pulled out a pen. I snatched a book. On its sleeve I stabbed in the words: I HATE HER! I HATE THE BITCH! I HOPE SHE GETS KILLED!

I paused for breath, and in that moment I saw her pale, worried face, paler and smaller now. I tore up my disgusting words, ripped them into many, many pieces. Then, lying on my bed, I imagined the crashing music and the dancing in the magic of shade and light. I imagined the tap on my shoulder and the glimpse of Eric before me. I thought about close dancing, about bodies melting one into the other.

Conversation with my father.

We knew mixing with boys and sexual relations would be the ultimate transgression. But it wasn't a subject you or Amie really discussed, not in the way other things were discussed. Were we all too embarrassed to mention it?

We're talking about these things because of your research, are we?

Yes.

'Ultimate transgression'? Hm. That's where the ethos of thinking, the values, the beliefs of the family become so aggressively sacred that it doesn't really occur to people to flout them.

Why is it that we discussed everything but never . . . ?

It's not a subject for discussion.

We don't discuss it and yet it constitutes an ultimate transgression, for females.

For males as well.

In Islamic terms, yes. In practical terms, you know that boys playing about isn't anywhere as serious as girls . . .

No!

Abu-ji!

211

You're talking to me. My view . . .

Amie didn't really discuss the subject with us. You – only to the extent of urging us always to remember who we were. I remember when Philip Lindley came to the door to deliver a Christmas present, you were extremely brusque with him. I remember thinking – what a mean way of carrying on. You made it quite clear what you thought about boys coming into the house.

I think the freedom to socialise with the opposite sex was never denied to my children, but it was on a professional level, an educational level. What was drilled into you, unobtrusively, was that the liaison between a male and female was the ultimate degradation.

Why unobtrusively?

It's not a debatable subject is it?

I want to hear your reasons . . .

I would say it was probably the idea of dignity which I, and your mother, tried to inculcate. I think you people understood that the physical surrender of a male to a female – or vice versa – is defilement.

We knew what izzat meant, how it was important. It was important to Amie. She lived her life by it. We certainly knew the importance of izzat. When I was fifteen you gave me your written reflections on women and sexual morality.

What are you trying to say? For your sixteenth birthday I gave you the works of Tolstoy and Pushkin. For your fifteenth, you're right, I wrote to you about the heinous calumny against Hadrat Ayesha. My reflections centred on that.

This has perplexed me – of all the crimes that could be committed by a female, of all the bad things that could be done, sexual transgression is the worst, a cardinal crime, worse than the taking of a life. Was that the big danger in your minds, in relation to me and Atiyya?

Of course not the only danger. It was considered to be a major thing, by me, and also naturally by your mother, because it was the defilement of the body, defilement of the soul. It's not a casual thing; much of European culture has made it casual, trivialised it. But it is major thing because once a man or woman lets slip, it's very difficult

212

for them, if not impossible, to recover their self-respect. They can force themselves to recover – human beings do survive – before they are buried. But it's tainted, it's a guilty, person. You can try to wash away guilt in life, you can do all sorts of things, justifying, but then you have to twist and distort the natural flow of morality.

What is 'natural morality'?

That which is fair and just. That which is naturally just. Natural justice is that all human beings are equal and that nobody should exploit the other. This applies also to sexual exploitation – male or female. We're dealing with the reproduction of life. Human beings are born.

Women can control birth.

If you respect human life, you can't muck around, you can't pursue sexual adventures. You can have only one relation in life – matrimony. One's love for one's children is based on the sanctity of sexual decency. Otherwise, what is there to hold anybody to anybody? 'Why should I love you? Get out! Off you go! I've done with you!' Why do I love my daughters? Why are you attached to me? Why do you show respect to me, think of me, phone me, worry about me? Because of this – I am your father. If you were married, if you had children, you'd be a mother. The point is, whatever your situation – whether you're a female, a male, a daughter, a son – purity equals dignity. I cannot conceive of a . . . it is psychologically impossible for a profligate female, and a profligate male, to be a good mother or father. Impossible. You came back at three o'clock.

When?

With that girl. Your friend at school.

Helen?

You walked all the way. You could have been raped and murdered. Slaughtered. I was restless, very restless. Your mother was crying. I can see her now.

Coming home at three? I can't remember.

You were walking all the way.

Where had I been?

I don't know. You gave me, you gave your mother and me, a lot of worry.

I had forgotten the incident. I remember it now. We'd been to the Roundhouse, hoping Eric would at last appear. All afternoon and all evening we had waited, and then Sarah asked us all to her house for an impromptu party. Her parents were out. Her cousin Jeremy would be there. So might Eric, I thought. But Eric didn't come. In the early hours of the morning, Helen and I walked home through the deserted streets of south London. My mother had been crying. I saw her red eyes, and her anger and relief, as I walked into the house. Silent, I heard her words breaking over my head.

My father has forgotten, and I have not reminded him, but for two whole weeks after that night, for two horrific weeks, he stopped talking to me. His behaviour was so bizarre, so unlike him. I felt my father's lack of interest; I saw my mother's pain. Imagine, I had forgotten.

Where did it come from, my mother's pain? My father had travelled far more than she; but it was Sabah who had moved worlds. Her first world was her mother's company. Until her wedding day – that glittering festival crowded with the English and American friends whom Ahmed had invited – she had even spent most of her waking hours at home. Her brothers went to school, and then, without distinction, to university. She received tutors at her father's house. While her mother looked on, she studied for her matriculation certificate. She worked hard at her studies: she could follow Keats and Iqbal; she could read and recite the Qu'ran. And she had other accomplishments: she could pick out the minutest defect in a carpet sample. She received relatives with extreme propriety. She discussed clothes and jewellery like an expert.

She liked observing people; she loved discussing their behaviour, in the smallest detail. For these reasons, weddings and festivals, and the long night-time conversations which followed them, were the highlights of her year.

This was her world. She knew something of others. Tutors carried to her secret proposals of marriage, and whispered the invitations they had been paid to offer. Less frequently, amazing stories reached her of other women her age, cousins of cousins, friends of friends, who had involved themselves in the politics of the new state. In neither way was my mother tempted. She waited, contentedly I think, for news that would change her life.

In 1953, when she was nineteen, my grandfather invited the broadcaster and newspaper editor Ahmed Iqbal Khan to stay at his house, and to meet his sons. They were related, distantly, and Muzaffer had noted the young, unmarried man's growing prestige.

They talked. He admired Ahmed's many-sided erudition and lucidity. My uncles were less impressed. They were learning at their university – so my father has told me many times – only a distrust of the intellect. Ahmed was an intellectual, they observed, and he was not, in their terms, rich. That he was educated was undeniable. He was as much at ease with the nineteenth-century novel as with the Persian classics, and almost as familiar with Aristotle and Plato as with interpretations of the Qu'ran. Muzaffer saw in him a culture he admired more than understood: an international man, whose knowledge might turn out to have a practical value as well as an impalpable prestige.

Ahmed had a national vision, too. Under the Raj, he had been a student leader. With independence, he became an under-secretary in the communications ministry. He had applied to join the Foreign Service: he wanted to do the best for his country, to make it as modern as it was Islamic, and he was ambitious for himself.

Twice my father applied; twice he was turned down. He discovered, so he told me, that others, with better connections, were appointed in his place. He resigned from the civil service and became a journalist. Now he was a regular visitor at Muzaffer's house. The girl, Sabah, was good and beautiful. He was going to marry her, and educate her, take her out of the past. The family's money would help him build a new career.

Where did it come from, my mother's pain?

In 1954, straight after the wedding, they moved to Karachi. She attended public functions with him there. His sisters taught her the chic way to wear a sari, the correct way to apply her Rubinstein creams. They told her to scent her skin not with attar, but with Chanel. Ahmed taught her French. He gave her English translations of Tolstoy. He told her of the real meanings of the Qu'ran, and its radical teaching on sex equality. She wondered why he had married her. She admired him. She was enraged by him. She was alone.

I was born in Karachi in the eleventh month of their marriage. A few weeks later, my father went to Harvard, talent-spotted by the US Government. I hardly saw him again until I was seven.

In America, he wrote articles, appeared on television, began to make himself a name. She wrote him letters. He wouldn't recognise Raisa, she had grown so much. Everyone was awaiting his return. She had not done anything important, but she was reading Maupassant, in English.

Ahmed, his scholarship over, and facing visa difficulties, decided to make his way home. En route, he stayed in London, where again he found a demand for his work. Four months after leaving the States, Ahmed was still in England. It was 1958.

Sabah waited. People talked. She loved her daughter more than her own life. She always slept with her, nestled, entwined. But now there were nights when she would push Raisa aside, to catch her breath. She would cry. She would scream at her brothers to stop castigating her husband. She would plead aloud for Ahmed to come home. She wrote to him three or four letters a week. She catalogued Raisa's illnesses; she complained about her brothers; she wrote of her own shame.

Ahmed was making plans to return. To build the most solid of bases for his family, and to escape from the necessity of Muzaffer's support, he had begun to think of a legal and political career, back in Pakistan. But his plans were shaken. In October 1958, the army took over in Pakistan. Ahmed read from afar of the attacks on peasants and the shooting of workers. He mourned their deaths and the lost, visionary gleam of an Islamic state. In a moment of clarity, he saw that Pakistan would not for many years be a land of opportunity, not even for those who had worked hard and honestly at excelling.

He would stay in England; he would study for the bar, qualify, and then return to happier times. He wrote to Sabah and to Muzaffer. Muzaffer trusted him, and sent him money. The brothers complained.

At the end of his first year's study, Ahmed returned to Pakistan. He had been gone four years.

Muzaffer welcomed him. Raisa, though an infant, sensed the glamour that surrounded her father. Sabah was relieved, happy, full of rage. She looked at Ahmed, a stranger and not a stranger.

He stayed a fortnight and was gone.

Sabah could stand no longer the whispering around her. She spoke to her mother; the two of them spoke to Muzaffer. Neither wanted her to go to England, but her situation was impossible. She had to join her husband.

And so, a year after Ahmed's visit, she left, driven by shame, unwillingly into an uncertain future. The woman who quarrelled so fiercely with me, her European daughter, was raging against her own destiny.

I loved my family. I would have died for my family. And I knew that the times I spent at late-night parties or the Roundhouse – as they really were – could never have been tolerated. But I, the loving and serious-minded daughter, was attracted to those very places. I felt the guilt; I felt the dissonance. I carried them with me when I met my circle of friends. Who was I when I met them?

I spent many hours with my friends and acquaintances – seeing them, thinking about them – and I argued with them. Mine wasn't a 'negative' identity, though. I didn't simply *not* have sex, *not* drink, *not* take drugs, *not* ignore world affairs. The sanctions against such behaviour were strong and powerful in my life, but I also had the objective facts to affirm the values of my family and background – sexual adventures trivialised relationships; drink and drugs were dangerous; an active involvement in the fight against injustice could make an impact on the world: 'Stop the Springbok Tour' was effective. I was able to say, I *am* celibate, I *am* teetotal, I *am* a fighter for justice.

I frequently talked about my views and argued with the others. My desire was to disrupt and change their ideas. The words that my friends thought glamorous were 'style', 'cool', 'hip'. These words carried specific meanings. It was cool, hip and stylish to have casual sex, to drop acid, to 'do your own thing'. I wanted to subvert these words and take over their glamour. It wasn't enough to find fault with *their* style, *their* idea of cool, *their* idea of hip. I wanted the words themselves, with their appeal and ability to impress and influence. I would use them in contexts other than their customary ones. I would make a show of my difference from the others, and with support from wherever I could find it – Helen here, Sarah there – I struggled to make my meanings dominant. 'It is cool, hip and stylish to take part in political discussion, to plan and support demonstrations against injustice, to keep away from debilitating drugs, to be celibate, and still to like Santana, Captain Beefheart, hippy clothes, late-night parties, wild dancing.'

And so, in the process of this challenge to my friends, I observed the creation of values that qualified my family's definition of the good daughter. It was fine to move around with girls whose lifestyles and views were so different; it was perfectly respectable to stay up all night discussing whatever topic with my female and male friends. It upset me, of course, that my mother was worried, and it frightened me that my father was angry. But I knew that as long as I stayed within the law and did not commit the cardinal crime, I was OK.

The dissonance was never quite resolved though.

The summer holidays had come to an end. We were sitting in the sixth-form common-room. 'Lay Lady Lay' was playing behind the chatter of students. Sarah mentioned, in passing, that Eric had gone back to Denmark, some time at the beginning of August, or perhaps it had been of July. She'd heard that he'd had VD. Helen said it was a pity he was gone, and carried on with her dancing. I said nothing. I pretended to carry on with *War and Peace*.

A November evening. Amie came home with her bag of shopping – she often came home with shopping – just cakes and things – she passed the bakery before it closed. My father gave her Azra Khala's letter. She washed, said her prayers and sat down to read it.

The last letter had been from her youngest brother. He had urged her to accept a cheque. They were being generous, he had written. They were heads of families, they had families to support. Hadn't she taken enough already – her large dowry, the comfortable years she and her daughter had spent in their father's house, the financial assistance given to her husband in his years abroad? My father had said that dowry couldn't be confused with inheritance. My mother had torn up the letter – why was he so interested in her inheritance? He left the room.

I watched her now. Tiredly, she opened her sister's letter. Azra Khala had accepted a single payment. So much for the brothers whom she had watched grow, she said to me. Look how money could break up even families. She was powerless and thousands of miles away. She had to tread carefully with them, her own brothers.

218

They wanted more and more and they found convenient arguments in their support.

Some evenings she would come home later. There was a backlog of work at the office. She spoke less guardedly about her work. It was becoming stressful, she would say. I would listen and wait for the subject to change. In better jest, she would describe her new future: a mazdoor toiling in exile – that was to be her lot! She, the first-born, could not look to the fruits of her father's efforts.

One day – yes, I did experience it like that – I looked at her and saw an ageing woman. She had shadows under her eyes; her hair seemed thinner; her movements were slower. She was writing to her sister. I told her to leave her job and forget about Nana Abu's houses and factories. Her health and peace of mind were more important. How could she do that? she asked me. My father's money wasn't enough to run our comfortable house, let alone allow her that freedom. She turned on me. What did I do besides give her more heartache with my wandering?

Her bursts of anger overlooked the change in me. Since September, the Roundhouse and the late-night parties had become things of the past. Tension at home, the passing of Eric, had dampened my interest. My only leisure now was talking to Helen – on the phone, at my house and, on Saturday mornings, at her house. Sometimes, when my mother would be shouting and my father making a display of his patience, I would wonder why they put up with each other. I would run up to my room and take out my strange and unfinished story.

On Tuesday, December 23rd, suddenly and without warning, in Wandsworth High Street, outside Woolworths, amid the busy Christmas shoppers, my mother died.

Many people came to her funeral. On a chill afternoon, in her living-room, they gathered. I, the eldest child, wandered amongst them, smiling here, speaking there, and thinking.

Dr Yacoub, my father's friend from Egypt, delayed his return in order to attend. Amie had liked his daughter. My father's colleagues and their wives were there. Amie was never comfortable with them. But all that was forgotten. Phuppo Razia and Phuppa Hassan came from Bonn. I looked at my father's sister, sitting there so elegantly and I remembered another time.

219

Five years earlier. Phuppo Razia was staying with us. Her holidays in London. She would laugh and talk with Amie for a short while and then, dressed and perfumed, she would leave to go out and about with her friends. Never did Phuppo Razia invite any of her friends to meet Amie; never did she take Amie with her to the dinners and the private Qawali concerts. The car always waited for her in the driveway. Once, a 'princess' did come to the door to collect her. Amie asked the woman to come inside, to have some tea. I heard the woman's hurry to be gone. She wasn't interested, I knew. It wasn't important. The sight will never leave me – Amie moving forward, outside and into the driveway; the 'princess' moving backwards, further and further away. Later that night, I spoke to Atiyya of the ugly kali woman who had come to the door with such airs and graces. Ugly and kali; and it was right – there were too many Pakistanis in the country; they gave us a bad name. My hurt had been deep; my anger was boundless. I understood the humiliation of unimportance.

And there was my aunt at my mother's funeral. Phuppa Hassan asked me if I was getting enough sleep. Phuppo Razia stroked my face. Would I like a few Mogadons? Half a tablet might help. I said I was all right.

My mother's brothers, all three of them, had come from Lahore. They said very little. I could see they were grieving for their sister. They couldn't have been the same brothers who had given her such pain. These were the uncles I had loved as a child. I knew them before I knew my father. Now they sat in their sister's house.

Two women were sitting near the family from Leyton. We had never met them before, we hadn't even known of their existence. I found their first names and phone numbers in my mother's address book. Denise from Jamaica and Maria from the Phillipines. It turned out that they had worked with my mother. Denise couldn't believe that Sonya – that's how they had known Amie – had lived in such a nice house. My father was a lawyer, was he? And my uncle an ambassador? Sonya hadn't said. They were with her minutes before it happened. They had left 'Jean-Pierre' together, and then parted at the top of Putney Bridge Road. Only minutes before, they had been with her. They saw my torment.

'We had some laughs together, you know.' Denise stroked my arm. 'We talked about this and we talked about that. We had some real laughs. You know, she must have been happy with all of you.'

Malik from Leyton sat in a group with his wife, sons, daughters and mother-in-law. His elder daughter came to sit with me. Her name was Mariam. She was thin and small, and her hair was pulled back into a tight, single plait. She asked me about school, and what I did with my time. We must carry on meeting, she said; we were like sisters. I must come to her house, and she to mine. We would carry on my mother's connection. I felt horrified by what she said. I didn't know her; I had nothing to say to her. She wore thin chooridor trousers, and she talked in her broad 'Indian' accent of becoming friends. It was my mother's funeral and she had come to join in my grief for her, and I wanted her to leave me alone. I was irritated by her over-familiarity.

I must have been polite with her, and she must have marvelled at my coldness – she was herself so friendly. I never met her again. She phoned a few years ago to tell us of her grandmother's death. My father answered; Atiyya and I were out. When we phoned back, she was out. It hurts me to remember.

Mariam didn't look much like Rezwana Shah, but the two sit in the same hidden corner of my mind.

My father called me to him. The time had come. I heard my heart beat. In my throat, I heard it. My mother was waiting at the mosque. Soon we would join her; we would pray for her; we would watch her brothers and her husband take her away, far away, to rest in Pakistan.

It must have been eighteen months later, just before my A levels. I was alone in the house. I opened my mother's cupboard. For the first time since her passing, I found I could go near her things. A strange impulse drove me now to touch her dresses, to hold her saris and her shalwaars next to me, to bury my face in her clothes. I searched for her smell. I found it in a beige raincoat, faintly, beneath the staleness of time: Madame Rochas, and Imperial Leather soap, and warmth: Amie's smell. I saw her then, watery-eyed from her wudu, head veiled for her prayers. My heart lurched at that, and at another image: Amie's face behind the glass window of the coffin, eyes closed and still, lips shiny smooth, skin synthetically fine of a new paleness. I was holding her coat tightly to my face; I was breathing deeply. I felt sick and I missed her.

I thought of her life with my father and her daughters. She was dissatisfied I knew, but was she unhappy with us? We never really spoke of those things; she shouted, I shouted back: that was all. She died when I was sixteen; I knew her no better than a child. The thought wouldn't leave me: was she unhappy with us, with me? Was she unhappy?

I touched a paisley-patterned skirt that she wore to work and I remembered one afternoon in summer. Long before Nana Abu's final illness, we were walking together along Fulham Broadway. We had met by chance at the Underground. She must have been coming from work, and I from school. She was telling me of her brothers' latest business blunder and their foolishness in thinking that they could run their father's business, when she stopped in mid-conversation. She lowered her head and walked quickly to the shop window. She told me to walk away from her. She was wearing a skirt, and she didn't want the couple she had seen, desi acquaintances, to recognise her. In her skirt, on her own, they wouldn't. And so she and I, mother and daughter, made our separate ways home.

Was that all part of her unhappiness – wearing the skirt, being pushed to becoming somebody that she couldn't be? My father had encouraged her. He'd said Islam wasn't about secluding half the human race behind a veil. I had been inspired by his words. Now, looking through her racks of European clothes, I recalled my mother's dissatisfaction.

On a shelf at the top of the cupboard lay the tan leather suitcase. I stood on a chair to reach it. Carefully, balancing my weight with the suitcase's, I carried it down to the carpet. The search – for what, I couldn't have imagined – had started. I pressed the locks open and lifted the lid. The silks and chiffon that she once had worn lay silently before me. I moved the top layers. Perhaps I would find some letters that would tell me about the Sabahs I didn't know – the daughter, the sister, the friend, the wife. There were no letters. Instead, hidden away in the soft folds of a lilac kameez, I found a small, red plastic box, a few inches square. It looked so garish in that case of pastel shades and rich fabrics. I took it out, a box that might contain a child's toy watch or some cheap jewellery. I opened it. Inside lay an embroidered handkerchief, folded tightly, and under it, pressed firmly out of sight, a tiny address book. It was Amie's, the one she had replaced years ago. I flicked through the miniature pages.

Names, addresses, phone numbers. Her writing. Her unique curly characters, so uniquely hers I heard her voice speak through them. I held the book and moved it in my hand. I felt its texture. Her warm hands had held it once, had touched the brown vinyl and the small embossed script – 'Shanghai, China'. The sleeves were slightly puffy; pieces of paper had been tucked into each one. I unfolded the three small sheets. On one, in a hurried scrawl – not my mother's – was written:

Monday–Thursday
   8.00–4.30   ½ hr lunch

Fri. 8.00–3.00
  10 min break

9th July
2 days time work
3/– hr
After piece work

On another:

SONY
Week ending 3/12/69

Fri. Time work	5½ hrs	16/6
Mon to Thurs piecework		
50 @ 8d		£1–13–4
2 @ 8d		1–4
9 @ 8d		6–0
61 TOTAL		£2–0–8

Should be producing
160 for 32 hrs work.

On another:

SUNAYA
Week ending 10/12/69

Fri. 14	@ 8d	9–4
3	@ 8d	2–0
20 csh	@ 7d	11–8
90 csh	@ 7d	£2–12–6
127		£3–15–6
1 hr owing last wk		3–0
		£3–18–6

Total weekly production
Should be minimum 5 cushions hour
40 hrs 200 cushions

At first I didn't understand. I knew the hidden slips of paper were important, but I didn't understand. The symbols, the figures and layout were unfamiliar. Then painfully I began to grasp their meaning. Amie had not worked in an office. She had not even been a simple clerk in an office. 'Jean Pierre' was a factory. My mother had worked in a factory where one week they thought she was 'Sony' and the next 'Sunaya'. They had given her a half-hour for lunch, a ten-minute break at some other time in the day, and sevenpence for a cushion. I looked at the quilt on my father's bed. The cushions and the matching quilts she had bought for our house must have been made in that factory. How much had they charged her to buy what she had made?

I looked back at the pieces of paper. They were telling her that she was not working hard enough. The wage slip was also a reprimand and a testament to her inefficiency. There must have been a productivity drive. Her hours had been increased. She wasn't well. Oh God, my mother couldn't have been well. The date on the last slip of paper was December 10th. She had a week left. The people who didn't know her name wanted her to work harder. If she had lived long enough, they would have sacked her.

For how long had she been working like that, I asked myself – my mother, Nana Abu's daughter? She had kept it a secret, even from her relations in Leyton, who worked in sweatshops of the same kind. In those last weeks, when her life was being worn away, she had offered us brief glimpses, and we had not understood.

I wanted the Jean-Pierres of the world to perish into nothingness. But there was also my father. How had he let her suffer that strain and humiliation? He was a barrister; he was educated: he should have been earning enough. And how could her brothers have been so greedy? They were also to blame.

Under all this, sat my own guilt. My anger would not sit one place; its target was the world.

My disgust at 'Jean-Pierre' would not leave me. Three weeks later, instead of going to school, I took the bus to Wandsworth. I travelled my mother's work route: the walk to the bus stop, the bus ride, the ten-minute walk to the factory. 'Jean-Pierre' was a squat two-storey building. The side facing the main road was covered with billboards. It could not have been more than thirty-feet deep and fifteen wide. The paintwork was peeling; two of the upper-storey windows were broken and boarded-up. I saw three women walking towards me and the front entrance. I looked away and hurried past them to the other side of the road. There I waited and imagined Amie among all the other women who were now walking to the factory. I looked for Denise and Maria. Perhaps they had already gone in – I was too far away to note anything other than general colour and general outlines, and most of the women were Asian or West Indian. I must have seen at least thirty-five; all packed in, soon to be working away.

Amie had gone in like them. There were mothers and sisters and daughters there, just like Amie. I was seeking consolation, and I found it. 'Why my mother?' had become 'Why not my mother?'

I walked away. Work had been unbearable, and Amie had put up with it. Sevenpence a cushion; she must have craved independence. I remembered Denise's words, 'We had some laughs together you know.' I remembered shopping with her and, yes, her interest in the cut and design of the skirts and dresses she had bought. She was 'Sonya' to her friends at work. There was more to Sabah Khanam than I, her seventeen-year-old daughter, could understand.

Perhaps I am being irrational in thinking that I was meant to find those wage slips with their harrowing secrets: they played such a decisive part in organising my loyalties and clarifying my sense of the just and the unjust. At the age of seventeen, sitting in front of my

225

mother's suitcase, injustice and my own life became clearly linked. South Africa, Palestine, Vietnam, Workers of the World Unite, took on new meanings, as did my Nana Abu's factories.

But clear understandings are not always lasting, for all kinds of reasons.

During those months – two years after he had left England – I thought again of Eric. I took up 'The Gaze' and tried to rework it. This time, I included what might have been, even as I knew it could never have been so. The arty circle thinned out, as new interests developed. Helen and I had drifted apart. She went to art school at the end of the lower sixth, and met her boyfriend. My life alternated between study and desire. Sometimes I would remember – a cold evening, the lights of a plane soaring into the darkness, my mother's final journey.

Tahira, you said to me, 'We don't know you' and, 'We're different from you.' Nasreen, you were silent. My letter is a response to those words and to that silence. Inshallah we will soon meet.

Raisa.

Twenty-seven

She had written to them a year ago. Nasreen had replied; Tahira hadn't. She had tried to phone Tahira, in those early weeks, but no one had answered her calls, and the months had passed.

The room would have been sombre, with its high ceilings and space and paleness, were it not for the books on the shelves and the windows looking on to garden and sky.

They hadn't met for eighteen months. Nasreen sipped her tea. Raisa sat beside her on the long sofa. Tahira had left, for good?

Yes. Nasreen's mother had only found out by chance. Mrs Khan mentioned it. They had left months ago.

Then Tahira hadn't received Raisa's letter! That was possible, wasn't it? Perhaps she hadn't received it.

Nasreen didn't know.

Raisa stood up, and then sat down again. Why to Chatham? Did they know anyone there?

They had friends there, and the uncle – the builder – had bought the shop at a good price. Mrs Rashid put her money into it as well – her mother had heard – and they were all working really hard. Seven days a week, from morning till night.

Mrs Rashid wanted to go back to Haila, one day. How could she now? And Tahira – did Nasreen remember? – had talked about evening classes.

Nasreen's fingers tapped silently on a cushion. How was Raisa's new job?

She didn't get it. A forced lightness in her voice. They gave it to someone else. He was more experienced – they had said – and interviewed brilliantly.

Nasreen put aside the cushion. She was finding it difficult at the sixth-form college, with her A levels and everything. It wasn't that she was stupid. It was just that what she knew, what she had to say didn't count; it didn't get her the high marks. She understood all that.

It was a good understanding.

Nasreen moved to the window. She had learned some important lessons in those last months at school. She had thought about things, important things.

That year, those months, had been a time of rethinking for Raisa too. A critical time. Still, people could so easily forget. The rush and fatigue of life, the distractions, could make people forget. Her voice faded.

She joined Nasreen at the window. The air was magically clear. She prayed that Tahira had not yet read her letter; and she prayed that she soon would. They must all remember the lessons of their meeting. She wanted them never to forget. Never. But Tahira had not contacted her, and wanting was not enough.

Glossary of Urdu and Punjabi words

aapa term of respect for eldest sister
abba-jaan my respected father (Urdu)
abu dad (U)
achcha all right (U & Punjabi)
amie mum/mother (U & P)
amma mum (P)
angraiz English people (U & P)
appa elder sister (U)
ayah nanny (U & P) Awaragard – tramp (U & P)
badmaash (male) 'villains'/outlaws (U & P)
badmaash (female) slut (U & P)
badtameez naughty/rude/bad-mannered/mischievous (U & P)
Barking Badmaash 'Barking Bad Boys'/'The Terrors of Barking'
baitai my dear son (U & P)
baitee my dear daughter (U & P)
baraadri 'clan' (U & P)
bichara/i poor thing (U & P)
bismillah in the name of Allah (Arabic, U & P)
burga garment covering face and body
chacha paternal uncle (U)
chamcha stooge/crawler/henchman (U & P)
dadi-ma paternal grandmother (P)
desi native/'eastern' (U & P)
dupatta head scarf (U)
Eid yearly Muslim festival (either for Ramadan or for annual pilgrimage to Mecca)
gora, goree, gorrai white man, white woman, white people (U & P)
gotta gold and silver tinsel for decorating clothes (P)
gunda/ais thug, gangster (P)
haji a person who has made a pilgrimage to Mecca (U & P)
haraam zaada kutta bastard dog (U & P)
inshallah as Allah desires (Arabic, U & P)
izzat honour; self-respect (U & P)

Asian Women Writers' Workshop
Right of Way

'Reflects the quiet but assertive confidence of a new generation of Asian women writers.' *City Limits*

This rich anthology presents a variety of subjects including old age, crime, union politics, abortion and a desperate escape from an arranged marriage. The stories are as diverse as the writers whose works is informed by their experiences on the Indian subcontinent and in Britain.

The London-based Asian Women Writers' Workshop was the first of its kind in Britain. Established in 1984, its aim is to reduce the isolation of Asian women writers and all the work in this anthology has been developed through a workshop process. Most of the members of the group are previously unpublished writers and the Workshop welcomes new writers who would like to work in this sort of forum.

Right of Way includes stories from the following authors: Leera Dhingra, Meera Syal, Rahila Gupta, Rukhsana Ahmad, Kanta Talukdar, Ravinder Randhawa.

Fiction/Short Stories   £3.95
ISBN 0 7043 4091 7

Ravinder Randhawa
A Wicked Old Woman

'Forget fiction. Real life is where the drama lies.'

Decked out with NHS specs and Oxfam coat, Kulwant
masquerades behind her old woman's disguise, taking or
leaving life as she feels inclined, and seeking new
adventures. Divorced from her husband, disapproved of by
her sons and mistrusted by their wives, Kuli makes contact
with Bahadur the Punjabi punk; with Caroline, her
gregarious friend from school days; with Maya the myopic
who can't see beyond her weeping heart, and with Shanti
who won't see, whose eyes will remain closed till her
runaway daughter returns to the fold.

A sharply observed first novel set in an Asian community in
a British city – a witty and confident piece of work from a
talented new writer.

Fiction   £4.95
ISBN 0 7043 4078 X